BREAKING THE BEAST

THE BEAST & THE BADASS

HOLLY ROBERDS

Cover Design: Holly Roberds

Editors: Theresa Paolo
Sensitivity Readers: The Havoc Archives & Wanika Kiana

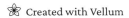 Created with Vellum

BOOKS BY HOLLY ROBERDS

Book 4.5 - Touch of Hell

Book 5 - End Game

* For recommended reading order, visit www.hollyroberds.com

To all the Vegas Immortals fans
Let's stay and play in this world a while

PROLOGUE

THE GOD OF THE DEAD

The elevator descended deeper into the bowels of the hotel, and with each passing moment, my unease grew. The humans didn't know that the Grim Reaper ran the most exclusive hotel on the Vegas strip. And no one knew what I kept in the basement far beneath the massive pyramid of dark glass, high rollers poker tables, and hottest night clubs. My greatest shame. And tonight, it called to me.

As the elevator doors opened, I stepped into a concrete room that extended out to either side. I met with a wall of steel bars, creating a structure similar to that of a zoo, but this held something far more dangerous than any jungle cat. The predator within couldn't be unleashed on this world. I had done my best to keep him content under lock and key, but I could not deny his request when he called.

Despite the harsh lights overhead in the antechamber, the cage gradually sank into darkness, concealing the truth of its depths. A voice called out from the shadows, low and lucid for once. "You came," it said, and a chill ran down my spine.

I loosened my tie, feeling the hot sting of power against my skin. It was wild, untamed, and as volatile as an atomic bomb. "You called," I replied, wary of what this encounter might bring.

As the god emerged from the shadows, hair fell over glinting silver eyes and sharp features. The power sickness surrounding him made it difficult to look at him. It grated against me and stung like lemon juice pouring into an open wound. My eyes burned from the onslaught of energy pulsating off him, but I didn't look away. I knew I had failed him, and it weighed heavily on my shoulders.

He grasped the bars of his cage, flexing muscles built on chaos and destruction. "The blade of bane, Grim. You found the blade of bane," he said, his voice holding a dangerous undertone.

"Vivien did," I replied, already aware of where this conversation was headed and trying to calculate a way to curb the outcome.

He grinned at the mention of my vampire bride. It was a terrible, sinister baring of the teeth. "Ah, the firecracker. We've met." The mirth evaporated from his face, replaced by cold ruthlessness. "Bring me the blade, Grim."

"The blade has bonded to a human, and only she can wield it now." Perhaps the god retained enough reason to understand why I couldn't bring her here. Why I couldn't let any mortal near him.

He cocked an eyebrow and tilted his head. "Then bring her to me."

"I can't do that either," I said, squaring off my stance.

Xander stilled. He seemed unnaturally frozen, staring at

me. Power crackled in the room, sizzling against my skin with anger and impatience.

My words came out low and careful. "Xander, she doesn't know how to use it. And she doesn't know how to protect herself. . ."

". . .from me," he finished. His voice became gravelly and raw. "Then bring her to me, Grim. And I'll teach her. And with any luck, she'll only need to learn once."

I turned away from him, running a hand down my face. "We both know your luck is shit," I muttered under my breath. But I owed him. I owed him what he asked, because even as the reaper of death, I couldn't give him what he needed. It was my ultimate failing.

Xander's silver eyes gleamed with warning as he bared his teeth. "Grim? If you don't, I'll break out of this cage and take matters into my own hands."

The threat hung in the air between us, and I knew he wasn't bluffing. We both recognized he was only in a cage because he let me put him there. As I stepped back into the elevator and the doors slid shut, I couldn't shake off the unease that lingered within me or the burn of his power from my skin. As much as I feared for Miranda's safety, I couldn't deny Xander his wish.

The elevator suddenly jerked to a stop, the lights flickering before going out completely. A cold, malevolent energy filled the air, emanating from Xander.

It was a parting warning. Bring the girl or the beast will come out to play.

Miranda had admirably dealt with the problems of gods, but the predator in that cage was far more dangerous than any creature she had encountered. Mortals shouldn't mix with monsters, and the beast I kept contained in the cage was more monster than god after all these years.

3

I could only hope that Miranda would quickly resolve this situation and absolve me of my ultimate failing. Otherwise, the beast would be unleashed.

CHAPTER ONE

THE BADASS

I sank into the hot water, submerging myself in the froth of lavender-scented bubbles. A low, contented sigh slipped out of me. I welcomed the caress of the water around me. Embracing the pleasure of a near-scalding bath was almost painful after the intense week. I was literally trying to melt my worries away.

I'd been waiting for days to find the time to get in my porcelain sanctuary and melt my stress with scalding heat.

Spillover from the supernatural world had twisted my

panties into such a tight bunch that I'd forgotten how to breathe properly for days. As if holding my breath would keep the bullshit at bay. There is that saying 'don't hold your breath' for a reason.

I closed my eyes trying not to think about the idiot group of demigods who tried to break into the antechambers below to see Amit, the soul eating crocodile god. Then a half-crazed, scared vampire got loose in the hotel, biting one of my maids where there were a dozen witnesses who had to have their minds wiped. And then there was a clashing of personalities at the check-in desk where one employee ended up relentlessly quacking at the other. That's right. Quacking.

Oddly enough there wasn't a handbook on how to handle immortal chaos, or jackass employees who mock each other in inventively annoying ways.

And yet I am the one who has to lay down the discipline, attempt mediation, clean up the blood, and come down on the dumbass demigods bearing the only weapon that will give them pause.

Not bad for a human, but hell if I didn't need two weeks' vacation on a beach somewhere after all that.

My muscles still fought release, even in the luxurious heat. So, I laid my head back and let out a deep breath, talking to myself in a low voice.

"Nothing needs to be done right now, Miranda. Just relax."

Again, a bigger part of me still wanted to fight it. Since Jamal left for summer camp a couple of days ago, my restlessness had flipped into overdrive.

But I made the serenity of my small bathroom irresistible with candles flickering all around the room. Lianne LaHavas crooned my favorite song, "Midnight," from my phone that I set on the closed toilet lid.

At last, I was lulled into some semblance of peace and relaxation.

I used the towel to dry my hands before reaching for my romance book.

Except my hands reached for an empty spot.

"Dammit," I cursed, rubbing my face. I had left my book and my glass of red wine in the kitchen.

Bubble baths were a self-care ritual I took incredibly seriously. It required all the right accessories from the choice of bath bomb, to the music, to the book.

And it wasn't just any wine sitting in the kitchen; it was a 1992 bottle of Pinot Noir from Celestial Cellars. It had been gifted to me by an actual goddess of wine who appreciated my assistance in training her hotel staff after a series of security breaches. I had tasted it once at my best friend's wedding, and it was the best thing to ever pass my lips.

Adjusting the cap holding up my braids, I sunk deeper into the water, trying to enjoy the bath anyway.

I don't need everything to be perfect to relax.

Who cares if I don't drink that ambrosia right now? I bet leaving it out will aerate it so it tastes even better!

But after I got out of the tub, the moment would be gone. The calm I felt in water didn't typically extend beyond the tub.

I scowled. My fingers flexed and relaxed several times as restlessness coiled through my limbs.

No. I can do this. I can relax without needing things to be perfect.

I sunk a couple of inches deeper, submerging my chin in frothy bubbles, my hands resting on either side of the tub.

My fingers began to tap. Tap, tap, tap on the porcelain edges.

Irritation mounted inside me as I kept envisioning the lone wine glass and book.

Water sloshed violently as I stood up. Yanking my towel off the rack, I wrapped it around me.

I opened the bathroom door, and left the small steamy room into the bracing cold of the rest of the house. Water tracks followed me as I went to grab my targets. I'd deal with the mess later.

With my spoils in hand, I stomped back to the bathroom, but the cool air was already pulling me out of the moment I had created.

A loud, obnoxious electronic beep preceded the house plunging into darkness. Ugh. Another brownout. Thankfully, I had candles lit all over the place, so I didn't lose total visibility, which meant I was less likely to trip and snap my neck.

With my son gone for the next couple of months, I wasn't sure who'd find my naked ass sprawled on the ground. At least we didn't have any cats to feast on the soft bits of my corpse.

Damn, that got way too dark too quick.

The house was way too quiet without Jamal brightening it up. Maybe I did need some kind of pet. A low-maintenance pet, like a guinea pig or a bird. Nah. My level is more like sea monkeys. Yes, that's more like it! I'll raise a hoard of sea monkeys in my kid's absence. When he comes home, he'll discover his mother had become a crazy sea monkey lady.

I tripped on the carpet, wine lurching dangerously to the rim of my glass.

I *really* needed to buy a generator. Maybe I should go get my laptop and –

I spoke out loud to myself, "Nope, you are not going to think about any of that. We are going to relax, goddammit."

A second dip back into the tub was not as nice as the first. The reentry of my cold, wet body chilled the water several degrees. Irritation raked along my insides at the inconvenience. At least I had managed to fill the tub before the brownout.

My beats cut out as my phone rang, and Vivien's face appeared. I scrambled to get up, clawing for my phone before settling back into the bath with a hard splash. Half the bubbles had disappeared from all my moving about. Just freaking great.

"Hey," I said, a little breathless.

"Hiya," Vivien said brightly. She was my best friend and also happened to be a vampire.

It took only that one word to let me know why she called.

"What do you need?" I sighed.

"My dearest, most awesome friend," Vivien said, laying on the syrup in her tone. "What makes you think I need something? Can't I just call to chat with you?"

Silence fell over the phone. I didn't bother to fill it, instead I smoothed a thin layer of pearlescent bubbles over my smooth, brown legs and waited. Waxing my legs at home was a messy, pain in the ass chore, but I didn't like shaving every day. I wondered if my vampire best friend had to shave anymore? Probably not, the lucky bitch.

"Okay, okay," Vivien burst out.

I knew if I waited a scant two minutes, she would crack. I was fairly certain if Vivien tried to hold in a secret for too long, she would explode into a cloud of blood, glitter, and sugar. The things I knew about her sex life alone were as detailed as they were vivid. Not that I minded since her stories of banging her equally supernatural honey were the only sexual thrill I got these days.

"It's not me actually," she confessed. "Here—" she said to someone off before I heard a shuffle.

A male voice came on the line. "Miranda?"

I straightened in the tub so fast, bubbles and water sloshed over the side.

"Mr. Scarapelli." Grim Scarapelli, aka Vivien's husband, aka the Grim Reaper himself. Though his original origins are more ancient and Egyptian, he is the god of the dead, once known as Anubis.

He used to prowl about in a monstrous jackal form and judge souls in the pyramids, but he'd modernized to the times.

Grim now wore expensive suits and owned the most exclusive hotel in Vegas, Sinopolis, a massive pyramid made of dark glass and filled with decadent luxury. He also happened to be my boss.

"Miranda, how many times do I have to tell you to call me Grim?" His voice was smooth as dark chocolate, and though he was my best friend's soul mate, I couldn't deny my attraction to him. But I learned not to take his magnetic effect seriously; every person had a little bit of a death wish. It helped to know it was a supernatural thing, and that I wasn't just a total scumbag.

"How can I help you?" I asked my boss.

There was a pause, and I imagined him pinching the bridge of his nose on the other end, a pose he fell back on when particularly pensive. While I waited for him to answer, I wondered why he didn't call or text me from his phone. It wasn't totally uncommon for him to contact me; I was head of security at his luxury hotel, Sinopolis, the most exclusive and upscale place to be on the Vegas Strip. Then I realized this wasn't business as usual. Going through Vivien meant it was personal.

"I know it's late, and I hate to impose, but there is something I would like to discuss with you."

I was already up and out of the tub with a towel wrapped about my soaking body. "Is it serious?"

"It is of a serious nature, yes," he said, hedging his words. "It's best if we speak in person. Is there any chance you could come to the hotel? Is Jamal at home? I'd be happy to send Timothy over to watch him while we handle our matters."

"I could watch him," I heard Vivien suggest in the background.

"No," Grim and I said in unison.

I wouldn't even trust my best friend with my imaginary hoard of sea monkeys. She'd either get distracted and leave them to die, or get some strange idea stuck in her head like feeding them sugar packets would supersize them somehow.

Translate these propensities toward a child and Jamal would definitely end up worse for wear. Nope. It was best my kid and the woman-sized child stay buddies rather than give her an ounce of power or authority over my spawn.

Pulling my cap off, I ignored Vivien's long whine that followed. A tumble of thin box braids fell down past my shoulder blades to my lower back. "That won't be necessary, sir. Jamal left this morning for camp."

My sweet, intelligent baby boy was eleven years old, and I missed him already.

"He'll be away for some time then?" Grim asked, trying to keep things light.

"Nine weeks," I answered as I finished snapping on my bra. He had been going since he was seven, and while I missed him terribly when he left, he loved the friends he made there. The camp was half focused on survival, and the other half was STEM education. My baby was a budding genius and got a special scholarship to this camp. Not that I was surprised. He got his wicked smarts from his mama. But his absence left me itching for a more exciting life. It sounded like Grim had something for me.

"So, you'll come then?"

I could tell it pained Grim to ask it of me. My pants were

already on, and I donned a forest green tank top. This didn't seem to call for formal attire.

"Of course."

"Good, good," he muttered more to himself.

Before I hung up, he said, "And Miranda, bring the blade."

My eyes tracked to my closet. I didn't lower the phone even after the call ended. I kept the Blade of Bane stored in a sheath between my formal dresses and my sweatpants. An unpleasant churning started in my stomach.

Whatever the god of the dead was about to ask me, I had a feeling I already wouldn't like it.

CHAPTER TWO

THE BADASS

" **M**iranda, you understand duty," Grim said, swirling a glass of brown liquor while avoiding meeting my gaze. We sat in his penthouse apartment atop the pyramid hotel, surrounded by upscale luxury.

My fingers grip the couch cushion beneath me. I feel like a kid who's been called to the principal's office even though my boss is in unusually informal shape.

Grim's usual pristine black suit jacket was carelessly discarded on a nearby chair, and his shirt was only partially buttoned. As he spoke, his fingers tapped restlessly against his thigh. To my surprise, he was barefoot, his feet planted firmly in the plush white carpet. I couldn't stop staring at them, which unsettled me.

"I suppose I do understand duty," I replied slowly. Needing to do something with my hands, I reached over and straightened a pillow.

Grim and I might share a sense of duty, but I found myself thinking of the person who linked us—Vivien.

Vivien often boasted that I was a badass because I used to be in the Special Forces and because I'm a single mom. But the military was a lifetime ago and being a single parent had made me softer in some ways. Although I would never admit that to Vivien, With Jamal away at camp, I found myself floundering for direction and orders. I enjoyed being her scary, tough as nails friend. Though sitting across from her husband, the god of death, I began to think she had a type she aligned herself with.

"I take my duties seriously," Grim said with a wry smile.

A deep line forms between my brows.

Grim was the god of the dead, and he was comparing our sense of duty.

How many feet of shit was I about to dive into?

I pushed back the cuticles on one hand. "I imagine sorting souls for the afterlife on a daily basis would require a certain level of commitment," I said, my eyes dropping back down to his bare feet.

He nodded, expression absent as if his mind was elsewhere.

I wasn't used to hanging out with my boss, and I didn't know why I was there. I moved to pushing back the cuticles on my other hand.

"And when I'm unable to perform my duties, it can...well, it eats away at me. I don't know if you can understand..." Grim said, sounding distracted.

"This isn't a sex thing, is it?" I asked incredulously, unable to believe I even had to ask.

"What?" He straightened and blinked. "No."

I sank back into the couch, relieved. "Oh good, because if the duties were in regard to my friend, I mean, she's kind of your problem now."

Grim seemed flustered. "No, there's no problem. I mean I perform with her just fine. That isn't what—"

I took the opportunity to reach for the glass of red wine waiting on the coffee table for me. It was divine, a testament to Grim's godly taste and wealth. But it wasn't a 1992 Celestial Cellers Pinot Noir, I thought glumly.

Grim rubbed his forehead and chuckled. "I feel I'm beginning to understand why you are so close with my sekhor."

Sekhor was an ancient word for vampire. While Vivien was a bloodsucker, she only had fangs for Grim.

My brain bounced like a strung out, hyper child, waiting for him to tell me why I was here. Again, my eyes fell on his bare feet. So wrong.

I put the glass back down, realizing I'd drained half the glass in one go.

This time Grim caught me staring and looked up at me, as if he was trying to gauge my thoughts. I quickly averted my gaze to his face.

"Yeah, we vibe." My knee began to bounce.

Why wasn't he getting to the point?

Vivien was already a vampire when I met her, and I may have tried to kill her at one point. She suffered from amnesia, having no idea who'd bitten her or who she was. She may have forgotten her name, but no amount of amnesia could downplay her wild, antagonist, and playful personality. She'd been put through the wringer when it came to immortals' business, and after a flood of humans were turned, she was the one dealing with the mess of newly minted bloodsuckers who didn't understand what had happened to them or what it meant.

It was also part of the deal Vivien made with the god Osiris. While Grim took care of the souls of the dead, Vivien shepherded the new vamps as the master vampire. She could control their will and keep them from harming anyone and help them through their transition.

"Right," Grim said, acknowledging mine and Vivien's close tie while setting his drink down as well. "I'm being obtuse. This can all be quite quick and over with." He stood abruptly. "You are the caretaker of the blade of bane. The only one who can wield it, correct?"

The sword lay on the couch next to me. My fingers rested on the hilt, as if needing to assure myself it was there. "Yes."

A jolt of warmth shot through my fingers and up my arm. The sword was like a living thing, humming with a subtle power that fused with me. I caressed the sleek, gold-inlaid hilt reverently, feeling its weight and balance. It felt like an extension of me, like an extra arm at times, and I knew it was meant for me and me alone.

Though I didn't really kill a god with it, so much as she threw herself on the sword's edge, not wanting to live anymore. It didn't feel right assisting her suicide like that. If I'd been faster or cleverer, I would have seen it coming and prevented the goddess Bast from ending her life.

Grim stopped in the middle of the room, hands folded behind his back. "I have a formal request of you as the blade's keeper."

"For cripes sake, would you spit it out already? I'm a big girl."

My hand clapped over my mouth as soon as the words escaped me.

Grim's golden brown eyes widened in surprise.

I couldn't believe I just mouthed off to the Grim Reaper. Not that I thought he would kill me. Or maybe a small part of me was all too aware that was a possibility.

I covered my eyes for a moment. "I'm just saying, you don't need to pussyfoot around me."

Grim unsuccessfully tried to suppress an amused smile. "You're right." Then he turned serious again and finally came right out with it. "I need you to kill a god for me."

Before I could even process that, he looked down at his feet before meeting my gaze with uncertainty. "And is there something wrong with my feet?"

THREE

THE BADASS

I artfully dodged the question about Grim Reaper's feet because thankfully there was a bigger topic at hand. Despite him being the god of the dead, Grim was one of the last people I'd expect to ask me to assassinate someone. When I asked for more information, he said it was better we take a short trip to further elaborate on the situation.

Whatever that meant.

My breath hitched in my throat, an eyebrow arching involuntarily when we got on his private elevator and a black button appeared below the column of three buttons like magic. Not *like* magic. It was magic. And I still wasn't totally used to it.

I'd released a small sigh of relief when I noticed he was now wearing slippers. For some bizarre reason, that made me feel a bit better, as if a modicum of order had been restored to my world.

Wherever we were going, it was a place below the chamber of judgement where Grim either led souls to the afterlife or fed the corrupt hearts to a giant crocodile god named Amit. I hadn't been to that level below the hotel, but Vivien had told me all about how it was like stepping into a pyramid chamber in ancient Egypt.

The doors of the elevator slid open with a ding that reverberated in the eerie stillness, putting me on edge. As soon as the doors parted, I felt an intense surge of energy. It was like a live current of electricity had replaced the air down here and enveloped me, making my skin feel raw and over-stimulated.

A prickling sensation ran up my spine, cold beads of sweat forming on my forehead. I involuntarily shrank back, every instinct screaming for an escape route from the pulsating power. Ghostly hands formed of pain and sickness traced patterns across my skin.

Grim gave me a concerned sideways glance. "Are you alright? It can be a lot for a human to be this close."

This close to what?

If the god of the dead himself was nervous for me, why the hell was I down here?

To kill a god, apparently. This Wednesday may be one of the weirdest yet, and I've cavorted about with vampires, and gods.

"What has he done?" I asked quietly, before stepping out, showing I could handle it. But could I? Could I really do this?

Kill a god? But if he was a threat, wouldn't it be better for everyone? Or was I just trying to convince myself?

A different male voice answered. "*He* has lived too goddamn long."

Something about the voice sent a shiver down my spine. While it had a masculine timbre, there was something unhinged about it. The cadence of his words bounced unevenly, irreverently.

Grim sighed and gestured for me to enter further.

The long, narrow room extended to either side of me. Ten feet in front of me were the bars of a massive cage. Inside the cage was mostly darkness, but the floors and walls in there were concrete like the entrance chamber.

I'm not one to shake in my boots, but I suddenly wished I'd worn flats or maybe heels instead of the lace-up shit-kickers I favored on off-hours because I was shaking in them now. Power pulsed against me, threatening to push me back and out of this place.

"So you are a god of your word, Grim," the same voice said from within the darkness. "Brought the mortal woman to kill me?"

"Is today a good day, or a bad day?" Grim asked in a gruff tone.

There was a trickle of creepy laughter before it halted suddenly. "I've had worse," the same mysterious voice answered in a dark, bitter tone. "Looks like it's about to get a whole hell of a lot better."

My grip tightened on the hilt of my blade. "I haven't agreed to kill anyone."

Silence fell, and my breath turned shallow. The little hairs on the back of my neck stood straight up as I stared deep into the darkness, but I didn't see anything.

Whoever, or whatever, was in there was dangerous. It was

ancient, and it melded into the shadows. The energy filling the room made my body feel strange, and the chaotic swirl made me feel dizzy and nauseous.

I edged closer to the bars, my heart pounding. I needed to see what was inside. Staring harder into the darkness, I tried to detect an outline or any movement, but there was only inky blackness.

CLANG.

A body slammed into the bars in front of me, causing me to jerk back. My heart leapt up into my throat. One moment there was nothing, and now there was a bare-chested man pressed against the bars. No, not a man. A god. A hazy glow surrounded the figure.

Ocean blue eyes captured me like a tracking beam. The air shifted around me as his scent invaded my senses—a potent mix of saltwater and sandalwood filled my nostrils. It was wild, invigorating, stirring a strange warmth within me.

His strong fingers gripped the bars. Wide nail beds. I found wide nail beds appealing. His abs formed a washboard and his navel was halfway to an outie.

Xander was as painfully gorgeous as any god. He had a body built for speed, dexterity, and power.

There were also the hundreds of scars across his chest. Like someone took a knife and sliced his flesh over and over again, leaving behind countless pale lines.

He was dangerous, there was no doubt about that, but there was something in his eyes that made my heart race for a different reason. An unseen thread seemed to weave between us, binding us in an intimate connection. It pulsed like a current, a magnetic pull I couldn't deny. *He's a god, Miranda. You are a mortal. All gods are beautiful and alluring to better sway you to worship them. Don't fall into the trap.*

But his eyes, so intense, unsettle me in ways unfamiliar and uncharted.

The air thickened around me and electric energy raced along my skin, each charge a reminder of the power that was trying to force itself on me. The electricity in the air surged and sparks spat out, sending searing heat through my skin. My muscles tensed as my instinct to flee was overruled—I had no choice but to stay put. I felt a magnetic pull towards him.

My eyes widened as I fought against it, but what I saw in his gaze made me clench my fists in fear. His blue irises bore into mine, trapping me in their depths. Their striations seemed to move and swell like ink spilled in dark choppy waters-- threatening to pull me under its cresting wave. I gasped for breath, struggling to keep my head above the overwhelming tide.

They ensnared me, drawing me into their depths with an intensity I hadn't expected.

Breathe, dammit.

While I couldn't pull out of the gravity of his eyes enough to even register the rest of the god's face, I saw curiosity, or maybe surprise, flicker in his gaze.

Don't step back. Do not retreat, Miranda. Remember, you are a badass.

"You won't kill me, then?" he asked in a voice laced with both hate and desperation, his fingers tightening around the bars of his cage.

My heart pounded as I tried to steady my voice, but it trembled slightly as I replied, "I didn't say that either."

I clenched my jaw, my grip tightening on the hilt of my sword. His words wrapped around my mind, twining my fears with my doubts. The power lashing at me added ten tons of weight to my mind and body. The invisible force seemed to crush me from all sides, pressing ever closer, until it felt as if I was surrounded by a sea of darkness. It was like drowning without even being in water.

The god's eyes bored into mine, and I felt like he was peering directly into my soul. The power around him danced like the northern lights, giving me a headache and causing my stomach to churn. It was out of control and...wrong.

"Tell her, Grim, tell her to run that sword right through me," he spat out the words with a maniacal cackle that made my skin crawl. Was he daring me to kill him or begging me to end his torment? I couldn't tell.

This time, I took a step back. His eyes may be the only grounding place to look, but in them, I found madness, chaos, and power.

When Grim spoke, he sounded weary and bitter. "I cannot tell her to do anything, Xander. She is the keeper of the blade. She was entrusted with the weapon, and she decides how it is to be used. But I did bring her here, so you could ask."

Ask?

I hesitated. "Wait, you want me to kill you?"

Xander commanded, "Leave us," with sudden force.

My heart leapt into my throat, but I tried to remain calm and composed. Grim hesitated, and I found the strength to tear my gaze away from Xander to look at him. For a moment, I didn't want Grim to go. He could protect me if I needed it, but as soon as the thought surfaced, I drowned it. I was the keeper of the blade; it was my responsibility. This was my business, and I could conduct it on my own. I gave Grim a curt nod.

"I'll just be. . ." Grim pointed up, and I gathered he'd be in the lobby or his penthouse.

My chest tightened as he started to walk away. Grim murmured as he passed by me, "Don't get too close," then added, "if you can help it."

The elevator dinged shut, and with that, any safety I felt in the room fled. But no, that wasn't true. This god was behind bars, I told myself.

"Why do you want me to kill you?" I asked, raising an eyebrow. My tone was both incredulous and skeptical. This whole thing felt like a bad setup, though I was sure the gods didn't go for candid camera gags. Or... I was *pretty* sure.

"Yes," Xander hissed, eyes glowing supernaturally. He shut them tight, his body curved back from the bars while still keeping a grip on them, as if he were trying to regain control. Twisting his head to the side, he looked as if it pained him to push down whatever was trying to force its way up from inside him. When his gaze returned to me, some of his feral had ebbed and it was a little easier to stand so close. A metallic taste filled the air, like an electrical conduit had a short and a surge of electricity passed through.

I tried to lick away the buzzing sensation from the sensitive skin of my lips. "I need to hear you say it."

There was something new in his eyes now. Pain. Deep, endless pain. As if he'd been a man tortured past his limits.

"Why do you want me to kill you?" I asked, raising my chin.

His glare was sharp, but I refused to retreat. I shifted my weight to one leg, adopting a more relaxed, in control stance. I wouldn't budge until I could assess the situation for myself. The ability to exterminate any being was not a light undertaking, and I'd been chosen to be judge, jury, and executioner.

Xander remained silent, choosing to glower at me.

"I know we just met," I began, forcing a calm I didn't feel into my voice, "but let me explain something to you. I don't kill indiscriminately. I have killed before, and I can again if need be. So you called me down here, interrupting my evening, to demand I kill you. Explain why."

It was far from a perfect night. But he didn't need to know that. A smirk twitched at the corner of the god's perfect lips, and my stomach suddenly swam up and down like I was weightless on a powerful ocean wave. That small twitch proved he was exactly like the other gods in one respect, as he was downright gorgeous under all the layers of chaotic power. And that scared me more than anything else. I refused to examine why.

"Bubble bath?" My breath hitched as his lips curved into a predatory smirk. I pressed my hand to my stomach, trying to quell the strange fluttering sensation that was suddenly there.

"How did you become the keeper of the blade?" Xander asked, his fingers caressing the bars in a far too suggestive manner.

Was he...was he *flirting*?

Ignoring the strange jolt of heat that his words sparked, I squared my shoulders. "Does that information matter to you?"

He shook his head, dropping the topic and whatever sensual web he had started to weave around me. "No, I suppose not."

As if it took great effort, the god released the bars of his cage. "I have lived down here for millennia, and I cannot die. The only key to oblivion and my release is in your hand right there. And I'm asking that you help set me free."

Xander's eyes traced the blade as it glinted in the dim light of the chamber. The weight of the weapon felt heavier than usual in my hand, as if it too was hesitant to be used in such a way.

"You're not going to do it, are you?" Xander asked, his voice barely above a whisper. Hope, anticipation, and disappointment all mixed into his question.

His gaze burned into me, the intensity of it causing my skin to prickle. A strange mix of fear and desire rose in my chest, and I found myself leaning closer to the bars without even realizing it. Then a sick wave of dizziness swept over me.

The power flowing off his body threatened to sweep me away.

"I didn't say that," I replied, my voice sounding unsteady even to my own ears. "You won't come back," I went on. "You won't return to the cradle of life and respawn in a hundred or a thousand years. You'll truly cease to exist."

His eyes met mine again, surprise evident. "A human knows so much about godly matters?"

I narrowed my eyes. It wasn't uncommon for someone to underestimate me, but I refused to ever get used to it.

Gods could die. When they did, their essence returned to the cradle of life. While I hadn't laid eyes on it, the description Vivien gave me reminded me of one of Jamal's video games that has a respawn point. But instead of instantly coming back to life, they stay there for hundreds, if not thousands of years before they emerge and rejoin humanity.

What I was less clear on was the consequences of them arising too soon. Vivien said it had something to do with being too powerful, or half-baked, like one of her cupcakes. My vampire best friend had a passion for baking, but that passion did not translate into any amount of skill. The cupcakes, cookies, or pastries usually came out burnt to a crisp, salty as the ocean, or a half-melted mess from being undercooked.

And a half-melted, salty god walking among us definitely sounded like a recipe for disaster.

I pulled the sword from the sheath with a sharp hiss. "This human knows how to use her toys."

The blade glinted in the dim light. To my surprise, intricate runes and symbols of ancient power glowed along it. Was it the god's presence powering the sword? I didn't know. But I did know if an immortal died by the edge of my blade, there would be no chance to respawn. It was game over.

Once more, his lips twitched—an action so subtly beautiful

that it felt like a physical blow, threatening to topple my carefully constructed defenses.

It was so unlike anything I had experienced before; I couldn't begin to explain it. Grim made me aware of the death wish I held in my soul, but this was a different power. His power, his eyes overwhelmed me, and part of me desired to be swept away. To be taken away from my life and thrown into another dimension where everything was fresh and new, including me. I both craved and feared it.

Despite the thunderous alarm bells in my mind, my feet drew me closer to him.

Xander leaned in closer. "Do it," he hissed, his voice an intoxicating blend of velvet and venom. His eyes blazed with a fire that threatened to combust. "End this eternal suffering."

His words stirred a maelstrom within me, sending a shiver down my spine that somehow ignited a comforting warmth in the pit of my belly. There was something in the way he looked at me, something that made me feel wanted, needed even.

Though my brain was screaming at me to stay back, to keep my distance if I wanted to live, I continued forward until a half foot of space and the bars were all that separated us. I grounded in those deep blue eyes as the energy pulsating off him accosted my body.

"Please, Miranda." His plea came out in a hoarse whisper. The way he said my name clawed at something inside me. "Kill me."

"Why?" I whispered.

Xander's eyes softened, and for a moment, I could see the pain and sadness in them. "Because I have endured eternal pain, because I am tired," he said, his voice barely above a whisper. "Tired of this existence, of this never-ending torment. I want to rest, to be at peace. And the only way to do that is through death."

A wave of sympathy for him crashed over me, but beneath it lay the unforgiving, jagged rocks of my duty. The blade of Bane had been entrusted to me for a reason.

I took a deep breath, steeling myself for what was to come. "I'll do it," I said, raising the sword high above my head.

Xander closed his eyes, and I could see his body tense up in anticipation. I swung the sword down with all my might, the blade singing through the air.

But at the last moment, I hesitated, my hand shaking. The blade stopped just short of Xander's chest, the tip hovering there as if suspended in mid-air.

Xander opened his eyes slowly, and I could see a fathomless depth of despair lingering in their depths. His mouth curled downward in a grimace of anguish, and his entire body seemed to slump with the weight of his resignation. For a moment, we just stood there, the sword still hovering between us. It seemed to fight me, wobbling in my hands. But it was likely just my own nerves.

Electricity crackled between us, and my heart pumped furiously. Our gazes locked as time stood still while I stood in the vortex of his power. The air was heavy with his scent of power, sex, and danger. I was drawn like a moth to flame, knowing if I got any closer, he would scorch me and leave me in cinders. Stranger yet, some part of me wanted to send him to oblivion with a kiss.

His gaze, now hooded, seemed to pierce through my defenses, devouring my unspoken thoughts. They dropped to my mouth as if considering the texture and taste of me.

How long had it been since this underground god had been kissed? Was it as long as it had been for me? Likely longer, though it felt like it'd been a thousand years since I felt the pressure of another's lips against mine.

"Xander?" I asked in a low voice. My palm turned sweaty around the hilt of the blade.

"Yes," he murmured, his body fully pressed against the bars now. As if he were straining to get closer.

"Wish granted."

My blade jabbed into his chest, cutting deep into his heart.

His eyelids flew wide as he grunted. First confusion filled them, as if he wasn't sure what was happening. Then face relaxed, mouth going slack, like he was experiencing immeasurable relief.

I yanked the blade out and Xander stumbled backward, hand gripping the wound in his body. Bright red blood covered his hand. Xander fell to the ground, dead.

The onslaught of abrasive energy disappeared, as if I'd been standing in a nuclear reactor that had been shut off. The silence, the sudden absence of his energy was deafening.

My body was drained, like I'd just been through a battle. I took a deep breath, trying to steady myself. The job was done, but the weight of it remained heavy on my shoulders.

I turned and marched to the elevator, my mind reeling with a mix of emotions. Guilt and regret were already creeping in, as I thought about the life I'd just taken. The elevator doors closed, and I hit the button to go up.

As the elevator ascended, I couldn't shake the unsettled sensation in my gut. I'd just killed a god, and it didn't feel like a victory. It felt like a tragedy. The world had been stripped of a powerful presence, and it felt as though, in fulfilling my duty, I had somehow hollowed out a piece of myself.

CHAPTER FOUR

THE BEAST

O blivion. Bliss. At last. Death swallowed me whole into nothingness, bestowed by the dark angel with the face of a seductress and the scent of berg-amot and lavender soap. Her eyes, her eyes were the last, most devastating beautiful thing I'd see.

But then, cold seeped into the skin on my back, and I blinked.

I blinked again, and reality hit me like a ton of bricks.

"Fuck," I grumbled, the ceiling of my cage creeping into my

vision, each cold and uncaring line a mocking reminder of my unending torment. My powers buzzed under my skin like a swarm of hornets, their relentless sting eroding the last vestiges of my sanity.

I sat up, gripping my hair as I set my elbows on my knees. Then I screamed. "Fuuuck!"

My cries of despair bounced off the confining bars, creating a symphony of agony as I convulsed, teetering on the edge of sanity. Death had briefly cradled me in her arms, a fleeting respite from my torment. Each shuddering breath felt like inhaling shards of glass, the pain a cruel reminder of the life I was bound to.

I had died, but only briefly. The wound on my chest had closed, and I had healed entirely. I had survived the Blade of Bane, something no immortal had ever done before.

To have come so close to what I wanted so badly made the failure a thousand times more painful.

I blinked back the wetness stinging my eyes, clenching my jaw so hard that I threatened to break some teeth. But they always grew back.

Staggering to my feet, a surge of raw emotion ripped through me, each pulse of my power a white-hot needle threading insanity into the fabric of my existence.. My senses were a cacophony of torment: the sight of my captivity, the taste of stale air, the rough coldness of the bars against my skin – all were sharp, maddening reminders of my reality. I stood at the precipice of my own mind, teetering on the edge of a freefall into the abyss of berserker rage

For once, I welcomed it. I wanted to lose myself to the oblivion of white-hot power searing through my brain, driving me right out of my mind. A roar of agony exploded from me, and the bars of my cage rattled.

Still, my frustration did not tip me over the edge. Hell, my surge of anger didn't even affect the lights. Normally they'd pop, spark, and plunge me into darkness.

Then I noticed it. A bit of my power was gone. It was as subtle as a missing spark from an inferno of power. Yet it was enough to keep me from losing control. A glimmer of hope dared to ignite in the black abyss of my despair.

And I did find oblivion, at least for a little while.

Excitement welled up inside me almost as fiercely as when I learned the Blade of Bane had resurfaced. This wasn't over. No, this was just the beginning. A grin curled on my face just as the elevator opened.

They revealed the impeccable silhouettes of Grim and his aide, Timothy.

Like Grim, Timothy donned exquisite suits, though his were always tinged with an extra flare, reflecting his taste for the theatric. His jet-black hair stood up in a perfectly gelled coif, offset by the deep purple suit he wore.

Grim had kept his tawny colored skin and strong Egyptian features, while Timothy spent many hundreds of years in China until he adopted Asiatic characteristics himself. We tend to adapt to whatever environment we immerse ourselves in. Down here, I grew pale, not having felt the kiss of the sun for I don't know how long.

Timothy's shrewd eyes narrowed when he saw me.

Grim looked surprised as well. "We thought you were dead."

"Yes, I was here to make plans for the body," Timothy announced in his uptight British accent. He fiddled with the cufflinks on his velvet, paisley suit:

Unfinished business made Timothy anxious. I'd been unfinished business for the past thousand years, and I knew it grated on the both of them. But this was about me.

"Believe me," I said, baring my teeth, "no one is more disappointed than me."

Grim's expression pulled into his usual scowl. "It didn't work."

I grabbed a bar up high. "Oh, it worked, just not how I imagined it would. Send the girl to me again. It turns out she and I might be stuck with each other for a while."

Grim and Timothy exchanged a wary look. When I explained it, I was certain they wouldn't deny me. The god of the dead wouldn't dream of denying someone death.

As I slumped against the cold, merciless bars, a chaotic symphony of thoughts and emotions raged within me. Among the discord, a single melody echoed above the rest - the dark angel, her cat-like eyes burrowing deep into my fractured soul.

She was like an alluring siren's song, and I the dangerous predator lurking in the depths, eager to disrupt her rigid composure.

Her warm, brown skin had a radiant glow that made me ache to touch it. Her hair, woven into intricate braids, flowed down her back like a waterfall of onyx silk ropes.

Miranda's cat-shaped eyes held a fierce determination, warning me not to cross her. They beckoned me, a captivating lure in the dark, tempting me to coax out the fire beneath her icy, no-nonsense demeanor.

She was a warrior at heart. I'd heard there were few warriors left in the world, but she'd been born one. My little badass. Beneath that tough exterior, there was a flicker of vulnerability that only made me more intrigued.

The thought of her provoked a visceral response: a thrilling shiver that rippled down my spine, causing my skin to prickle and my muscles to tense in anticipation. Miranda possessed a magnetic attraction that I couldn't deny. Despite the fact that she had come closer to killing me than anyone else, the idea of being tied to her, even in a dance to the death, was both terri-fying and exhilarating.

A sly smile slithered across my lips, the first genuine show of amusement I'd felt in an eternity. I had two things to look forward to: the inevitability of my death and another chance to meet the beautiful woman who would be the author of my demise.

CHAPTER
FIVE

THE BADASS

S ix AM the next morning, I sat at a table by Perkatory, the hotel's café, my hands wrapped around an over-sized to-go cup of coffee. I tried to shake off the chill that had settled into my bones, but even the piping hot, bitter liquid flowing down my throat failed to warm me up.

I used to work at Castlegate, a neighboring hotel, where garish colors and boisterous families were the norm. Sinopolis, on the other hand, offered a stark contrast. Here, the onyx marble floors shimmered like a moonlit abyss, while gold accents punctuated the surrounding walls and ceilings like gilded poetry. Amidst this luxurious setting, Grim had created a sanctuary, with lush green plants surrounding soothing indoor waterfalls.

The lobby of Sinopolis resonated with echoes of an ancient Egyptian oasis, reminding me of the grandeur and power of the god I had recently slain. It felt as if the hotel itself reflected his immense power and storied past. How long had he been confined in that cage? Did he yearn for the black sands of his true home?

Perkatory was nestled amidst large, exotic plants, offering a semi-private space within the lobby. It allowed me to be aware of the hotel's activities while finding a much-needed moment of peace and solitude.

But today, I found it difficult to access the serenity I usually found in my morning routine. As I sipped my drink, there was a nagging whisper telling me I had just crossed a dangerous line into the world of the gods, where power and danger were intertwined.

I knew that treading carefully was the key to surviving in this new world, but I couldn't help but feel drawn deeper into it.

Xander's words echoed in my mind, the desperation in his voice as he begged me to end his existence. I knew I had no other choice, but that didn't make it any easier. It wasn't every day that someone asked me to kill them. I hoped it never happened again.

Though admittedly, I felt as though I'd performed an important duty. My job as head of security at Sinopolis gave me purpose, but I couldn't help but feel like something was missing. With Jamal's absence, it was harder to deny I was lacking a certain satisfaction in my life.

My eyes closed for a moment. Xander's face haunted my

dreams, and still remained behind my eyelids every time I blinked. The sharpness of his porcelain features, the way he looked at me through the wild hair half covering his eyes, like he was a predator studying me. And there was the way he held himself with an air of confidence and power – it all drew me to him in a way I hadn't expected.

I pushed those thoughts away and opened my eyes, bringing myself back to reality.

A sudden heat wave coursed through me, causing my forest green suit jacket to become suffocating. I rolled up the sleeves, but it didn't help. I wouldn't clip on my nametag until I officially started work for the day, which wasn't for another thirty minutes. I took a deep breath and downed some more coffee, hoping to find some clarity in the chaos that had become my life.

"Morning, Viv," I said, taking another sip.

A petulant groan came from behind me. The auburn-haired vampire wearing blood red lipstick and a tight leather dress dropped into the chair across from me. Vivien put the vamp in vampire. "How do you always know?" she complained.

My lips curved around my coffee cup. I'll never tell.

"Looks like you've got a long way to go before you graduate from ninja school," I said in a lofty tone.

Vivien glowered at my taunt. "Yeah, well, you better watch out for my ninja stars." She made whooshing sounds while miming throwing some at my head.

I snorted. "Like anyone is dumb enough to let you wield anything sharper than a butter knife."

"Eh," she shrugged, "Who needs 'em?" She flashed her fangs at me. "As the only master vampire, the newly turned primarily rely on my diplomatic skills and my ability to control their will if any of them get out of control. Isn't that a laugh? Me using diplomacy."

Vivien had clearly just learned the word diplomacy and was swinging it about as if it were a large appendage between her legs. Good for her.

The usual string of leather was wrapped a dozen times around her neck, hiding the bite of the master vampire who turned her. Thankfully, he was long gone.

Little lines of exhaustion snaked out and around her eyes. They hadn't been there a couple months ago. The beginning of my day was the end of hers, being a night dweller. Weirdly enough, the lack of windows in Vegas hotels made it safe for her to stay up past her bedtime when the sun came up.

"How is it, managing the newly turned?" Vivien had been appointed by Osiris— an Egyptian god so powerful he wasn't on our plane— to be the shepherd of the vampires. When humans were turned, they were scared, hungry, and sometimes reckless. My vibrant, rebellious friend was now in charge of handling all those situations.

She frowned. "A pain in the neck." She rubbed her neck as if someone had tried to bite her. Maybe they had. "But you know what really chaps my ass?"

"Do tell," I asked.

Vivien's fingers curled around the edges of the table. "Grim and I got into an argument the other night, and do you know how he ended it?" Fire blazed in her eyes.

"With sex?" I guessed. That was the usual method.

She waved a hand. "That was later, so yes, but no. That uptight bastard had the gall to hit me with a pillow. Right in the face." Her words came out an indignant screech.

"That bastard," I responded in an even, dry tone.

Vivien stood up, hands still gripping the table. "He thinks he won the argument, but now he's started a war."

The maniacal gleam in her eye should have scared me. The

fact that I was only amused probably meant I was deranged as well.

"So have you retaliated yet?"

She settled back into her chair. "Oh, I've got plans. Don't you worry, I've got plans." Vivien might as well have been drumming her fingers together like a James Bond villain. Lord help us all.

"You realize this war you've declared is likely a coping mechanism and distraction from being the only Master vampire, right?" I blinked at her innocently.

Her eyelids flickered as her head tilted. Time was momentarily suspended as she absorbed the weight of the words. The little men running Vivien's brain seemed to freeze up, as if they hadn't considered it before.

When the gears finally began to work again, she sniffed. "So what? It doesn't hurt to indulge in a little play, a little escapism. So I don't have to think about the grief of a vampire who realizes she'll outlive her entire family." A shadow passed over her eyes for a moment before she snapped out of it and put all her focus back on me. "Speaking of immortals, tell me what happened last night."

I squirmed in my seat.

"W-what are we t-talking about, ladies?" Aaron asked. He twirled the third chair around and plopped down in it, handing a blended coffee drink piled high with whipped cream to Vivien. Vampires may subsist off blood, but my friend had a sweet tooth that was out of control.

There were few people milling about the Sinopolis lobby this early in the morning, making it perfect for us to have a mini hang first thing. Our little threesome morning chats had become one of my favorite rituals.

"Grim asked Miranda to kill a god last night," Vivien explained without preamble.

"Way to put me on the spot," I hissed at my traitorous friend.

No one was around to hear the insane summation, and what human would believe us? Still, it didn't settle well.

Aaron's eyebrows shot up. He wore his black smock with the skull design encircled by the café's name. The logo read "Good to the Last Breath."

Aaron brushed the wild mane of blond hair, naturally bleached by the sun, from his glowing, tanned face. Vivien and I agreed he resembled Patrick Swayze from the surfer heist movie, Point Break. When we told him of our conclusion, his blinding white smile nearly cracked his entire face. We noted to be careful not to feed his ego too much in the future.

It didn't hurt that Aaron was an avid surfer from California and an adrenaline junkie. While he wasn't near the waves anymore, he spent most of his time rock climbing, skydiving, or learning to fly a helicopter.

Aaron was also one of the very few humans to know gods, vampires, and more lived among us in plain sight.

"D-did you? Kill him, I mean?" he asked me. Years ago, he got hit in the jugular with a surfboard and was left with a permanent stutter, but it didn't seem to skin a single slice off his confidence. In fact, with speech therapy, his stutter had lessened slightly.

"I did," I confirmed, interlacing my fingers around my cup. Then my phone vibrated against the table. I picked it up to find a picture of Jamal with a toothy smile, arm flung over one of his camp friend's shoulders. Another couple of pictures followed. The counselors led them on a sunrise hike, and Jamal took photos of mountains backed by brilliant purples and shocking oranges as the sun appeared over the horizon.

My heart squeezed hard. I missed my little man, but it was great to see him having such a good time.

"And. . .?" Vivien tried to dig in, forcing me to put my phone back down. "You aren't going to share details?" Vivien's brows furrowed, her eyes scanning my face acting like magnets attempting to draw out my secrets

"Are you okay with it?" she asked in a sincere, low voice.

I shrugged. "I'm fine." Strange feelings rioted in my chest. The replay of Xander's death began to start up again in my brain. A mixture of pain and gratitude etched into his sharp, beautiful features. The unnamed chemistry that lingered in between as he studied my mouth in those last moments.

Aaron and Vivien exchanged a look. "You are definitely not okay," Vivien countered.

Maybe that's because I killed a god, my brain informed me.

Rude. I was just trying to make everything normal. Why was my brain a traitor?

I brushed the thought away like a buzzing fly. "It's fine. Like Grim said, I understand duty. Duty to honor the mantle of Bob's responsibilities."

"Bob?" Aaron asked, rearing back.

"The Blade of Bane," I explained. "Their nickname is Bob."

"Their, not his?" A line formed between Aaron's brows.

"Bob is a nonbinary blade," Vivien chimed in. "So we use gender-neutral pronouns."

Vampire or not, Vivien got me. She went on. "So you respect your duty to Bob to slay gods as fairly as possible. It doesn't mean you aren't shaken."

I was shaken. Killing someone wasn't a small thing, no matter how much I tried to rationalize it. No matter how much he wanted it. It sat heavy in my gut.

A wave of queasiness washed over me, twisting my stomach into knots. I left him there, slumped on the ground. Alone.

In that moment, I longed for some of Vivien's playfulness.

If I could combat the trash feelings churning inside me with a lighthearted, err, bloodthirsty pillow fight, maybe I'd feel better. But I left the playing to Jamal. I got a kind of vicarious fun from watching him animatedly play video games or talk about the basketball game he played at school that day.

Between living through him for fun and Vivien for her sex life, I started to wonder when I was living for myself.

You had that bubble bath last night, I tried to argue with myself.

Yeah right. Despite my claim to Xander, my bath time had been far from perfect. I couldn't even wind down enough to enjoy the few minutes I had before I was called to work. I all but leapt at an opportunity to have a mission of some kind.

I'd almost think I needed a vacation, but I wouldn't even know where to go or what to do.

"Miranda, just the person I want to see," a British voice announced behind me.

I knew who it was before I turned. If not for the voice, Aaron's eyes rounded and went glassy as if looking upon a prime A-grade steak. He all but drooled, hungrily.

I twisted around to face Timothy. The man's style was as fierce as it was flawless. Like all the gods, he was painfully beautiful from his high cheekbones to his long dexterous fingers. Timothy tried to keep his dark, narrow eyes averted from Aaron, but the magnetism was always palpable when they got within striking distance of each other. The uptight god and the surfer bro human. I guess opposites do attract.

"What do you need?" I asked. In a few minutes, I planned to head to the security office to start my duties for the day.

"A word, alone." He stressed the last word for Vivien's sake. She leaned back in her chair and sucked vindictively on her frozen coffee, hating to be left out of things.

Timothy studiously ignored both her and Aaron. I gave my

two best friends a nod before following the god of literature, science, and wisdom.

He led me across the lobby, ensuring we wouldn't be seen or overheard. Timothy's question came out with a held breath. "We need you to do it again."

"Do what?" I asked.

"Kill Xander."

My heart pounded inexplicably. "I don't understand. He's dead."

Timothy shook his head, lips thinning. "Not exactly. He was for a time, but woke up, revived and healed."

Kaboom. Mind blown. I was surprised I wasn't thrown off my feet, but I managed to stay upright.

"But the blade kills gods, immortals," I stuttered. "How can he be alive?"

That familiar line formed between Timothy's eyebrows as he fiddled with his tie. "Xander is a. . . special case. He is very powerful, too powerful."

That I easily believed. I was shocked to find out my eyebrows and eyelashes hadn't sizzled right off my face in that basement.

"But Xander requests you return today to do it again," Timothy said.

That piercing gaze entered my mind's eye, and I suppressed a shiver.

"Will you do it?" Timothy carefully studied me.

"I don't know what good it will do if it didn't work last night," I said. "And I really don't want to kill two nights in a row, even if it's the same person."

Especially if it's *that* god. Something in me knew it was best to stay far far away, if not for the burn of his power, but because of the magnetic intensity that seeped into my every pore, urging me toward him.

There was a gentle intensity in Timothy's eyes as he regarded me, his gaze now filled with empathy. "It would be a great service to both Grim and me. You can't know what a burden it is to serve the transition from life to death for so long and encounter someone who can't make the same sacred passage. Believe me, you are a benevolent force here."

Aw damn. He was appealing to my feelings. While I liked that I exuded a hard-shell exterior, it served me well in covering up that I had a gooey center. But I'd been through the ringer in the past with Timothy when it came to immortals and end-of-the-world stakes. This classy sonofabitch knew exactly what a softie I was.

"Low move," I growled.

He gave me a weak smile. "So you will?" Without waiting for my answer, he went on. "This takes precedence, and Grim and I realize this, so consider this your primary concern. No need to handle security matters. Javier can handle things for a while."

A spike of panic went through me. While I implicitly trusted my number two, and good friend from the army, I didn't want to be replaced.

"I still need a job."

If I refused to kill Xander to keep my job, would they accept that? Instantly, I knew I couldn't do that. Damn, Grim knew exactly what he was saying when he said I was bound by duty. And I didn't take that responsibility lightly, being the only one with the power to permanently eradicate any god.

Timothy's eyebrows shot up. "Oh, you misunderstand me. You would, of course, keep your current pay and compensation. But seeing as you are handling immortal matters, we view this as no less important than the service you provide this hotel. Far more so, in fact."

Oh.

"If it's all the same, I would like to keep my regular duties," I said.

Timothy seemed confused, so I shrugged. "It didn't take long to kill him. But I still don't understand how he—"

The tablet under Timothy's arm began to chime with notifications, ending our conversation as he whisked off to take care of the entire world, humans and immortals alike.

But I had more questions. Did Timothy intend for me to take the day off or more? It seemed like this could be a lasting situation. And why did they believe I could have any effect on Xander's immortality if I didn't succeed in killing him last night?

I had a feeling the person, or rather the god, who could explain was currently caged and waiting for me to kill him...*again*. A shudder ran down my spine. I wasn't sure what caused it—the prospect of facing his out-of-control, searing power, or my uncertainty about how to handle the way he looked at me, or the way he made me feel.

I clipped on my nametag and headed to the security office. Though I didn't relish the thought of returning, I knew I had to pull myself up by the bootstraps and murder a god tonight.

SIX

THE BEAST

T he elevator binged, announcing the arrival of my angel of death. A jolt of feverish anticipation sent spikes of exhilaration through my veins, electrifying the otherwise stagnant air of my cage. I'd been unbearably restless, pacing in the shadows for hours.

"I was beginning to think you weren't coming," I said from where I hid in the darkness.

Gods, she was more alluring than I remember. Miranda's face was tight, full lips pursed together. The muscles of her body grew tighter with each step she took further into my own personal hell. Either she had a rough day, or she was girding herself against the waves of power that arced and flowed off from me like the sun.

If you think that hurts, my little badass, try being me.

An insane titter escaped me. I worked to swallow down the power, not wanting to scare her off. The feral, wild side of me longed to be free of this cage, to unleash my power and show her the full extent of my madness. To explode with all my pent-up energies. But if I shifted or went berserk, I would scare her off. I couldn't afford that.

"I had to go home to pick up this," Miranda explained, lifting the sheathed blade of bane. "I don't typically carry it with me on a normal workday."

She lifted the blade of bane, and a surge of hunger swept through me. I craved death, and she held the power to grant it. My heart raced. The sheer force of her presence unleashed a whirlwind of emotions, cascading over me like a waterfall of exhilaration. I grew dizzy from the thrill of being near my dark angel.

Gone was the athletic goddess of yesternight, in a tank top and leggings that embraced her every toned, muscular curve. Today, she was a figure of authority, clad in the formal armor of her station. The forest green of her jacket made her eyes appear lighter, more luminescent. Or maybe I was hallucinating again?

But I knew underneath her garb, she had a body like a battle-axe. I couldn't forget. That same body danced around my dreams all last night, taunting and tempting me. Beckoning to bend her, break her, claim her until she killed me.

It had been a long time since I had seen such a beautiful woman. Maybe I had *never* met such a beautiful woman. Maybe I had never met *any* woman.

I clenched my fist instead of using the hand to knock sense into my rattled brain.

"Since you've brought it all this way," I said, trying to remain coy. If I weren't in my cage I would have hurled myself at her and upon the blade she held. To contain my erratic desires, I gripped the cage bars so hard they groaned.

Miranda eyed my white knuckles.

Steady, Xander.

Instead of coming closer and stabbing me as she'd done yesterday she asked, "Why didn't it work?"

Oh for fuck's sake. They didn't tell her? They couldn't bother to save me the trouble?

"It did work," I answered.

She raised an eyebrow at the same time she cocked a hip and set a hand on it. I was struck by the amount of sass she packed into that posture. I absolutely loved it.

More more more. Lick her sass, make her yours, my brain singsonged.

Then I remembered yesterday how for a moment I thought she was going to kiss me. I knew the effect I have on humans as an immortal, enough to not take it seriously. Her attraction to me was a byproduct of being a god. But for a heart stopping moment, I almost gave in despite knowing better. I wanted her to close those seductive eyes and surrender those impossibly seductive lips to me.

But then she gave me an even better gift. Death.

"I died for a little while. That's never happened before, no matter what I've tried. I always stayed in perfect consciousness."

Her lips twisted into a scowl, the sass in her eyes replaced by a look of confusion. "They said you had too much power."

I nodded and stretched, leveraging myself against the bars, and a vertebra popped. Miranda's eyes flitted to my flexing arms before returning to my eyes. I knew it must be painful for her to be down here, this close to me. Yet she still put off the relief she'd get from killing me right away to assess the situation. She certainly was unusual.

"Yes, far too much power. But when I awoke after regenerating, some of it was missing. I believe you killed some of it off when you stabbed me."

"Oh," was all she said, her hard gaze back on my face. I flexed my muscles to see if I could draw her attention even if for a moment.

Her eyes swept down my bare abdomen, her mouth parting ever so slightly.

Heat rushed south as I felt something I hadn't in years. Pleasure. My mouth instantly went dry. I was hungry for her. Starving.

Miranda cleared her throat and looked away. Even as she swallowed hard, I knew she wanted me. The crazy god in a cage. Any mortal would likely have the same reaction, but she fought it.

It made me want to push her further until she gave into the desire swirling around her. Let it off the tight leash she had on it.

I was a god. She must want to worship me. But I wanted to worship her. Feel the soft touch of a woman again.

My curiosity and pleasure shattered abruptly, replaced by pain. Buzzing assaulted my brain. I shut my eyes, my head snapping to the side as I braced myself against it. Retreating, I clutched at my ears. I unleashed a primal howl, a vain attempt to drown out the onslaught. Every nerve vibrated like a tuning fork, the agonizing ache radiating throughout my frame. *No. No. No.*

"It's coming, it's coming, it's..." The words spilled from my lips, a mantra of impending doom, their meaning lost in the cacophony of my spiraling mind.

My muscles swelled as I tried to ground against the wave of pain. The beast wanted to come out. It wanted to rage. Human fingers transformed into long, lethal talons. The world around me pitched and rolled as though I was at sea, the strobing lights a frenzied whirl of color that threatened to consume me until there was nothing left. I carved the claws into the floor, grasping at anything that could anchor me and keep me from floating away in a sea of agony.

"Xander?" I heard a voice call. I forced my eyes open, not realizing I closed them.

Miranda stood inside my cage, then outside of it. She teleported back and forth.

No. Get out of here. I don't want to hurt you.

"Xander," her command sliced through the chaotic fog. I grabbed at the anchor of her authoritative voice and pulled myself toward it.

At last, the tumult eased leaving me shaky and exhausted. As long as I could remember, my flesh had been a battleground of unrelenting agony, leaving me feeling hollow and depleted. I was trapped in a never-ending cycle of suffering. The weight of it suffocates my spirit, fueling a bitter resentment towards a life that seems to revel in my torment.

Miranda had taken several steps back, still well behind the bars. Thank fuck. Both her hands strangled the hilt of her blade. The radiance in her eyes had dimmed, her normally warm brown skin paled several shades.

Fear shone in her eyes. Bitterness swallowed me up as it usually did. I wanted to rip the bars off this cage and impale myself to the wall. Punish myself for losing control.

Good, better she's afraid. It will just give her another reason to run me through.

Still, nausea and disgust filled me. There was no escaping this prison of meat and bone.

Except that wasn't exactly true anymore.

Gritting the words out through my teeth, my voice rougher than before, "I need you to come back here and kill me, every day, until I achieve true death. Based on yesterday, I expect it will take some time."

My eyes were drawn to her sword once more as I sidled closer. Oh gods, I wanted her to kill me, so bad. I could practically taste the edge of the blade.

Please my angel of death. Carve a new fate in my flesh. Cut out the pain from the organ of my heart.

"This is. . ." she seemed to search for the word, "unusual."

I couldn't stop the cackles escaping me then. The sound of my own laughter helped fight off the buzzing in my head. When I finished, I couldn't help but grin at her. Though it probably appeared like I was baring my teeth. "You wield an unusual weapon."

Miranda tipped the blade at me. "Fair point."

Impatient, and unable to wait any longer, I snapped. "Well, do you agree? Will you come down here every day and kill me?"

Miranda's frown deepened. I wanted to lick her cheek up to the frown lines gathered on her forehead. Was that a normal response? I couldn't say anymore.

I bit back the next batch of crazy giggles that threatened to escape me. I needed her focused on the task, not on my crazy. Though the need to climb the bars to swing and rail against them and my miserable fucking existence was overwhelming.

She strode across the room, approaching me with purpose. On instinct, I pressed my chest hard to the bars, so hopeful, I could barely breathe.

Kill me, beautiful.

"Wish granted." Then she stabbed me in the heart for the second time.

In that moment, I fiercely loved her more than anything in my entire damned existence. My lips twisted in satisfaction and pain as they mingled in the most intense manner.

She was so close, I breathed her in with my last breath — bergamot oil and her unique scent — inducing an insatiable hunger. My mouth watered. I almost wished I had a second breath to inhale her one more time.

But that blissful black haze engulfed me.

My last thought was bless the goddess of mercy before me and the invention of bergamot.

CHAPTER
SEVEN

THE BADASS

Every day after I'd completed my security work, I headed down to the god of the dead's basement, and stabbed a god straight through the heart. Then I went home, poured myself a half glass of red wine and called it a day.

After a couple of days, I'd gotten used to the strange ritual. It had become the new central gravity of my life.

Though I never got used to the feelings Xander aroused in me with his intensity and power.

His cerulean eyes said so much more than his lips did. And

if we were speaking the same language, he was saying he wanted the bars between us to disappear along with our clothes.

Usually right at the moment I ran him through, leaving me more than a little confused by the riot of emotions he inspired.

Kill me. Fuck me. Thank you.

A hot shiver raced up my spine. I tried to ignore it. This was a simple job. Nothing more.

While I'd grown use to our strange routine, it was becoming harder to kill Xander. The blade seemed heavier every time I returned. My aim had even failed me. Once I sliced in just to the left of his heart and it took a second strike to finish him off. Embarrassment flooded me, but he never said anything other than the grunt of pain at impact. His expression was only of gratitude and desire.

I was grateful he didn't bring up the mishap.

Nowadays, I brought the blade of bane with me to Sinopolis. I had to keep it on my person at all times, so I started to wear the black duster jacket Vivien gifted me for May twenty-second. She said she probably should have waited for a holiday, but she decided May twenty-second deserved some celebration as well. Yet again, I found myself envious of her whimsical nature.

Vivien said it suited me, and I had to admit that I absolutely loved it. The best part was cheetah print lined the inside of the black vegan leather. She said it was exactly like me. Badass on the outside, extra on the inside.

Considerate friend that she was, Vivien also had a designer add a holster to the inside of the jacket for Bob, so I could hide the sword underneath. No one said anything about my change in attire at work, and I wasn't sure if it was because they were used to strange things happening at Sinopolis, or because I scared everyone.

I asked my number two, Javier, who not only came over from Castlegate hotel with me, but we were also in the special forces unit back in the day. He didn't even look up from the surveillance monitors as he affirmed, they were all, "scared pissless" of me.

Today would be no different. I waved a hand over the buttons of Grim's private elevator to make the secret fourth one appear, and pushed the black circle.

I entered the entry chamber and Xander was there as usual. But instead of his usual positioning, pressed against the bars, eager for me to run him through, today Xander sat further back, mostly covered in shadow. Light from my side of the cage slashed across him, illuminating only his mouth and half of his body. His lean, muscular arms encircled his legs where he sat on the ground.

My ears and face buzzed. Coming down here, still felt like entering a nuclear reactor, but some of the painful sizzle had ebbed. Presumably because I'd been killing off pieces of his power. Soon there would be nothing left to kill.

I'd have nothing left of this except the ghost of his blood on my blade.

Xander still hadn't gotten up.

"Hi," I said awkwardly. Typically, we don't speak. It's enter, stab, leave.

There was a long pause.

"What's in the bag?" he finally asked. Xander's voice seemed raspier than I remember.

In one hand I gripped the blade of bane, and in the other I carried my purple reusable lunch sack. I didn't need two hands to kill him, so I hadn't planned on putting it down.

Wow, I really had adjusted to the weirdness fast.

"Lunch."

I'd planned on walking straight to my car after this and

scarfing down some of the food to ease the hunger pains rumbling in my gut.

"Busy day. I missed my chance to eat." I couldn't keep the exhaustion from my voice. One of the high rollers in the poker room got caught cheating, I found a cocktail waitress skimming money because her abusive scumbag boyfriend pressured her into it, and a rock band partied straight through the morning, trashing a hotel room and terrorizing the staff. It had been a lot for one day.

Not that I couldn't handle it. In fact, with Jamal gone, I welcomed the chaos. I could make order of it. Help the waitress, soothe the staff, and kick the ass of everyone out of line. But admittedly, I worked until I was too tense. There would be no Jamal when I went home to lighten the mood, to tell me what cool new stuff he learned today, or put on some ridiculous cartoon and giggle until I had to join in.

At least I had Vivien and Aaron in the mornings to break things up. Though Vivien was busier these days between helping new vampires and plotting Grim's demise by goose down. The great pillow war raged on.

Over a caffeine and sugar, she victoriously recounted how she jumped Grim while he was in the shower. The bedding popped, and he ended up wet and covered in fluff. He'd been displeased, as she put it. If she weren't immortal, I'd be worried for her life.

I really did envy her whimsy.

In the shadows, Xander's outline nodded. "Busy day? Or hard day?"

We didn't talk like this. We didn't talk at all. "Yes," I answered, in the affirmative to both. The admission added an extra ten pounds of gravity to my body. I was bone tired and hungry as hell. I had to readjust my grip, the sword seeming impossibly heavy as well. Or was I getting weaker?

Was I getting weaker around *him*?

The moment of pause between us was heavy and long.

"Me too," he said in a low voice.

I could hear it. His voice sounded like it had been dragged over a long road of gravel and ash. He was either exhausted, in pain, or both.

He gestured to a chair off to the side of me. "Why don't you take a seat and eat something before we get to business?"

I looked at the chair, then back at him.

"I'd prefer you have all your strength if you are going to kill me properly today," he said. My cheeks heated, knowing he referenced my double stab mishap.

Before I could tell him we should just get on with it, my stomach took that moment to emit an obnoxious gurgle. One corner of his lips curved up.

Though I'd rather stab and run, something told me he also needed a moment before we got to business today.

Before he died today.

Yep, my life was really fucking weird.

"Okay," I conceded, and went to settle in the single metal chair against the wall and opened my lunch tote. I pulled out a container of sliced apples. As I chewed, the awkwardness of the situation began to creep in on me. Usually I don't mind silence, but something about it seemed so wrong right now.

"What *is* your job?" Xander asked, breaking the silence and granting my wish. For a moment I wondered if he was a god who could read my mind.

Pickles, pickles, pickles.

Okay, if he could read my mind, he certainly would have reacted to the barrage of pickles spewing from my brain at him. I figured I was safe.

Swallowing my bit of apple, I said, "I work for Grim. I'm head of his hotel security."

Then I wondered if he knew he was at the base of a hotel. Did he know what a hotel was? He said he'd been imprisoned for a thousand years. Maybe he had no concept of time or space.

"What?" he asked.

"What what?" I asked back.

"You have a look on your face, like you want to ask me something."

Pickles pickles pickles pickles.

Nope, guess he really did just read my expression.

"Do you know what a hotel is?" I asked.

He barked out a laugh. It wasn't like his usual broken, crazy laugh that set my teeth on edge. It was sardonic, and I liked it. "Yes, I know what a hotel is."

"Oh." I crunched into another slice of apple.

"You're still frowning," he said.

My hand instinctively reached up to touch my forehead. "Am I?"

"You have more questions."

I did have more questions. He was all but inviting me to ask them. I shifted in the seat, feeling caught between two desires. "Maybe it's better if we keep this professional."

In the darkness he elongated his arms, stretching them out from his body. He never wore a shirt or footwear, only the same dark loose set of pants. Unlike Grim, his feet didn't weird me out. I needed my boss to fit into an orderly box, that included his feet. But it seemed right for Xander to be like this, half naked and feral. In fact, I couldn't imagine his feet being covered by socks or shoes. They were long and attractive.

Inwardly, I cringed. Sweet baby Jesus, did I have some kind of secret foot fetish going on?

"Keep it professional," he echoed in a lofty tone. "Worried you are going to fall in love with me?"

I was the one to smile this time. "Hardly."

He rocked back and then sprung forward up onto his feet with all the grace of some kind of jungle cat. Deft, silent, and positively lethal. A shockwave of unexpected heat hit me.

He sauntered out from the shadows. "Come on, I'm irresistible. Afterall, I'm a god."

"And just as humble as the rest of the gods I see," I taunted. "Real sexy."

Unfortunately for me, I'd taken another bite of apple and when Xander fully came into view, I inhaled a piece, choking hard. Even as I fought for my very life against that bit of fruit, my heart ripped itself up at the sight of him.

I dropped the bag to the floor. Xander looked positively ill. Deep dark circles surrounded his hollowed-out eyes. His cheeks were sunken, and his normal golden pallor was a sickly grayish green. Fresh deep slices decorated his exposed chest. As if a rabid animal clawed at his chest over and over again. His chest was a mess of exposed muscle. Anyone else would be bleeding out from wounds like that.

"See? I take all the ladies' breath away," he said with a wan smile.

I somehow managed to glare at him even as I coughed violently, tiny apple pieces flying from my mouth. If I were vainer, I'd worry about how I looked spewing little chunks. But this was duty, not pleasure. I wasn't here to impress a god. Just kill him.

When I got a hold of myself, I stood. "What happened to you?"

"I thought you wanted to keep this professional?" he taunted, throwing my words back in my face.

Fuck. He had me there.

Xander's sickly smile widened into a grin. "Your glower is even more appealing than your frown."

"I'm not—"

He interrupted. "I'll save the trouble of defending your ire and tell you that I did this to myself." He waved a hand over his grisly chest.

In less than a heartbeat, he'd thrown me off entirely.

As if some magnet pulled me forward, I took several steps closer to his grotesque form. Seeing him like this pained me in a way I couldn't describe. "Why?"

The mirth bled from his eyes and face, leaving something stoney in its place. "Like I said, it's been a bad day."

"I've had a bad day too, but you don't see me taking a razor to my arm," I said, anger vibrating in my voice.

Xander's face smoothed in surprise. "Are you—are you mad?"

Why did it bother me so much to know he'd torn his own flesh open? Was I just taking the stress of my day out on him? Admittedly, a secret part of myself felt like I was letting off steam by going after him.

"Mad you mutilated yourself? You're fucking right I am. I thought you were a god who'd lived for millennia, not a moody teenager who thinks this is the solution." I waved a hand at his wrecked flesh.

Xander's eyes darkened. An oppressive force closed in around us like a pressure cooker, sealing all of the air inside. His skin seemed to ripple before my eyes, as if he were made of liquid that morphed and changed with every breath we took. My heart pounded in my chest like a galloping horse, and my breathing was rapid and shallow as fear slowly flooded my veins. I could almost taste the electricity in the air around me; feel the danger radiating from his pores.

In the blink of an eye, Xander had morphed before me into a scary, unpredictable god. And that was very, no good news for me.

He snarled and leapt onto the bars, several feet above me. The movement was as fast as it was erratic. He craned his neck at an unnatural angle, continuing to meet my gaze. "How dare you compare my pain to that of some pissant little teenager. You know nothing of pain. You sit there with your perfect neat little life and judge how I handle this shitty existence I'm enslaved too? Sweetheart, you don't know what pain is."

Despite my galloping heart and skittish nerves, I couldn't take that lying down. I met him with an unwavering gaze, and took a step toward the intimidating, unhinged god. "You don't know anything about me. You don't know anything about my pain or my life."

He raised an eyebrow, still sneering at me in a way that made my blood boil. Slowly he slid down the bars, coming closer to my level. "You clean your boots every night, don't you?" Neither of us looked down to confirm what was obvious about my footwear. He went on.

His toes touched the floor, hands dropping from the bars. "Not only is your lunch bag neatly written with your address, that food container is also properly labeled with your name."

"What's wrong with that?" I challenged.

Xander shot me a wicked grin that heated up my blood in a totally different way. "From your head to your toes, you are as neat as a perfectly licked envelope. And I can see inside that envelope you shove all your feelings because you are so busy calculating them. Pain means feeling and you work very hard not to feel, don't you?"

I stiffened. That blow landed as true as an axe splitting a log. "Are you calling me a robot?"

"If the tin heart fits, sweetheart," he purred, stretching his arms up and grabbing the bars over his head. His arm muscles flexed. My stomach turned fluttery and weightless in response.

"Do you even know how to have fun?" The tip of his tongue touched his top lip in a lewd manner.

"Do *you*?" I shot back at a loss for words. The way his satisfied grin deepened; I knew I'd said the exact wrong thing.

"Why don't you open the door, come in here and I'll show you." He scanned me up and down with a look so hot my skin burned. The sudden twinkle in his tired eyes told me he was trying to get under my skin.

It took a minute to fully swallow.

"That's right, sweetheart. Come in here and I'll show you how to lose control." He opened his arms in invitation. "I bet we could have some fun. I could split those pretty legs and lick up your yummy slit until you beg me to fuck you. We could go all night, until you have screamed my name so many times you've forgotten your own. I think that could be *fun*." Slowly, his hand slipped down the front of his pants. His fingers disappeared under the fabric, creeping toward an evident bulge growing in his loose slacks.

My throat turned as dry as a week-old scone, but I still managed to get out the words in my sternest tone. "Watch your language."

Xander's smile was half amusement, half disbelief. "What are you, my mother?"

His hand receded from his pants. Thank god, because it was inspiring far too many images in my head. Ones that made my heart beat faster and generated a liquid heat in my lower belly.

"Maybe that's because I *am* a mother," I shot back. "So I have no problem calling bullshit on someone when needed."

Shock registered on his haggard face, brows climbing up his forehead. "You. *You* are a mother. What are you nineteen?"

My cheeks grew hot. Was I flattered or insulted? Usually, I knew. "No."

He looked at me with renewed interest. "You seem *so* young."

Okay, I was definitely insulted now. I knew I looked damn good, but people tried to underestimate me based on my looks, and youth was one of the many stigmas I had to prove myself against.

The fire gave me enough fuel to push away the strange mixture of arousal to volley back to outrage.

I touched my forehead with the tip of my finger. "Maybe you haven't heard this because you've been a sad old man trapped in a cage, but black don't crack honey. I'll look this good until I'm ninety." If I lived that long. Because this strange banter/fight was more dangerous than I was probably giving it credit.

Sure Miranda, scold a god. Pick a fight with him, this will end well.

A voice in my head assured me, *we can take him.*

At the very least, I should back away out of reach. All he'd have to do is thrust his arms through the bars and snap my neck, rip out my jugular, or. . .or other things he mentioned.

My thighs squeezed together.

Xander's eyes took more of an interest in perusing me from top to bottom. "Black don't crack," he echoed in an amused voice. As if I'd given him a new idea he enjoyed playing with, like a cat batting at a ball of yarn.

His gaze flitted away before meeting mine again. "And what does your husband think of our arrangement?"

Something flashed in his eyes that I couldn't identify. It could have been raw power, or maybe...jealousy?

No that's ridiculous.

"My husband died years ago." I said it as a point of fact, because it was. Jamal was still in diapers when Rashon died serving his country. It hurt. It hurt knowing we'd lost our future, but between both our deployments, Rashon and I never got to know each other on as deep a level as I would have liked. In fact, the pain that should have throbbed in my heart at the thought of him remained silent and still.

"Lucky him." Xander's words were laced with dark jealousy.

Oh no he fucking didn't. What didn't hurt before, suddenly roared to life with pain.

I smacked one of the bars by his head with an open palm. The strike of the cold, hard steel felt good in contrast to the heat of my anger. "You sonofabitch. How dare you say that to a widow."

The god seemed unphased. "I wasn't implying he should be deprived of your wonderful company. I simply meant I am envious of his situation."

Before I could further comment on the inappropriateness of his demeanor, he asked. "How did he pass to the Afterlife?"

The way he phrased it struck me. Since learning Grim was god of the dead, I knew invisible reaper dogs fetched the souls of the dead and transported them to the afterlife. Which meant that's where Rashon went. It was both comforting and unnerving to know that now.

I stuck my chin up. "He died on foreign soil, serving his country."

"A hero's death then," Xander said bitterly.

"What is your goddamn problem?" How dare he make light of the sacrifice my husband made, of the sacrifice his family had to endure?

Xander's body seemed to fill the space around him, and I wasn't quite sure if it was his physical body or his power doing it. "My problem is I have no such luxury as your late husband. My problem is I am stuck in this prison."

My gaze naturally went to the bars.

"Not that prison, sweetheart." He gave me a humorless grin. Trailing his hand over the open wounds of his chest, they traveled down the pronounced muscles of his abdomen before his thumb hooked into the edge of his pants. "This prison."

While he was making a rather gruesome point, I couldn't help but follow the track of his hand too closely. The front of his slacks dipped under his thumb, exposing a vee of muscle that led to his groin.

His 'prison' stirred things in me. Things that threatened my good sense. His lewd suggestions sent them rioting in a way I hadn't felt for years, and I resented it. I prided myself on good sense. But still, my nerve endings strained, wanting to touch his solid muscle, and take his idea of 'fun' for a test ride.

He was oblivious of my sudden shift in mood as his expression darkened with loathing.

"Live a thousand years of power and pain in a cage and let me know what you do then, sweetheart," he growled.

Instead of acknowledging his point or my sudden arousal, I shot back, "Don't call me sweetheart."

He cocked his head to the side. "Again, are you worried about falling in love with me if I call you sweetheart? Afraid you'll believe you *are* my sweetheart."

I shot back a vicious grin as I pulled Bob out from my duster. "This just makes it all the easier to kill you, beast boy."

He neared the bars but didn't press his chest against them like usual. "Beast boy, is it?"

How had our conversation escalated so quickly? Part of me was excited by the way he needled me. Was I always secretly looking for a fight?

Xander puckered his lips and sent me an air kiss. "Then why don't you just do it, my little badass."

I couldn't decide which I hated more: his nickname or the

way it made the liquid heat intensify at my center. Bob plunged into the already broken flesh on his chest.

"Wish granted," I said through bared teeth.

I yanked the blade out, and Xander smiled at me. I couldn't help but smile back just before he fell and died...again.

As I gathered up my sack lunch, something light and almost whimsical fluttered in my chest. Like a hoard of butterflies taking flight. The heaviness of the day no longer clung to my body or mind. There was satisfaction from a day of hard work that wasn't there before. From the security work, or killing Xander? That question could fuck a girl up.

But not as much as the excited anticipation I felt at the prospect of killing him tomorrow.

CHAPTER
EIGHT

THE BEAST

W hen I woke from my temporary death, the smell of bergamot clung to the inside of my nose. For all these years I'd been obsessed with one thing. Death.

But now I had two obsessions.

Getting to my feet, I smoothed my hand over my chest, over the healed sword wound. I retreated into the shadows of the cage until I reached the back door. Pushing it open, I descended the stone steps to my chambers.

I wanted to see her again. I wanted to breathe her in. I wanted to touch Miranda's skin and feel her warmth. No, fuck that. I wanted her hot and out of control.

I meant what I said. I would be happy to school Miranda in fun, in exchange for her deadly services. That is, if I weren't worried I'd go crazy and kill her.

I shoved down my pants, kicking them away as I grew hard. I followed one of the rocky paths to the pool of water. Slowly, I stepped into the cool water, immersing myself. As soon as I touched it, the water bubbled, heating up from my energy. I sunk in until it reached my chin. My hand fisted around my cock and I groaned.

The fantasy of Miranda falling apart under me played over in my mind as I stroked myself. Could I fuck away her worries, the inner workings of her mind? Could I make her eyes glaze over, and kiss her with such bruising force her already full lips would turn swollen from my abuse? I wanted her screaming and begging, mindless with need.

She'd fight me on it. She'd fight me every step of the way, vying for control and the upper hand. It was her nature. My hand moved faster along my straining, rigid flesh. Pleasure rippled through my spine, gathering in my balls.

Again, I had to question if I was reacting to her because I'd been trapped in solitude for so long. Was this about any morsel of flesh I could get my hands on?

No. I'd seen Grim and the other gods through the years. I'd even met Grim's firecracker of a woman. But next to my angel of death, the sekhor was a mere muted spark.

Miranda was delectable in her own unique way. She shimmered and shone like a diamond and was even stronger than the precious gem.

An orgasm built at the base of my spine as I furiously

pumped my engorged flesh. My pleasure wove in with my anger and bitterness. Two fires fueling each other. Dueling for release in my body and release from this existence. And now I felt imprisoned by my need for Miranda. She trapped me in a way I hadn't expected. I wanted her. I wanted her all to myself. A monster taking his maiden back to his lair where I would treat her like a queen. But it would still be a prison and I would still be the beast.

Something crackled at the back of my mind, my senses overloading with power. The water glowed blue from my energy.

I panted as images tumbled through my fractured mind. Tying her up, making her feel as trapped as I was. Before touching, kissing every inch of her soft, luxurious skin. Tasting the bitterness of her scowl, until I coaxed out her sweetness, her screams for more. The world would splinter around us as I thrust home into her inviting body. I'd be surrounded by her strength, grounding her even as her foundation shook to pieces.

A rock shaking roar exploded from me when my release reached its precipice. The lights flickered. I released myself over the edge of the boiling spring.

As soon as I was spent, the vision swirling in my head shifted into a nightmare. Under me, Miranda was no longer a willing participant. Her face was a mask of horror, terrified I would hurt her.

The lights continued flickering, as if scared for her.

This time, another roar, more powerful yet mournful ruptured from my throat. I longed for death more than ever before if only to escape the visions of Miranda's fear and disgust that circled my brain.

I burst from the spring, water surging up with me in a

powerful blast. My rational side disappeared as pain engulfed me. Rage and agony pulsated like a pack of clawed demons gleeful to torment.

Then my agony folded over like a piece of paper, again and again, thickening with layers of Miranda's fear, her revulsion of me.

Her sword carved through my flesh over and over again as the landscape shifted into sun baked black sands, then into the searing yellow light of the cradle of life. Tumbling, flying in agony until there was no beginning or end.

But it did finally end. Eventually, I found myself blinking on the floor. My muscles were stiff and frozen. I hadn't died, but I was trapped in a body struck by rigor mortis.

Getting up slowly with great deliberation, I grunted through the pain to stand. I pushed the hair back from my face, taking everything in.

Fuck. My chambers were destroyed.

Usually I could make it to the cage before losing all control, but the episode had come on so quick. I hadn't the wherewithal to get to the barred room. I'd found Miranda carved enough power off me that I couldn't turn berserker even if I wanted to for hours. But the desire I had for her, along with the fear-fueled hallucinations, pushed me over the edge. The thought of hurting her was unbearable.

I limped over to the wall with a control panel. I pressed the button Timothy referred to as "room service."

This is when I would normally wallow in the broken mess I'd created, let myself stew in it. The shadow images of Miranda in pain haunted me like dancing demons, refusing to give me relief. I needed to see her. I needed to know she was okay. That my craziness hadn't somehow stretched out beyond these bars and hurt her.

Miranda would be back tomorrow. I might be on my way out with every thrust of her blade, and I was determined to die like a man, not a beast.

THE BADASS

In the elevator, my heart quickened, and a hot flash of excitement possessed me. Our verbal sparring yesterday had opened up something in me. I wanted more. I wanted to talk to Xander more, fight with him more. All day, I'd been thinking about the scarred, broken god and his sharp tongue.

He illustrated a little too well what other things that tongue could do. I dreamt of the image he painted, waking up with a sheen of perspiration on me, and an insistent ache between my thighs. But I didn't have time to give myself any relief.

I didn't need it. I'm fully in control of my baser desires, I told myself. If I was being honest, my being able to hold off my own needs was a point of pride. I only broke down a couple times a year and pulled out a vibrating aide to help me release the sexual tension I'd stored up.

The moment I entered the basement, I knew something was wrong. My arousal evaporated instantly as I dropped into my body, coming into the moment. My hand automatically gripped Bob's hilt. The energy of the room was wrong. It pressed against my bones like a heavy cold cloud. Something crackled in the darkness, a lethal power that could destroy me. My mouth dried and sweat popped out on my forehead, fear flooded my instincts, forming a sour patina on my tongue.

Every nerve-ending shouted at me to back right up into the open elevator and leave. The fragility of my humanity was all too real right now.

"Xander?" I called out. The word came out hoarse. The air grated against my throat with something toxic and raw.

Something panted in the shadows of his cage. But whatever was making the sound couldn't be Xander. It didn't sound human, it sounded like an animal. My eyes tracked the movement of the something in the cage. The outline was so much bigger than Xander's.

Oh my god, had something gotten in? Had it hurt Xander?

The elevator doors closed behind me, and I took a couple steps into the room. He had to be alright. He couldn't be dead. Not until I killed him anyway.

"Xander," I tried to call out again, but it came out even weaker than last time.

The thing inside the cage growled; it was a guttural,

menacing tone that emerged from the depths of what had to be a monstrous throat.

Goosebumps broke out on my skin, and ice chilled straight to the marrow of my bones. My adrenaline pumped so hard and fast; I could barely take a breath.

"Xander?" This time it was a whisper.

"Get out." The words ground out like gravel. Then a deep monstrous cry of pain pierced the air. Each sound made me recoil as if I'd bitten on tin foil.

Jesus, it wasn't some new beast, it was Xander in there. I neared the bars, a half inch of my fear melted away. "Xander. What's happening?"

A strange cackling laughter cracked through the air like a whip lashing against my senses. "He's crazy. He's crazy. He's crazy."

I could barely discern it was his voice. The pitch shot up and down like a roller coaster. "Eat his heart. Wet his lips. The trees aren't happy. The trees aren't happy, so we are all angry here. We are blacks and reds and blues. All of us here."

My instincts ripped me in two. I was painfully aware of how much danger I was in. If I valued my life, I'd get the hell out of here. I'd go find Timothy, or Grim maybe. But the other half of me couldn't. His pain, his power was palpable. It grated against me like course sandpaper, but Xander was the one at the epicenter.

Xander's growls and monstrous cries tore at my soul, but I couldn't leave him like this. I forced myself closer to the cage.

His rambling cut off suddenly.

Soft whispers began. All the hairs on my forearms stuck straight up as if someone were speaking directly against them.

"She thinks, she thinks she can. She thinks you won't. She thinks you won't, but you will."

"You will do what?" I asked, carefully. If he came closer, I could kill him and stop whatever this was. Help carve a piece of his power off and release him from this madness.

The whispers layered like a hundred demons, scaring me even more. "She thinks you won't eat her up, yum yum, like a dish of meat in the bowl where the tongue licks and ticks and licks."

I didn't understand. Maybe there was nothing to understand, but I kept thinking if I kept him talking, I could crack the code.

"Xander," I tried to keep my voice from shaking. My hand wasn't nearly as steady. "I need you to come to the bars so I can. . .help you." I had to get through to Xander, to break through the madness and reach the man I knew was still there. The thought of killing him in his current state made my stomach churn, but it was a necessary evil. I would do anything to save him, even if it meant taking his life.

He whined out the words like some metal machine, "The blade doesn't like my blood. The blade doesn't want to bite me."

"Xander," I said softly as if speaking to a child. "Please come here."

A cackle of laughter filled the air, and I had to resist covering my ears in protection. Then it stopped.

A creature slammed into the bars, bursting into supernatural blue light. My mouth parted in a silent scream as my chest seized up.

It was Xander, but not. I recognized only a trace of his likeness. His body had expanded into a massive eight-foot monster. His skin turned into black lava rock but cracks in it revealed a supernatural blue glow that also radiated hatefully from his eyes. Slate gray hair flowed upward as if underwater, defying gravity. The azure glow wafted off the top of his head and surrounded his body like an aura. The power was electric, painful, and I had to close my eyes against the burn.

My skin sizzled.

A massive boom forced my eyes open. The beast in the cage slammed against the bars. Arms reached toward me with massive rocky fists that opened and closed. He was trying to get at me.

Fear paralyzed me. I couldn't sort out all the painful sensations in my body. It felt like I was being irradiated. And Xander's new form made me want to ball up and scream for help. But instead, I gritted my teeth.

The monstrous voice called out my name before he slammed into the bars again. The room shuddered and the lights went out. My stomach dropped out of my body as I was plunged into darkness. Only Xander's blue energy illuminated the room. It wafted out toward me like inviting hands of death.

Hands shaking, I swallowed hard and took a step back. Every primal part of me wanted to scream and run. His ancient uncontrollable power pummeled into me.

I needed to kill him. I needed to kill his power before it hurt me, or anyone else.

Forcing my feet forward, I started toward the beast. The monster slammed against the bars again, his long, muscle roped arms reaching for me. "Miranda."

This time the voice still held all the menace and danger as before, but underneath it, I could swear I heard him pleading with me.

If I got any closer, he'd be able to grab me.

The Xander-monster said he'd eat me up. Would he try to kill me? Every instinct told me he would crush me before licking the meat from my bones. Xander wasn't just powerful, he was out of his mind.

I could leave. Or at least, if the elevator didn't work, I could hide in there until it started working again, then run home with my tail between my legs. Later I'd come back and give him what he wanted, after he calmed.

"Miranda," he pleaded again. That sonorous demonic voice was so sorrowful it ripped at my insides.

The power wasn't only painful to me, it was agony for him. And I couldn't leave him like this.

"Xander," I said, using my best authoritative voice. Blood rushed in my ears so loud, I'm pretty sure I screamed it. "Stop!"

What sounded like tumbled gravel came from his throat, but he stilled. His arms were still outstretched.

I drew closer.

You got this. You got this, a voice softly in my head chanted. For once, my sword felt light and sure in my hands.

When I stepped inside the space between his arms, my alarm shot through the roof. I was in the most vulnerable position possible. I looked up into his illuminated blue eyes and found agony in their blaze. Despite my fear, his arms remained still.

"Kill me," he gurgled.

"Wish granted," I whispered, before thrusting Bob into his chest.

Xander threw back his head, an excess of electric sparks shooting up and out from his eyes. The sparks landed and prickled painfully on my skin. Releasing the blade, I retreated back across the room, fleeing the white-hot energy.

He crumpled to the ground, blue energy dimming where the sword still protruded from his chest. The harsh lights in the room flickered back to life with an audible hum.

Suddenly the explanation for all the mysterious brown outs in the city became clear to me. It was him. He was causing them.

I neared the cage again, needing to retrieve Bob. I crouched down and stuck my arm through the bars. My fingers reached out toward the hilt, but a blackened hand intercepted mine. My heart shot up and lodged itself in my throat as he gripped my hand in his hard, rocky hand. I met his tortured gaze even as the blue blaze faded, turning them human again. Intensity shone from those cerulean depths. "Thank you," he rasped.

His head fell back with a thud. Xander's eyes remained open and sightless. I held his cold, lifeless hand as he fully returned to the shape of a man.

I don't know how long I stayed crouched there with him, but at some point, I became aware of the tears on my cheeks. Xander was dead. For a little while, anyway. But I didn't want to leave him there all alone. His torment, his pain, his gratitude and then relief, they all seared their way into me like a brand.

No one should have to endure that much pain.

The stark reality that he'd been caged down here for millennia, unable to control his power or his pain hit me like a brick in the face. I'd known, but. . .I hadn't truly understood until now.

Eventually, I gently laid his hand down and straightened. My knees were stiff from crouching for so long. I pulled the sword out from his torso, making his body jerk. A sick feeling lurched in my gut. I tucked Bob back into my coat and wiped the tears from my face before heading toward the elevator.

My body started to shake. I needed a bath so hot it could melt my bones. But it wouldn't erase what I saw, what I felt.

I was inside his storm of torment, terrified it would swallow me up. And for a brief moment, I was inclined to let it. Just so he wouldn't have to be in the vortex by himself.

I wrapped my arms around myself, suddenly more scared of myself and my feelings for whatever *this* was.

But no matter what I felt, I had to return tomorrow. I could only wonder, would I face the god or the monster?

CHAPTER
TEN

THE BADASS

"What's wrong, boss?"

I jerked up at Javier's question. He'd turned from the security monitors to face me.

"What? Nothing."

This morning we'd already worked security details for the high roller guests that would show up tonight, as well as helped track down a woman's miniature schnauzer that got loose in the hotel. Everything was perfectly ordinary. Except today I felt zero satisfaction in bringing order to the ongoings of Sinopolis.

Javier's serene eyes studied me closely. With a closed mouth he licked his teeth, causing the small mustache on his upper lip to push out for a moment. Javier was born in Mexico, but his parents managed to get into the US when he was five years old. He never lost his accent though.

More often than not, Javier had a steadying silence about him. It was that steadying silence that got me through our tour in Afghanistan. It was his strong, silent presence that gave me a modicum of strength when Rashon passed and I still had to take care of my toddler. Javier showed up at my door every morning, made breakfast for us, and watched Jamal until I could pull myself out of bed, which for several months, was never before eleven am.

"You steady?" he asked.

It was our code. When shit got rough, too rough, we checked in. The code was sacred and unbreakable. No lies, no bullshit.

Was I steady? After yesterday, seeing Xander like that...it shook me. I could admit that.

Because he scared the shit out of you with his god-likeness?

I'd seen it before. Grim and the other gods all had one. I'd personally seen my boss transform into a massive jackal monster to fight off other gods. So, this should not be that big of a deal.

But it was.

I'd seen Xander completely out of control. I saw his pain, his power, his misery, and it shook me to my core. That's why he was caged.

No surprise when I got home, my neighbor emerged to inform me we'd experienced yet another brownout. She was getting sick and tired of it and went out to buy a generator right then.

My insides quaked as I stepped inside my dark, hot house. Without the A/C the Vegas night heat seeped inside.

How many times had I also been inconvenienced by the brownouts since moving to this area?

But now I knew what the cause of them were. Xander's suffering.

Of course, I'd been terrified of him. Grim was scary but Xander was beyond, what with his power beating on me, trying to sear the flesh away from my bones. The pain had robbed him of all sense and he was an animal.

My fingers slowly curled into my palm as I thought of how long I held his cold, dead hand. I wanted him to wake up. I needed him to wake up.

What if that had been the last blow that took him out?

I realized I knew too little about him. The god I was killing nightly.

I'd wanted to keep things professional, but was I really just trying to protect myself from emotionally attaching to Xander?

The way he groaned out my name in a plea, begging me to kill him, still tore at me.

What had I really gotten myself into? I decided then and there I was going to find the fuck out.

"I'm steady," I finally said to Javier.

He nodded, accepting my answer and the amount of time it took to consider before answering.

The door to our office opened and slammed shut. I was shocked to find Vivien standing there, dark circles under her bloodshot eyes, her back pressed against the door as if barring anyone who wanted to enter.

"What are you doing up? It's daylight?"

While Javier wasn't nearly as entrenched in the business of

immortals as I'd been, he'd been privy to Vivien fanging out among other strange occurrences. He handled it like a champ. Which also made it easier for us to work as an effective team in running a not-so-normal hotel.

"I know, I know," she said breathlessly, her eyes wide and wild with fear. "But I'm on the run, and you gotta hide me."

Javier and I exchanged a glance, both of us preparing ourselves for whatever catastrophe was about to come knocking on our door.

I got to my feet and took hold of her shoulders to steady her. "What's happened?"

"H-he was judging someone's soul, and I'd already snuck into his chambers and was in hiding."

My fingers tightened on her. "Vivien, you didn't."

Despite my highest hopes, she nodded her head. "Right as he was about to cast judgement—you know, the part where he whips out his big magic scales and weighs the heart of someone against the feather of truth—I exploded from behind the pillar and swatted him right in the face with a pillow."

I scrubbed my face with my hands while I heard a scoff from behind me. That was the closest I'd heard Javier to giggling.

"It's not funny, Javier," I said. "She's led him right to us."

The small smile on his face vanished.

"What fucking possessed you?" I demanded of my insane friend.

"The need to win?" she shrugged. "And I knew he would have to stay there and finish out the judgement of the soul and couldn't follow me."

"Yeah, not right away. But he'll be done eventually," I said, pointing out the huge hole in her plan. It won't be long before he surfaces from his ancient Egyptian chambers below this very hotel. And when he comes, he'll come hunting for the troublemaker.

Her eyebrows scrunched together, her lower lip popping out as she grabbed me by the shoulders, giving me a slight shake. "I get that now! I didn't think it through. What else is new? You've got to hide me."

I suddenly knew why people got the urge in old movies to slap someone who was hysterical.

The room suddenly got darker, like someone dimmed the lights to fifty percent. My eye caught on the bits of black smoke that seeped in from under the doorway.

"In the utility locker," I said, immediately rushing to unlock it and push aside our sensitive equipment to make room for my friend. It was well over eight feet tall, and was organized in a way that she could easily fit.

Vivien didn't hesitate, cramming herself in. "Lock it behind me," she ordered in a harsh whisper.

"Duh," I said, shutting the door in her face and locking it again.

A knock came a moment before the door opened. I'd only just slipped into my chair as Javier easily became engrossed with our work.

Fear prickled the back of my neck, causing all the fine hairs to stand straight up.

"Where is she?" a low, inhuman voice grumbled.

I swiveled around, my face cleared of any and all emotion.

"Mr. Scarapelli, nice to see you. Are you here to check in on the ongoings of security?"

My boss was already a dark hulking mass in his black suit, but he seemed bigger right now. Black smoke poured off his shoulders as if he was literally seething.

"Where is she?" he repeated.

I casually toyed with my pen. "Where is who, sir?"

"Where is my wife?" he said the last word through gritted teeth.

My eyebrows knitted in apparent confusion. "Why, it's daylight. I imagine she's up in the penthouse fast asleep. She's a vampire."

He opened his mouth as if he were going to yell at me, but then his jaw clicked closed.

Instead, his words came out delicate as glass, like if he bit down on them too hard they'd crunch under the pressure. "I was in the middle of determining whether someone's soul should either be admitted access to the Afterlife or condemned to Amit where their soul would be consumed and destroyed. A very serious matter. When I was attacked by my wife. It was upsetting to say the least. Now please answer carefully when I ask again, where is my wife?"

Javier's face gave away absolutely nothing. As if he'd never done anything his entire life. Like before Grim entered, all he'd been doing was sitting here, since the moment he was born. Not touching anything, just being.

I mimicked his expression.

"Haven't seen her," I said.

Grim continued to scrutinize the two of us, but we stared placidly back.

Finally, he said, "Then can you please explain why there are five reaper dogs currently in this room?"

"What are reaper dogs?" Javier asked.

I turned to him. "They fetch the souls of the dead and take them to the Afterlife, to Amit the crocodile god who eats souls, or to Grim for judgement. We can't see them because we aren't dead."

"I see," he said, nodding his head.

Our conversation was casual and lofty, a contrast to the intensity of the god demanding answers from the doorway.

Javier turned to Grim. "No dead people in here."

Only undead, I thought to myself.

Grim let out a huff, the black smoke having reduced to wisps coming off his shoulders. "As my security team, I expect you to inform me of the location and ongoings of people in this hotel."

He was pulling the "I'm the boss" card. But our duties were to protect the ongoings of operations above ground. His antechamber of judgement was below the hotel and out of our jurisdiction.

"Of course, sir," I acknowledged.

"Always," Javier agreed.

Grim's gaze bounced back and forth between us for another minute before he turned and shut the door behind him. The lights in the room instantly brightened, and it suddenly felt like I could breathe again.

While Grim adored his wife beyond measure and would never truly hurt her, I could only imagine the special brand of revenge he will exact when he finally catches her.

A muffled voice came from inside the utility cabinet. "Thanks guys."

CHAPTER
ELEVEN

THE BEAST

"Who are you?"

I looked up from where I sat in the corner of my cage. After last night, I hadn't expected Miranda to ever return. Yet I dragged my ass into the cage, prepared to make my disappointment all the worse.

Miranda couldn't see me, where I was hidden in shadow. I liked it that way. I liked the shroud around me as I saw my personal angel of death shine under the bright florescent light.

The fierce yet compassionate look in her eye made my breath catch. The badass had returned.

She'd seen me lose control, saw the beast I truly was. It both sickened and disgusted me. I'd never felt this way before. The comings and goings of my sanity and power were what they were. Yet around Miranda, I wanted her to see. . .me. I wanted to be a man around her.

A strange feeling swirled in my chest. It made me feel vulnerable and powerful at the same time. But I was always fucking vulnerable and powerful. Whereas she stood before me, as perfect as any goddess. Dare I say, more so.

"I'm no one," I finally answered.

"They wouldn't put *no one* in a cage. What kind of god are you?"

My earlier thoughts echoed. I wanted to be a man around her. Not a god. But I was what I was.

Pushing to my feet, the usual cold bitterness about my situation spread like an infection from my heart.

"I am the kind of god you should kill." I pressed my chest against the bars.

Miranda didn't move. As the tension thickened, her gaze remained unyielding, a defiant spark igniting within her eyes. She was dissecting every nuance of my fractured being. This mortal was always thinking, always calculating like some kind of threat machine. But I wondered if she ever just *was*. Was there a moment she was relaxed, simply in the moment?

Suddenly I craved to see that. I craved to yank her scheming mind into the present. Make her see me, really see me. No. The god I used to be wasn't good enough. I wanted to *become* something new for her.

"Tell me," she requested in a quiet voice.

It was the softness in her tone that snapped my barrier like a twig.

"I once was the god of the seas and oceans." My words came out hoarse, as they were laden with the heaviness of the past. "I ruled the tides. My most favored was the Mediterranean." My heart squeezed painfully with aching and longing. "I brought balance and bounty to everyone with my oceans."

"Like Poseidon?"

I couldn't keep my lip from curling. "Yes, that is a name I've been called, though I never sported a white beard and trident. The myth spiraled far away from the man," I held open my arms. "Originally, my worshippers knew me as Nun."

Miranda snorted. Her eyes flew wide as she clapped a hand over her mouth. "I'm sorry."

"What?"

"It's nothing."

I scowled. "It's not nothing. You are clearly on the verge of some kind of fit." Her outburst and the way she covered her mouth was highly abrupt.

She shook her head, her palm back over her mouth.

"Miranda." I drew her name out in a dangerous tone.

With great reluctance, she dropped her hand. "It's just I'm surprised you didn't tell me your name was Nun earlier."

I cocked my head to the side.

"Nunyabusiness," she added. The grin on her face was as absurd as it was infectious. She burst into laughter. Waving a hand, she tried to get control of herself. "I'm sorry, that's my son talking through me. Or maybe Vivien. It's ridiculous. I think it's a sign I'm crumbling under all the pressure."

Her laugh. I'd never heard a real laugh from her. It was like being kissed by a thousand butterflies and warmth spread through my lower belly.

I didn't join her, but I watched her, drinking in this new side of her like it was some kind of rare liquor. And I was intoxicated by it.

We fell into silence as her laughter trailed off.

Composing herself, she got back to business. "So Nun, why are you down here?"

The utterance of my true name acted as a catalyst, unleashing a surge of raw, agonizing power that ripped through my body like a bolt of lightning.

I gripped the steel bars to brace myself. The air vibrated painfully around me, threatening to send me over the edge. If anyone didn't need a super charge, it was me.

"Please," I said through bared teeth, "do not use my ancient name. Call me Xander."

I caught a flicker of surprise in her eyes, a subtle widening and a brief parting of her lips, as if my unleashed magic had taken her off guard.

Me too, sweetheart.

Trying to sound calmer and more reasonable, I explained, "The old names still hold power, and as you know, I have an excess of that. In ancient times, whenever gods became too powerful, we were forced to change our name and move to another locale. It upset the balance. Eventually, Osiris forbid any of us from being worshipped." I cracked my neck to the side with a loud snap.

Though now that I think of it, a couple days ago and such a slip would have sent me into a raging blackout. She'd slowly been carving slices off of my power, and with each jab the pain was a little less, and I was a little more in control.

She frowned. "I wasn't worshipping you."

I'll show you how you can worship me, sweetheart.

While I could not take her fealty and prayers, I wanted to make her moan and scream to the heavens as I fell to my knees before her.

My hands slid up and down the smooth metal while thinking of her warm, pliable body. Miranda tracked the movement, her mouth parting slightly. For a moment, I thought I caught a trace of lust in her eyes, but it was gone in an instant.

I dropped my arms and took a couple steps away. "To answer your question as to how I got here, I died of course."

"How?" She neared the bars once again.

"By the hands of my enemy." A snarl sprang to my lips.

"Was he a vampire? A sekhor?"

I shook my head. "He was another god, a sun god. He burned me to death."

"Who was it?" Miranda suddenly asked in a demanding tone. "Is he here? In Vegas? Running one of the hotels while you sit down here and rot in pain?"

When I looked up at her, I saw fire in her eyes. A smile tugged at the corner of my lips.

"No. He's long dead and gone." I nodded to her. "By the very blade you hold in your hand there."

Miranda studied her sword with renewed interest, as if she could see the ghost of my nemesis there.

My tone turned dark as I paced along the edge of my cage. "He was insane, out of his mind, the power hungry son of a bitch. I tried to warn the others, but no one believed me. I told them he would burn everything to the ground until he was the last one standing." I opened my mouth to say his name, but then closed it shut. Ancient names held too much power, even though he'd been vanquished by the very blade I was trying to end my existence on. The irony was not lost on me. It was like he was still here, sending me to my death for a second time. Winning after he was long dead and gone.

"I faced him alone, and we battled. I tried to drown him, he boiled my seas, and in the end, he was the victor."

I fell silent, the echo of my last words lingering in the air. Then, with a sigh, I continued, "But my death was the catalyst for the uprising against him. Timothy regaled me with the events after my godly essence returned to the cradle of life. Gods, fae, and man fought him alike, until he was finally vanquished with the blade of bane."

Miranda had listened intently, but now she asked. "But why are you here? Why are you like this?"

I shrugged. "Like I said, I was killed and returned to the cradle of life. But my repose was cut short. I don't know why. I don't know how. It was far too soon. I had not lain long enough."

Miranda expanded on the issue. "Gods need to lay in there for years, even hundreds of years before they can emerge again."

I nodded. "At first, our energies are too volatile which is why we must rest until we are in control again."

"But Vivien called Grim out from the cradle within a matter of days and he wasn't...out of control. Or at least not after a while."

I stopped my pacing, my heart thumping wildly with anger over the injustice. I knew he'd been revived along with some of the details. "Indeed," I said in a dark voice. "He did not suffer the same effects as me." My words came out crisp and bitter.

"Why?"

I shrugged, trying to bury my anger and resentment in indifference. "Who knows? Perhaps he is more controlled than me. Perhaps I am being punished."

"Is that what you think?" She came within arm's reach.

I stepped back up to the bars again, inhaling her scent. It both calmed and infuriated me. I wanted her. I could never have her, if for nothing other than the fact I was a monster.

"Look at me, Miranda," I said, my words harsh. "Do you see where I am? I am far from any ocean because my simple presence makes them boil. Grim moved to the desert of North America to help sequester me. I am kept behind bars. There is nothing but endless pain and solitude for me. I am not an omniscient god, but I understand punishment when I'm in the midst of it. Osiris cannot or will not account for my current state. So perhaps some even larger entity rules us all and saw fit to make me suffer. Perhaps my enemy is still somehow pulling the strings on my pain long after his demise. Either way, will you do me the kindness of running me through and giving me a modicum of relief until I am finally dead and gone for good." It was then I realized I'd yelled the last bit.

Miranda's lip trembled as she shrank away from me.

At first, I thought it was my power flaring, hurting her. But no, I hadn't unleashed anything for once. She was simply experiencing some strong emotion. From the look in her eyes, I couldn't guess if it was pity, fear, or maybe disgust. I was a monster last night, but most of all, I hated the bitter creature I was right now. It almost made me long to return to my gnarled, deformed god-likeness so she wouldn't see me like this.

Just as I was about to retreat to the shadows, Miranda stepped even closer. A mere inch separated us. A shaking hand raised up. My brow furrowed as she reached through the bars and ran her fingers through my hair. A hard lump formed in my throat, and it was as if someone tightened screws in my chest. Both sensations loosened at her touch, and I swallowed hard.

Fuck. When was the last time I'd been touched in affection? Had I ever?

A bottomless chasm opened in my chest even as her touch softened the hardest parts of me.

I drew in a shuddering breath as long forgotten sensations overwhelmed me. The warmth of flesh. The unique healing power it possessed when pressed against another's. Immortals may possess magic, but did mortals understand the power of touch?

The soft pads of her fingertips grazed my scalp. The sensation threatened to pull me under, drown me. I could drown in her. In the solace she somehow traced into my mind with the scrape of her short nails.

What would it be like to feel her touch all over? To hold her warm, pliant body to mine? To smooth away the worries from her troubled mind?

Her hand dropped away, and my insides railed at the loss as a deep sadness consumed me from the inside out. It was not meant to be. It could never be. There were only two fates for me. Existence and pain. Or death and oblivion. But Miranda would live.

She withdrew her sword. "Wish granted," she said.

The painful strike of the sword was a welcome sensation after she stopped touching me. And it helped cut up my rush of affection and need for Miranda. I wanted more. So much more.

I couldn't remember the last time I wanted more. I've only wanted less, less breath, less life. But those enchanting fucking eyes made me want to drop to my knees and promise her anything she wanted as long as she touched me again like that, looked at me like this. Like she gave a fuck about me.

CHAPTER
TWELVE

THE BADASS

The next morning, I bought a redeye from Aaron — a large cup of coffee with an espresso shot thrown in on top— and sat at my usual table at Perkatory.

Aaron was hard at work, steaming milk and pulling shots for the long line of bleary-eyed guests who stayed up way too late last night, indulging in all their vices.

Vivien wasn't back from her evening yet. I finally broke down and texted our group thread after waiting for ten minutes.

You coming, Viv?

Ugh. I can't today. I'm dealing with the BS.

These days, BS was synonymous for bullshit *and* blood suckers.

What now?

The dot dot dot of her texting appeared for a long time before the message downloaded.

One of the new baby vamps is having an emotional breakdown. I've been here most of the night trying to assure her immortality isn't the worst thing in the world. Hard when she has a husband and kids. Had to hold the bitch back with my vamp powers to keep her from turning them too. Have a dollop of whipped cream on your coffee in my honor.

I swallowed hard. I couldn't even begin to imagine the trauma of being bitten and turned immortal without having a say in it.

But maybe it was for the best she wasn't here. I'd been warring with myself on what or what not to share.

How could I tell her I couldn't help but reach into the beast's cage and touch him? How could I tell her I couldn't figure out the monster, the man, or the god? How could I allow myself to share the excitement and anticipation fluttering in my stomach at the prospect of seeing him again tonight? It seemed so. . .silly? Awkward? Bizarre?

Don't worry about it, I wrote Vivien back. *Take care of baby vamps. That's more important.*

After another dot dot dot. *More importantly, after my shower attack, Grim used his powers to float pillows to surround me before they bombarded me. That sonofabitch. I told him no powers allowed. Though now I'm thinking about mind controlling all baby vamps to attack him with pillows.*

A smile threatened to disrupt the firm line of my lips. Aaron barked out a laugh. People were still waiting for coffee, but he'd clearly read the message on our group thread too. We traded a knowing look across the room. She was crazier than a squirrel's nuts, but we loved her.

The clack of heels against the black marble floors jerked my attention away from my thoughts. A figure rounded the high wall of lush plants. A frothy pink robe, lined in feathers, fluttered all around a woman who looked like a pinup model from the 1940s. Flaxen blonde curls fell in a soft cloud around her perfectly beautiful cream face. The woman was the definition of femininity, and I'd met her before. The goddess, Hathor, otherwise known as Bianca, seemed to be on the hunt for someone or something.

When her crystalline blues alighted on me, I knew she'd found her target. My fingers curled around my coffee cup. Uh oh.

Before I could even guess as to why she was looking for me, Bianca floated into the seat across from me. The air carried her heavenly fragrance, a blend of cotton candy sweetness intertwined with the gentle essence of blooming flowers.

"There you are, Miranda. I'm so glad I found you," she said with a tight smile. The goddess was normally the picture of ease, but there was a tension around her eyes. As if she'd been up worrying all night.

"How can I help you?" I asked, putting my business voice on. Bianca owned the Parisienne hotel further down the strip. This could be a hotel matter, but the twist in my stomach told me it wasn't.

"Miranda," she said my name again as if preparing both of us for what she had to say. "It is urgent I speak with you about your. . .recent activities."

"Recent activities?" My gut clenched as a guilty conscience kicked up. But no. There's no way she could know the feelings I'd been having recently, and there was even less of a chance she would care whether or not I was experiencing some kind of sexual awakening.

Little lines gathered between her eyes as she looked at me in earnest. "Yes. The task Grim has assigned you. It isn't safe."

Something cold snaked through me.

"I'm afraid you'll have to be more specific," I said carefully. Grim and Timothy never told me my job with Xander was a secret, but I'd be damned if I assumed and let something important slip out.

With another tight smile, as if understanding what I was making her do. "Killing Xander," she said, confirming my suspicion for sure. "You have to stop."

"What?"

She shook her head mournfully. "It's my fault you see. I told him. I told him you had the blade. I saw his death. But it was meant to be a warning. You must trust me, Miranda. Under no circumstances should you try to kill him."

I looked away from Bianca, down to my cup of inky black caffeine. "Why not?"

Her delicate hand covered mine, pulling it off my cup, forcing me to look into her eyes. "Because it will bring about the end of the world."

Well fuck me sideways on a rollercoaster.

"What did you see?" I asked, my voice suddenly hoarse. Bianca was an oracle and had visions about the future, but from what I gathered, they weren't always clear or as literal as her interpretations.

Bianca's head tilted as she closed her eyes, like she was sending her vision inward. She wrinkled her brow as if trying even harder to see something. "Chaos. Blinding light."

I slid my hand away from hers to hold my coffee cup again. "No more detail than that."

Bianca frowned. "Miranda, you must take this seriously."

My hackles rose at that. Of all the people she could accuse of not taking things seriously... That was my problem. Hell, my identity. Everything was a dire event that needed me to be the strong leader who cleaned up everyone else's mess. Without Jamal, what little humor and sense of play dried up into a raisin. To insinuate anything else, grated. Maybe I should have been taking a back seat to all the shit, maybe I should spend more time messing around or screwing off. Then I wouldn't be so pissed off by her comment.

Even though it wasn't Bianca's fault she'd hit one of my hot buttons, my blood boiled. "Of course, I'm taking this seriously. But your vision doesn't seem to tie coherently to Xander. How can my killing Xander create what you are seeing? How do you know they are connected at all." I couldn't control the steel edge in my words. She wanted me to take this seriously? I'd show her how critical I could be about all sides in the matter.

Bianca shifted in her seat and looked away, her cheeks flushing. "It's more a feeling. Visions aren't a science."

Trying to calm my tits, I said in a slightly softer tone, "Is there a chance you are wrong?"

Bianca shook her head slightly as if in amazement. "You are so intent to kill him? I don't understand, why?"

I licked my lips, preparing my answer. "Because he is in pain." At her reaction, I realized she knew it too. "Do you want him to be in pain for eternity?"

"No, of course I don't," she said with a tired sigh. "But Miranda, the very future of immortals and humans is at stake if you kill Xander. I don't know how. But I know they are connected."

And I believed her. Or at least, I believed that she believed. Bianca was a caring, compassionate goddess. There were few people I trusted, and even fewer gods. But Bianca proved to be pure of heart, with the interest of mortals at the forefront. A rarity among the immortals, from what I'd learned.

However, that still didn't make her right, did it?

Wow Miranda, you are going to go with your gut over a god who can literally see the future? Don't you think highly of yourself?

No. Of course I recognized the Oracle was an authority to be taken seriously. Still, I didn't feel right about this. Not about leaving Xander in his prison, out of his mind with power and pain.

And if it was such a bad thing, why would the god of the dead himself direct me to kill him? I trusted Bianca, but I trusted Grim even more. Still, the math didn't add up.

Maybe I was the wrong person to be the caretaker of the blade? Maybe it required someone with cold calculation to sort through all this. Yet, my heart was getting in the way, telling me I couldn't just let Xander suffer like he had.

A migraine started at my temples, even as a dull sucking ache throbbed in my heart.

Bianca pulled my hand off my cup again to give my fingers a squeeze. "I know you are a good person. I know you want to do the right thing. Please, Miranda. Do the right thing."

THIRTEEN

THE BEAST

I'd been waiting for Miranda. It felt like an eternity between her visits, and our evenings had become my favorite part of the day. Before her, I didn't have a favorite part of the day. Before her, my life was knitted together by moments of excruciating pain.

I could try to tell myself her arrival, triggering my heart to gallop and throb with excitement, was only because I looked forward to dying. But it had become more than that.

Our verbal sparring woke up parts of my brain that had slumbered so long I'd thought they died before the rest of me could. When Miranda's cat-like eyes flashed as her body squared off, preparing for a fight, tendrils of warm blood snaked through my body. Scratching at the paint on her perfect veneer, trying to get underneath to the real her, had sparked an obsession.

Perhaps I'd get to peel away some of her armor before I died my final, true death.

I inhaled a shuddering breath of anticipation, my eyes fluttering close.

Death.

Every day I neared my true, perfect end. Freedom from flesh and bone. Oblivion.

"Well, Ms. Badass. Aren't you going to kill me today?" I asked, letting a grin curl my lips upward.

She stared at me for a long time as if trying to figure something out. The smile slid off my face. My gut churned with anticipation and foreboding, a sickly charged sensation.

Before she could respond, her phone rang with an ear-splitting shrillness that felt like a physical blow. Panic raced through me like a lightning bolt. The air shimmered like a place over hot coals and the blaring in my head felt like a river of water being pulled through a pinhole.

My fists balled into shaking fists. Teeth cracked when I clenched my jaw, in an attempt to gird myself. I couldn't afford to lose control. I couldn't afford to scare her off.

I wanted to die today. I *needed* to die today.

"Make it stop," I growled.

Miranda fumbled for the phone, but it slipped from her fingers.

Do dee do dee do.

The jarring melody continued to drill into my senses. The notes blasted through my ears, shattering my fragile mental defenses. My hands shook, my veins popping out as my skin twisted and morphed into a blackened shell of rage. Unholy fire ignited inside me, a raging inferno ready to scorch the world and anyone unfortunate enough to be standing nearby. It would be so satisfying to grab her and thrust her hard against the bars until the noise ceased. Technicolor violent fantasies drove my insanity to dangerous heights.

No, I absolutely would not fucking hurt her. No one hurts my dark angel, not even me. My fear of hurting her or scaring her surged faster, outrunning my crazy. Still, I didn't know how long my need to protect her would keep my senses intact. If I fell over the edge, she'd see, see me for what I really was. She'd never come back.

I gripped the bars so hard they shuddered. "Turn it off!" I roared.

Miranda winced. Her fingers wrapped around the phone, and she went to dismiss the call.

"Oh crap," she muttered as a face appeared on her screen. She whipped the phone away so whoever it was couldn't see me.

"Hi mom," a young voice chirped.

The bell clanging in my head fell blissfully silent, and I sagged against the bars. *Fuck, that had been close.*

"Hey kiddo, sorry, I actually can't—"

But the boy interrupted. "Mom, we had the best day ever. They let us assemble actual robots. It was the coolest. Have you ever done anything like that?"

I focused on the steady beat of Miranda's heart. On the voice of the kid. I slowly but surely reeled in the power that almost took me entirely.

"No Jamal, I haven't but I need to—"

Again, he interrupted her. "You need to have more fun. You don't have enough fun. Maybe you should ask Vivien and Aaron to play board games with you. We have a whole day for board games coming up. Oh dang, I got to go. They just brought out the pizza. Love you, bye!"

The call went dead.

"Love you too," she muttered. Then she blew out a heavy breath. "I'm so sorry. I didn't mean to answer."

Jamal. Knowing her kid's name, hearing his voice, somehow gave me another piece of the woman I saw every day. There was something I instantly liked about Jamal. In the brief moments he spoke to his mother, he exhibited a candidness and maturity that matched hers. More than that, he seemed somehow unruined by life. As if the heavy weights of living hadn't yet crushed any vital part of him yet. I wondered how much of that was his own indomitable spirit, and how much was Miranda's wisdom and guidance.

"It's alright," I assured her, though my voice was hoarse now. I was spent from holding back the surge of power. "Are you going to take his advice?"

"What?"

"Are you going to practice having more fun?"

"Don't fuck with me," she said in warning. She thought I was trying to mess with her about her kid.

"It's good advice, you know."

"Oh really?" she snorted in disbelief. "Are you down here playing ping-pong by yourself?"

"I knit," I said without pause.

"Har har."

"Your kid know you are a badass blade wielder?" I asked, my curiosity getting the best of me.

"Unfortunately, he knows more about the supernatural than anybody should have too. Grim saved his life once when some vampires used him as a pawn. I'm very grateful he is unusually mature, but he is still a sensitive soul."

The distress on her face kept me from asking any more questions about her son's knowledge of gods and monsters.

Then she walked over to the lone chair and opened her lunch sack. She pulled out a prepackaged bag of chips and ripped it. Her face rearranged into an unreadable mask.

Why wasn't she over here stabbing me through the heart? She seemed to be considering something, very intensely.

Something was wrong. Very wrong.

"What is it?" I asked, trying not to crawl out of my skin.

Why was she so distant?

Miranda waited until she finished chewing and swallowed a chip. My fingers twitched, desperate to rip the bars apart and shake her until she told me what happened.

"I'm not sure I can kill you," she said quietly, dispassionately. Her eyes drifted across the room.

Inside my skull, a storm of panic raged. Lightning bolts of fear struck at the core of my thoughts, threatening to shatter my fragile equilibrium all over again.

I began to pace back and forth, never taking my eyes off her. "What the fuck are you talking about?"

It would have been better if she yelled it, if she dug her heels in and faced off with me. But Miranda turned off like a switch, so cold and distant.

"Can you calm down first?" she asked in an even tone.

"No, I can't fucking calm down. You just said you aren't going to kill me."

"Please," she said, wincing.

The lights flickered. My power was going berserk and hurting her. Before I could register the impact I had on her, I found myself up on the bars by the ceiling. I didn't remember climbing up here. Instead of reacting, she continued to stare at me impassively, as if waiting for me to get over my fit. Like I was some kind of child.

I leapt off and landed silently on my feet, reeling the excess in, though it pained me to bite back all the energy and pain I wanted to let explode out.

"Explain," I ground out.

Miranda lowered the chip bag. "Bianca came to me. She said if I kill you, something terrible is going to happen. End of the world terrible."

My teeth cracked under the pressure of my clenched jaw. They would heal later. And I would hate even that. I was broken and I wanted to feel every piece of my brokenness. Chop myself up into little pieces until I looked how I felt. Box my bits up, send them to Miranda with a red bow. The tag would read, "I go to pieces."

My crazy runaway train of thought jerked to a halt, bringing me back to clarity. I would never do that to Miranda.

I was struck by the miracle of that. When I started to spiral there was usually no bringing me back from the precipice. But I'd already recovered once today, saved by the need to protect the woman across from me.

Miranda must be some kind of enchantress.

Or I simply knew she was the key to my freedom, one death at a time.

"Miranda. Please don't do this."

"I can't be responsible for ending the world." Even as she said it, I saw regret and uncertainty in her eyes. The door hadn't fully closed on my salvation, not yet. And I planned on digging my claws in and ripping it back open.

I stepped up to the bars and encircled the cold metal with my hands. "Bianca's visions aren't always as they seem."

Miranda didn't say anything.

"Did she say how it would happen? How my death would lead to the end of the world?"

After a pause, Miranda shook her head.

I let out a sigh of relief. "How could my death possibly bring about the end of the world?"

Miranda dropped her lunch sack to the ground and pushed off from her chair. "I don't know. You tell me." Frustration edged her words. "I'm trying to do the right thing here."

And she was. I knew it. Miranda was like Grim in that she was trying to protect others. Yet she somehow missed how terribly delicate and fragile her own humanity was. I coveted her humanity, and the power she held in her delicate being.

"Killing me is the right thing, Miranda." The lights flickered and Miranda stepped back from my flux of power. Without thinking, I grabbed her hand and pulled her to the bars.

Her brown eyes widened. They were a couple shades lighter than her skin, making for an irresistible contrast of color. Like sparkling brown sugar irises set against rich walnut. And I wondered, not for the first time, if she tasted as sweet as she looked.

With my other hand, I reached through the bars and caught her face. My thumb stroked along her jawline, trying to ease the pain I caused her. She inhaled sharply but didn't move away. "Miranda, if I thought there was a chance my demise would end the world—would end your world—I wouldn't ask."

I sunk every bit of meaning, of feeling into those words. I needed her to believe me.

Maybe I'd been cut off from the world outside too long, but Miranda somehow connected me to it again. It hadn't taken much, but it was true all the same.

"How can I tru—believe you?"

I realized there was something more here for both of us.

Something pulsating. Something alive. Something connecting us.

Her body pressed against the bars, meeting my hard chest with her soft curves. My fingers trailed across her cheek. Fucking hell her skin was so smooth, so soft, over a bone structure that would make any man hard to gaze upon.

But she was more than skin and bones. So much more. My little badass. Who was free to live her life, but I could see invisible chains around her. She held herself back, and I wanted to rip away the constraints so very badly.

My gaze dropped to her lips. Full, inviting lips made me forget how to breathe. "Miranda. Please," I rasped, caught in a whirl of desire and desperation. I wasn't sure what I was pleading for anymore.

Her breath hitched, shallow and fast, and I could almost hear the gears turning in her mind, could see the battle waging in her eyes.

"Wish granted," she murmured, her voice as sharp as the weapon she plunged into my chest, a cold, keen contrast to the heat brewing between us. The breath hitched in my throat, as my heart split under the blade.

The pain was immediate, intense, yet it wasn't enough to tear my eyes away from hers. There, in those beautiful depths, I saw conflict, uncertainty – a mirror of my own.

Her indecision stabbed me sharper than any blade. I'd placed this burden on her, forced her to bear the weight of my death. Guilt gnawed at my conscience, but it was too late to take it back. Instead, I reached through the bars, pulling her face to mine.

I kissed her right on those gorgeous fucking lips. I told myself it was gratitude, but as soon as my lips met hers, I knew it was so much more than that.

She froze under me like a deer in headlights, but she didn't move away.

I kissed her in slow, soft laps, the tip of my tongue flicking over her decadent mouth. Finally, her soft, wet lips slid against mine, her head tilting to press in, to kiss me back. I moaned at the sensation, her lips so soft and inviting, like they were made for me.

Lips parted and I swept my tongue in her mouth. *Fuck.* She was sweeter and more intoxicating than the wildest of fantasies that had haunted my solitude. My little badass was exquisite, erotic.

Something split wide inside me and reached for her with greedy phantom hands.

I needed more. More Miranda. More of her hardness, more of her softness. I'd drink every last drop of her, no matter how bitter or sweet. Heat and tingles whipped around inside me, stirring an insatiable hunger.

When my gaze met hers, I found the same intense passion mirrored there. Her hooded, lust-filled eyes, usually composed, were wide with an emotion that echoed my own – a raw, wild desire. An affirmation that she, too, was lost in this whirlpool of shared intensity. The sight of her, so unguarded, did unspeakable things to me. I knew then that our passions were intertwined.

Her shuddering breath puffed against my lips as her fingers burrowed into my hair. She kissed me like she had never kissed anyone before, like she was discovering a new world.

I tasted her fear, her pleasure, her deep dark passion.

She wasn't close enough. The hand cupping her chin moved to the base of her skull, while my other one grasped her sexy hip. I pulled her closer, which pushed the sword deeper into my heart. I grunted as I felt life bleed from me faster, but it was worth it to get closer to her warm skin.

Though I tried to ignore it, the darkness closed in around me, relentless, pulling me away from Miranda's sweetness. For the first time ever, I wanted to cling to life, just for a little longer.

The last thought I had before succumbing to oblivion was I hoped this was my last death rather than never taste her again.

CHAPTER
FOURTEEN

THE BADASS

The next morning, I lay in bed, until almost seven AM. It was my day off, but I was still usually up and at 'em by five.

Maybe I was getting sick. That was the only explanation for what was happening in my body.

Unless your kakuchie can catch cold, this is not that, my brain informed me.

"Shut up."

Last night, Xander kissed me.

Since I'd stepped into that basement, Xander excited parts of me I long thought dead. He turned me into a puddle of liquid heat, but I never let it compromise me. Even though I'd traced the outline of his perfect lips with my eyes, I never expected him to lay them on me.

When he did, it changed everything. The moment his lips pressed against mine, I went from being a bystander in a muted life to the strongest yet most vulnerable version of myself. It was like coming back to life, as I served him death.

My finger pads ghosted over my lips, chasing the phantom pressure of his, trying to rekindle the sensation. Or maybe, just maybe, I was attempting to understand how one man's kiss could cause such a seismic shift in me.

Was the kiss so intense because he was a god, or because it had been so long?

Years, my judgmental brain whispered.

"Shut up. I've been busy raising a son and working," I said out loud again. Still, a gnawing sensation ate at my gut, demanding attention, or the very least, a name.

Loneliness, my brain whispered again.

"Arrgh," I cried out even as I paced the living room. "How dare you think that. You don't need anything else. You have friends. You have a son who is amazing, kind and smart."

But no matter what I said, I felt the effects of a need I'd tried so hard to shove away. And I fucking hated it.

I would have called a friend, but it was daylight and Vivien was likely already asleep, and Aaron was off rock climbing for the entire weekend. There was no one.

There's someone, my stupid brain said again.

"Nope, I'm not going to him." I laced up my tennis shoes, prepared to do the only rational thing here. Burn it all off at the gym.

My tablet rang and buzzed on my dresser table. Normally,

I'd leap to answer it, knowing who it was. But I was moving slowly today. Still, I was no less happy to answer and see the smiling face of my kid.

Jamal grinned from ear to ear. "Hey mom."

"Hey my baby, how is camp going?" I settled in the small cream-colored sitting chair by the window. I bought the comfy seat with the hopes I'd read books and sit in peaceful silence, but I somehow never found the time to do either.

That was all it took for Jamal to launch into stories about the high ropes course they traversed the day before. His best friend, Jun Hie, who came all the way from Tokyo to take advantage of the program as well. They'd met last summer, and they'd picked up right where they left off, bonding over the latest in robotics and astronomy.

I lived for that toothy smile on his face. To say I was grateful for the program and scholarship, so he could attend, was an understatement.

"You okay, mom?"

"Of course, baby. Why do you ask?"

"I don't know," he said, studying me as close as he could through a camera. "You seem. . .sad. Are you taking care of yourself?"

My kid. The eleven-year-old going on forty.

"Of course, I am," I said, a little too defensively.

"Are you taking time to have fun?" He spelled it out for me as if I didn't understand his original question.

I rubbed my forehead. "Baby, you know I gotta work." And these days, work was killer.

Ha! I could be funny when I wanted to be.

Jamal frowned. "You don't work all the time. And if I'm not there to make sure you have fun, you should go play with Vivien and Aaron."

"Who's the parent here?" I asked, failing to suppress a smile.

He shook his finger at the camera dramatically, before breaking out into laughter.

Then Jamal turned serious again. "Mom, are you lonely?"

A spike stabbed through my heart. "Of course not."

If we'd simply been talking over the phone, I would have missed the stink-eye he gave me. "You know you always tug on your hair when you are lying."

I released braids as if they were made of fire.

Jamal took a deep breath. "I need to go in a couple minutes here, but it's time we had the talk."

I straightened in my seat. Oh god, he's barely eleven. Why would he need to have the talk now? I wasn't ready. It was all happening too soon.

"I think it's time you started dating again."

I would have been less surprised if he slapped me across the face with a live fish.

"Baby, I—"

His tone was stern and far beyond his years. "I can't be there all the time, and someone else needs to treat you like the queen you are."

"Hey Jamal," a voice called from the background.

"Sorry mom, I gotta go. We are preparing to go on a backpacking trip where we can do some serious star gazing. It's gonna be the coolest."

I barely had a chance to say goodbye before he hung up.

There I continued to sit, in the stark silence, chewing on what my kid just said.

He wants me to date?

Well, dammit. I'd been using Jamal as a smoke screen to keep myself unavailable to relationships, and now my own kid ripped away the safety blanket I had, leaving me exposed. I could run from my own feelings, but it was a hell of a lot harder when he held up the mirror, showing me all the parts I'd been avoiding.

Just because he told me to do it didn't mean I had to.

If your own kid thinks you need to get laid, you need to get laid.

"That is *not* what he was saying."

He may not get the mechanics, but he gets the mood, and he knows you are too uptight.

I hadn't felt uptight yesterday with Xander.

Standing and stretching my legs, I didn't think the answer is fucking a half feral god before I kill him for the umpteenth time.

Stopping at my bathroom door, I scrubbed a hand over my face.

Oh fuckity ducks. I'm going to have to start dating again.

Before I could think about it too much, I grabbed my phone and downloaded three different dating apps. I didn't do anything halfway. Which meant I had a whole other mission to complete before Jamal came home. Go on at least one date with a perfectly normal guy.

But before I tackled that, a trip to the gym was still in order.

AFTER LIFTING weights for thirty minutes, I wound my braids up into a bun and crossed to the boxing gym that was attached. I paid extra for the access, and ever since I started having to fight off gods and vampires, I found it a wise investment.

Finding myself an available bag in a corner, my fists slammed into it until sweat dripped into my eyes.

Loneliness.

Pow pow. My knuckles crashed into the bag over and over. I tried to beat away the feeling.

I'm not lonely. Loneliness wasn't a factor. It was just a feeling and feelings couldn't control me.

I'd learned that after Rashon passed.

Xander's words returned to me.

Pain means feeling and you work very hard not to feel, don't you?

Pow pow.

My breathing turned shallow as I tried to punch his words away. Tried to fight away how quick he cut to my core.

"Jeezus, Miranda, you pissed today or what?"

I pivoted to find myself face-to-face with Amos, the boxing gym owner. A massive wall of muscle with a shaved head that gleamed. His skin tone was rich as midnight, with bluish-red undertones. A crimson shirt stretched across his powerful barrel chest. Amos had the warmest smile, gave the best hugs, and punched like a beast. Not that he'd unleashed that power fully on me when we were sparring, being so far out of my weight class. But he was helping me level up little by little when I could fit in one-on-one sessions with him.

"I'm not pissed," I responded, winding a couple braids back up that had fallen out of my bun.

He held his hands up and chuckled. "Sure."

Okay, so I even said it like I was pissed.

"Just don't go breaking my bags. They are hella expensive." Then he seemed to think better of it. "On second thought, break the bag if you want. It will only make the others train harder, and they'll think I'm responsible for your badassery." He tossed a look over his shoulder to where a couple of guys were training. One of them pretended he hadn't been staring at me, while the other gave me a suggestive grin. I wouldn't be surprised if he approached me to ask if we could spar in an attempt to get my number.

Should I say yes if he did? I did just download dating apps to my phone.

The idea made my skin crawl and something at the pit of my stomach longed for the feel of someone else's lips. My already pumping blood ran hotter. The way he groaned echoed in my ears. My mouth hungered for his salty masculine tongue sliding against mine. How he pulled me closer even as it sunk the blade in further. Like I was worth all the pain in the world, if he could get me a little wild. A throbbing kicked up at my center like a heartbeat.

Nope. I'm choosing to ignore all pangs of desire for a completely off-limits immortal.

The pangs didn't fucking listen.

"Then if I break one of your bags, you owe me a month of one-on-ones," I said, trying to bargain.

Amos squinted at me. "Deal." Then he turned back to his clipboard and walked off, leaving me to it.

My clothes clung to my soaked body, and my muscles had turned into overcooked noodles. Not to mention the buzz of arousal still ran through me. It was time to throw in the towel. I checked the big clock hanging over the sparring ring.

Two fucking PM? Would this day ever end? Maybe I could just go into work?

No. I needed to try and relax. I promised Jamal before he left that I would try to have some fun. I'd humored him at the time, but now I realized how spot on my eleven-year-old son was.

Flipping open one of the dating apps, I easily set up a profile. Three pictures, one of me in a dress for church last Easter, one of me and Jamal at the beach, though I cropped out his face as it was thrown back in laughter, and the last an old one of me in my army fatigues. I found men were often bothered by my service, so it was best to weed those ones out right away. I quickly typed that I enjoyed working, working out, and hanging out with my son. In no time at all, I was swiping on the faces of men who lived in the area.

Thankfully, I was far away enough from the Strip to get actual residents of Vegas, but still, none of them really piqued my interest. None of them had burning sapphire eyes or a presence that jumped out of my phone. None of them had a smirk that both irritated and excited me.

Realizing I was being too picky, I swiped right on a couple I found mildly attractive. Almost instantly I got matched. I had no idea what came next. Messaging? Dates? I clicked off my screen. I'd figure it out later.

But first, I needed to swing by Sinopolis and take care of the business of the day. Killing a god. Releasing my braids so they could dry, I grabbed my bag and headed out. The Vegas sun-baked air immediately began drying the sweat on my body.

My eye caught on the back of someone slim in an orange hoodie near my car. Wait, they were trying to break *into* my car.

"Hey!" I called out.

Something clanged to the ground as the person bolted. I broke into a run after them but stopped at my car. One minute the hooded person had been there and next, they'd disappeared. On the asphalt lay a slim jim.

"Fucking car jackers." I picked up the flat piece of metal. "I never cussed this much before Jamal left. Guess that means I'm chilling out."

"What was that?"

I jerked my head up. A guy getting into his vehicle a couple cars away stood by his opened door. He thought I'd been talking to him.

"Uh, nothing. Just talking to myself." I hadn't done it this much since Rashon passed away. Another sign my stress was getting the best of me.

The guy gave me a strange look before getting into his car.

I sagged against my Jeep, feeling the weight of more than I could express into words. Glancing through the windows of my car, it occurred to me the attempted jacking might not have been about taking my vehicle.

Bob lay in their sheath, on the back seat.

Are you an idiot, Miranda? Leaving something that important out in the open?

I slid into the front seat, putting Bob up in the passenger side next to me. I managed to resist the urge to buckle them in. Now that would have been crazy.

I turned the engine on.

Side-eyeing the blade, I reached over and snapped the buckle in.

As I pulled out of my parking spot, I said, "I really am fucking losing my mind." Though something told me Bob was grateful to be extra secure.

CHAPTER
FIFTEEN

THE BEAST

T he ding of the elevator had me as excited as one of
Pavlov's dogs. Whether it was the strike of her sword,
or the slant of her mouth, the unrelenting pain that
usually gripped me had become less potent. The searing agony
that once clouded my thoughts and haunted my existence had
dimmed. The debilitating bouts of madness, the blackout
spells had been remarkably absent in the past few days.

It was as if the edges of my torment had blurred, faded at

the seams, turning from vivid scarlet slashes of pain to muted hues of manageable discomfort.

Miranda, had begun to transform my endless torment into bearable stretches of anticipation.

Come kill me again, sweetheart. Kiss me again as you do.

Miranda emerged, her skin glistening more than usual. Tight fitting workout clothes clung to her muscular, tight body. I had to bite back a groan. Fucking hell, she was gorgeous. And fierce, and smart, and a hard-ass. I could *definitely* see what a hard-ass she was in those pants.

And I couldn't wait for her to kill me. She really was my personal angelic badass.

Before I could even open my mouth, she held up a hand. "You can't kiss me. Not ever again."

Some part deep inside me growled at my acquiescence, not wanting to promise any such thing. After all, hadn't her own spawn told her she needed to have fun last night? I could help. I could help her have *a lot* of fun.

Kissing her had been a hell of a lot more than just fun. It had been a revelation, a cataclysmic event that set my world ablaze. I'd been swept away in a torrent of raw emotion, of sensations I didn't know I was still capable of experiencing.

Her taste, her touch had seeped into the hollows of my existence, filling the spaces I hadn't realized were void. Her kiss was not just pleasure—it was a lifeline, an anchoring force that momentarily tethered me to the world of the living.

But I was, after all, a man on a direct course to death.

Though I selfishly didn't want to spend the rest of my life —short as it may be—knowing what she tasted like and not having her again.

Her eyebrows lifted expectantly. She was waiting for an answer.

I blinked. "Okay."

Her posture visibly relaxed.

"You're early," I pointed out in a gruff tone, trying to pretend I didn't care about what she just said. That it didn't rankle me, and that I instantly wanted to haul her up against the bars and kiss her until she lost it.

Calm down. You need her to kill you, not run off in a huff.

"It's my day off." She said it as if she'd been walking on a bed of nails and sucking on lemon juice the whole day.

The urge to laugh rose in me. Not a crazy explosive cackle, a genuine laugh. But I bit it back.

"And looks like you're enjoying every minute of it," I said.

Miranda pulled the blade from her coat and neared my cage. Every hair on my body rose with excitement. For my oblivion?

I inhaled deeply.

No. For Miranda. I was excited to be near my angel of death. Especially with the close call, I wanted to bury myself in her, lose myself in her and forget the monster I was.

She stopped inches away from me.

Sweet fucking reaper dogs, how does she smell even more delicious? If I didn't watch myself, my tongue would loll right out of my mouth, as I panted in lust like a cartoon character.

"Someone tried to get the blade," she confessed in a low tone.

All humor and attraction froze before cracking into a million pieces. I gripped the bars. "What happened, exactly?"

Miranda told me about the person in the orange hoodie. She couldn't even tell if it was a man or woman, or how old they were. They were slight of frame and fast as hell.

"They could have just wanted my car," she said, unconvincingly.

Panic gripped my chest in a vice before crawling up my

throat like a gang of worms. "Miranda, you can't let anyone get their hands on that blade," I said.

She pushed some of her braids back in frustration. "You don't think I know that?"

"I'm serious. The consequences could be dire."

She got right in my face. "You seriously think I don't know? Of course, I know beast boy. I don't intend to let anyone take it from me."

My eyes trailed from the blazing fire in her eyes to the blade at her side. "Do you even know how to use that thing?"

Her lips quirked in displeasure as she cocked her hips in that way when she was annoyed or impatient. "I'm pretty sure I've proven that more to you than anyone."

I shook my head. "I mean, do you know how to wield a blade, sword fight?"

Uncertainty crept into her eyes.

So that's a no.

"See that panel over there?" I pointed to a box of electronics with buttons and levers. "You can open the door and come inside. I'll teach you how to use it so no one can ever take it from you."

"No fucking way."

My eyebrows shot up. "No fucking way?" I echoed. "Sweetheart. You need help, and I'm very invested in giving you that help."

"Oh yeah, Miranda," she mocked, "Why don't you walk into a cage and trap yourself with a feral, overly powerful god. Nothing could possibly go wrong."

I honestly couldn't tell if she was talking to herself or me.

"Miranda," I said sternly. "I won't hurt you. I promise." And I'd never been so certain of anything in my life. In fact, lately I calmed when she was near. Her mere presence drowned out the pain I experienced day in and day out. I couldn't account for it. It was more than my daily deaths. It was her.

Miranda eyed me. No one I'd ever known could pack so much suspicion or sass into one look. It devastated me in ways I hadn't expected.

"I can take lessons from someone else," she said finally.

I shook my head. "If a god is crazy enough to go for a snatch and grab of the blade, risking you'll stab them, you'll need to know how to fight them off using what you have. And you have the blade that can hurt them the most."

She shifted her weight onto the other foot. "I don't know if it was a god who tried to break into my car."

"It doesn't matter. If someone is trying, it will only encourage others to follow."

Miranda pursed her lips.

Wild, untamed energy rose in me. I wanted to rip the bars away. But not because I was losing control, it was because I wanted to get close to her. I wanted to get inside the clockwork gears of her mind to give myself a fighting chance.

Don't abandon me now. Let me in.

After what felt like an eternity, she raised the blade, pointing it at me. "If you step out of line, I'll kill you."

I let out a sigh of relief, my crazy levels dimming back down. "Perfect," I said in agreement.

"When should we start?" she asked.

I grinned. "What are you doing right now, sweetheart?"

WHEN SHE HIT the button to open my cage, and the bars slid to the side, I backed up, giving her ample room to assure her safety.

I jerked my head toward the controls. "You might want to turn the lights on too."

She did as I suggested, without taking her eyes off me. She didn't trust me. But I wouldn't be so callous with her safety.

Or maybe I was simply too desperate to get even close to the woman whose narrowed eyes could have sliced through me.

The kerchunk of the overhead lights was as abrasive as the sudden blinding light. "No wonder you prefer them off," she muttered, blinking against the assault. "And here I thought you were just playing at being Batman." Miranda froze, her eyes widening. "I'm sorry, you probably don't know who Batman is."

I frowned. "Of course, I know who Batman is."

Miranda waved a hand at my cage. "How? You don't even have a toilet in here."

Dammit, I had to suppress a smile again. "This is not the entirety of my quarters."

Her brows furrowed and her luscious lips deepened into a pout.

I pointed at the elevator. "I get notified when someone is coming down to my level and come out to this." I looked at the barren bars and sighed. "Greeting chamber."

"So where are your quarters?" she asked, coming closer to me. Then she looked over her shoulder.

"Worried, sweetheart?" She should be. With so many deaths, it was easier to control my power. But that didn't mean she was entirely safe. I was playing a dangerous game. But to protect the blade, it was worth it.

You won't hurt her, I assured myself.

Her head snapped back to me. "Don't call me that."

"Afraid everyone is going to figure out the badass has a sweet heart?"

Miranda rolled her eyes.

As she did so, I lunged forward and plucked the blade of bane from her hands.

"Hey," she cried out. "I wasn't ready."

Flipping the blade and offering the hilt back to her, I said, "That's the point, sweetheart. Now why don't you try to keep your hands on the most important weapon in the world and stab me if I come at you?"

"I don't want to hurt you," she said, taking the weapon back.

I blinked. "You kill me every day."

Miranda shrugged, clearly uncomfortable. "That's different."

I stepped closer to her, forcing her to look up several inches to meet my eye. We were so close. I could taste the kiss from yesterday and it sent a hot rush through me. "Maybe I deserve it."

Gods, was she really as painfully gorgeous as I believed, or had I just been away too long?

"I can be the judge of that, what did you do?" she said, her voice lowering. The moment somehow turned intimate.

Nothing separated us. I could sense her fear. But there was more than that. Excitement.

Was she thinking of that kiss yesterday as well?

My eyes lowered to those impossibly full lips. I regretted that I didn't get to explore them more yesterday. I didn't get to nibble on them. I didn't get to push my tongue past her teeth and taste the depths of her already intoxicating mouth. But then my imagination started to take things further. There were more places on this hot little human I'd like to probe and penetrate.

This close, I heard her heart rate speed up. My mouth quirked, trying to hold back a smile.

"Well? Are you going to tell me why you deserve to be punished?" she asked, before licking her lips. She asked one question, but her energy was nothing but excited, inviting.

I snatched the blade as easy as taking candy from a baby and backed away with a teasing grin.

The seductive energy about her evaporated instantly. I shoved her right back into frustration and mission-mode.

"I'm going to teach you how to use this thing, so you don't screw things up for both of us." The words were meant to be menacing, a dire warning, but I couldn't help my grin. I suddenly felt like I was a cat who'd been given a toy after eating a bunch of catnip.

I WRENCHED the blade from her hand for the thirteenth time in ten minutes.

"You're still too slow." I spun the weapon in one hand. Vaguely, I wondered if she was impressed.

A growl of frustration rumbled from her throat. My scary little badass was getting worked up.

"Bob, you traitor," she muttered.

"I'm sorry. What was that?"

"Bob," she said, holding out her hand. "It's what I call the Blade of Bane."

My twirling stopped abruptly. "You named the most powerful weapon that can decimate immortals. . . Bob?"

Miranda pushed some braids back over her shoulder. "That's its name," she said impatiently. "Blade of Bane? B. O. B. Bob."

I observed the weapon in my hand, trying to swallow the moniker.

"Give it back," she said, her voice suddenly serious as a

heart attack. Concern tightened her eyes, her shoulders squaring off.

I flipped the sword over, offering her the hilt again. Miranda took it and turned her back on me to walk to the other side of the cell.

"I don't even know if I should be doing this," she said, and I couldn't tell if it was for me or for herself. "The blade was given to me and only me. I was told I wasn't to allow it to fall into the hands of any immortal and here we are practically playing catch with the damn thing. I'm an idiot."

"You're not an idiot." The words came out harsh. Miranda's gaze flew up to meet mine. "And better me than someone who really wants it."

"How do I know you don't?" she accused.

"What?"

"How do I know this isn't some ploy to have Bob all to yourself?" She clutched the weapon tightly. "That you aren't luring me into a false sense of security so you can wield this weapon and slay gods and reap power?"

Extending my arms out, I said, "Miranda, the only one I want dead is me." That only made her frown deepen. "You're too serious," I observed.

"*I'm* too serious?" Miranda let out a scoff before crossing the distance back to me. "I have a duty. A duty to the blade to protect immortals and all of mankind. I have a duty to Bianca to take her seriously and not to destroy the world. And I have a duty to free you from your pain."

"Oh well then, I didn't realize you were so important."

She pointed Bob at me.

For fucks sake, was I really calling it Bob now too?

"That's not what I said."

I stalked around her slowly, in a circle. "Sure you did. You are the most important person on this earth, and you have zero time for pleasure or fun."

She twisted to keep her eyes on me. "And you are down here having a barrel of fun every day. Oh wait, that's just because you have zero responsibilities to anyone else but yourself."

My smirk fled faster than my good humor. "Don't compare us. We are not the same."

"No, no, go on. You can criticize me for trying to do the right thing, but I can't point out your hypocrisy. You don't have a pot to piss in, buddy. I may be struggling to figure out how to wield a power that could help or hurt the entire world, but you are only concerned about yourself. Would you even care if your death did trigger the end of the world? Or are you so selfish that you wouldn't give a damn? Maybe I should rethink this entire situation."

I stopped in front of her again. Power began to churn in me, responding to the bait. "Don't toy with me, Miranda."

"Why? Aren't you having fun? Isn't this the fun you are talking about? Don't you enjoy toying with me anymore, beast boy?"

A growl escaped my throat. "I'm helping you right now, protecting your precious little status of savior of the world."

"Excuse me?"

"You want to be a superhero, wielding Bob against the evils of this world? Well, I'm helping you right now. How is that selfish?"

"You are only doing it so the key to your freedom doesn't escape you," she shot back.

Okay, that was true, but the situation had become more complicated than that. I genuinely cared about Miranda's ability to protect herself. But she'd hit a hot button, and I wasn't up for admitting that.

Foolish little mortal scoffed at my attempt to help her? A million other people would beg for the chance to be favored by me. And she threw it back in my face.

"You're damn right. I don't want you fucking things up for me because you are too proud to get help. And that's what I'm doing, helping you." I said the words with as much condescension as I could muster. Fire flashed in her eyes. I'd pushed her too far.

"Please, you have nothing better to do. Is this really about making me spend time down here with you, so you don't feel so lonely?"

She might as well have cut me through the heart.

The instant look of regret told me she knew she went too far.

"You're right. I don't have anything better to do. Maybe I do just want you down here, trapped in this cage with me. I want you for entertainment, Miranda. Because I'm so bored and lonely." I laid the sarcasm as thick as a slab of butter on toast. Even so, I slunk toward her in lazy strides. Her back stiffened as she watched me approach.

"Although if I wanted you to help me pass the time, I could think of far more fun things to do than sparring." I looked her up and down, not bothering the hide the hunger I felt.

"Stop," she said, her tone stiff.

Even from a distance I could hear her heartbeat kick up. Fear? Or excitement?

"Maybe we could spend our time more pleasurably between deaths?"

What was I doing? Acting like a sexual predator, and I couldn't even blame my crazy on this one. Miranda had simply frustrated me into wanting to cross lines. I wanted to cross all her lines. It was only fair, wasn't it? A prisoner's compensation?

I studied her from top to bottom. From the absolute perfection of those long, tight braids, to her luscious lips, to the fullness of her breasts, the flare of her hips, and to the impossibly white sneakers.

This anal-retentive woman needed someone to shake things up for her. She was as brittle as a twig from all her pent-up emotions, and she had no idea. And fuck if I didn't want to be the one to break her.

Blood rushed south as I imagined what it would be like to get her to lose control. Could I get her to scream, to beg for more, as I pounded into her tight body?

Miranda's gaze bounced between my crotch and my face. The loose pants did nothing to hide my sudden arousal.

"Don't make me kill you," she warned, holding Bob up. Fear shone in her eyes. Was she scared of me? No, she was scared of what our argument had morphed into.

"You are going to have to, or Miranda," I said it slowly, licking my lips, "I'm going to kiss you so deep, I'll taste your soul. And then there will be no hiding from me."

Pain speared through my heart, taking my breath. We'd had quite a bit of time to recover from our sparring match, but Miranda was breathing as hard as if she'd run a mile.

Copper filled my mouth, and though I'm sure I looked gruesome, I couldn't help but smile. Because I learned something Miranda may not be fully aware of. She wanted me. She wanted me badly.

CHAPTER
SIXTEEN

THE BADASS

W hat the fuck was I doing?

"A date, Miranda." I muttered to myself. "You are going on a date. Like a normal woman with a normal life."

My phone turned over and over in my hand. Last night I found one of my online matches was amenable to meet me for lunch.

The Mexican restaurant had brightly colored chairs and tables and mariachi music blared from the speakers. The place was relatively empty for a weekday at noon. It was my second day off and I'd found a totally new way to spend it.

After tossing and turning, dreaming of Xander, his hard body sliding against mine, in tandem with blood spurting out of his mouth from being stabbed, I got up extra early and hit the gym again. I'd gone until I'd exhausted myself, then cleaned up and showed up at the restaurant fifteen minutes early.

This is the right thing to do, I assured myself. You need to start dating and you absolutely cannot be thinking about a particular god who you killed to keep from kissing you.

I only killed him because I was terrified of how much I wanted him. If Xander kissed me, I don't think I'd let him stop.

When I saw him again tonight, I was determined to be on a totally new level. A new Miranda, in fact. The best, most exciting part of my day wouldn't be murdering the hottest, craziest god who clearly wanted to do bad, naughty things to me before I stabbed him to death.

New Miranda had a life outside that basement.

Maybe this guy I met would be so interesting I would think of nothing but this nice normal man after this date? Maybe I'd want to assault him with pillows and introduce him to my son?

My stomach lurched so I grabbed another handful of corn chips, hoping the food would help calm my nervous guts.

Catching sight of a tall man walking in, I paused my demolition on the bowl of chips. He was handsome, with neatly styled hair and warm brown eyes. His white linen shirt accentuated his tan features. He was attractive in a clean-cut way, just like in his pictures.

I smiled up at him as he held out his hand for a handshake. "Miranda, it's so nice to meet you in person. I'm Jim." He smiled brightly at me, and I could tell he was pleased with me in real life as well. No cat fishing here.

As we sat down, something similar to a bell, signaling the beginning of a wrestling match, dinged in my head. Let the date begin.

We ordered some tacos and shared about our families and our careers. He was a single dad, divorced, and worked in tech. He loved his two golden retrievers and golfed whenever he could. More than that, he was genuinely interested in me. He respected my time in the service without being intimidated or weird about it. He asked all the right questions about Jamal, relating my stories to that of his daughter, Abby.

Even though the conversation was nice enough, I couldn't help feel like something was missing; something intangible. Was this really a date? It had been so long since I'd been on one. I wondered if they were all just pleasant lunches with strangers until one lunch you suddenly wanted to bang their brains out.

Jim was nice. Perfectly nice. Uncomplicated, respectful, and...and, oh fuck I was bored. I was so bored I wanted to cry.

My thoughts slipped back to Xander's wicked grin and intense, ocean eyes; and that kiss he laid on me. Somehow, the ghost of our one kiss burned my lips as if reminding me of what I truly wanted.

Good luck, Miranda, I could almost hear him taunt in my head. *Think he can help you have fun?*

I shifted in my seat as hot liquid pooled in my lower belly.

"Are you alright?" Jim asked.

"Uh, yeah, sorry, I'm just a little distracted today."

Instead of getting offended, he leaned his elbows on the table and laced his fingers together. "Oh yeah? What's on your mind?"

It was a perfectly reasonable question. It was sincere and the right thing to say.

However, telling Jim I was counting down the minutes to

when I could visit my crazy, feral god in the Grim Reaper's basement would not be an appropriate response.

"Work has been very intense lately," I supplied lamely. Jim didn't need to know I killed a guy to keep him from kissing me because I freaked out and worried I'd like it too much.

Or worse, that I was thinking I would have to do it again.

When the check came, I insisted on splitting, and Jim didn't protest.

His hand reached across the table, covering one of mine. "I really enjoyed this, Miranda. You are a beautiful, interesting woman, and I'd like to see you again."

The feel of his warm, dry palm on my hand should have been comforting. It should have felt good, like his words. But all I wanted to do was pull away. I somehow managed to keep it there on the table, stiff as a board under his.

"Thank you, Jim. That's very nice of you, but I don't think that would be a good idea. You are very nice yourself, but I don't feel that...spark. You know?"

It was like a switch flipped inside him. His warm brown eyes suddenly became cold and distant. His hand retreated.

Before I could take a breath of relief, he pushed away from the table and stood up abruptly. "Women," he muttered, shaking his head as he grabbed his coat off the back of his seat. "Never knowing a good thing when it's in front of them."

And with that, he turned and stormed out of the restaurant without another word.

I sat there for what felt like an eternity, stunned at what had just happened. Xander might be crazy and unpredictable, but at least I knew it.

This was beyond. For fuck's sake, was this what online dating was going to be like? Rubbing my forehead, I couldn't help but think this probably wasn't the *fun* Jamal had in mind for me.

SEVENTEEN

THE BEAST

The next evening when Miranda came to see me, I had something new in mind.

"What is that?" she asked, blinking at my little setup. Her shoulders were stiff and her face was an unreadable mask. Miranda had turned stone cold again.

Because we'd broken a barrier and she came inside my cage? Because I kept taking Bob from her without much effort? Or because she was worried I would threaten to kiss her again, or worse, actually follow through with it.

Though I could see why she would find the setup in my cell strange today.

I looked at it again to make sure it wasn't. With my hallucinations, who knew what I'd pulled up from my chambers. It had required a special delivery from Timothy.

But no, I hadn't mistakenly laid out a banana and a pair of underwear, or something equally ludicrous from a delusion. It was a table with two chairs. On the table, a game was spread out.

"It's Monopoly," I said, stating the obvious.

"I know what it is. What's it doing here?"

"Why, sweetheart," A wicked grin slid onto my face. "You look as terrified as a lamb being led to slaughter. You aren't afraid of a little...fun, are you?"

"Don't be ridiculous." Her body stiffened further. If she tightened up anymore, the rod in her ass was in danger of breaking.

"I'm afraid I'm usually hysterical," I countered. "But I'm deadly serious about this, sweetheart. Taken on your son's advisement, you'd best start having fun. So we are going to fit a little game in before our sword training from now on."

Her gaze bounced between the board game and me with abject terror. "We don't need to do that."

"I suppose your tin heart couldn't handle a little game. You might be in danger of enjoying yourself, and we can't have that, can we? You are so very busy and important that there is no time for enjoyment."

Her lips thinned. I'd hit my mark, and my grin widened as I knew I had her now.

Miranda stomped over to the control panel and slammed her hand on the blue button, and the cage door unlocked with an audible crack.

ONE HOUR later and neither of us were having fun. Miranda and I wore twin expressions of grim determination.

Not five, anything but a five. I can't get a five. My little ship can go anywhere else and I can survive if I just don't roll a five.

The dice fell from my palm, rolling across the board.

As soon as the cube settled, Miranda's eyes lit up with a vindictive fire. "Ha! Boardwalk baby." She pumped her fist before pointing at me. "You can't even afford it, honey," she said in an exaggerated tone that rankled all my chains.

A growl ripped out of my throat as I surged to my feet. The board went flying, sending her tiny hat and all the money into the air. The round table crashed on its side before rolling out of the way. Miranda jumped to her feet as well, facing off with me wearing a positively evil grin.

"How?" I yelled. "You must be cheating."

"Maybe I'm just that good," she countered.

Even though a part of me wanted to respond with a lascivious comment to that, I was far more aggravated about the loss. "How were you cheating? That is the only way you could have won!" I was shouting now.

"What? You can't believe a mortal can beat a god? Get used to it, beast boy."

"No," I said, tugging at my hair. "You can't have won because *I* was cheating."

Her victorious snarl evaporated as she stood there stunned. "*You* were cheating?"

"Yes." My fists clenched at my sides. "I was sneaking money from the bank the entire time. So you must have been doing so, as well. Or maybe you were cheating in some other devious way?"

Miranda's eyes narrowed. "You dirty little snake. Well guess what? I don't need to cheat to beat your ass."

Another growl of frustration emerged from me.

"Are we having fun yet?" she taunted, spreading her arms out. "Is this the fun you wanted to have? Because I'm having loads of it. I feel like a gleeful child again."

Tension flared between us, and the danger of the moment struck me.

Cold fear shot through me as I realized I was about to lose control and hurt her. Stressors far less than this had sent me into a raging blackout. Any second energy would plume and lash out in painful waves.

Yet it didn't come. A palpable current thrummed between us, but I wasn't teetering on the edge of sanity. The pain of my power had been reduced to a shockingly bearable dull roar.

Bob killed off even more of my power than I supposed. A wave of gleefulness mixed in with my combative, hot-blooded state. My emotions were always mixing swirling vortexes, but I was starting to enjoy this. Fighting with Miranda while staying in control.

Every movement of hers, every flash of her eyes, every sharp word that fell from her lips acted as a stimulant, heightening my awareness. This newfound sense of control didn't just keep my powers at bay, it fucking thrilled me. It actually thrilled me. Our combative tussles reminded me of two lions play grappling and it left my chest heaving and my dick hard.

As I pondered this new level of being, Miranda smashed her lips against mine.

Heat and arousal exploded in me. I met her kiss with my own ferocious energy. My tongue pushed its way past her lips and we both groaned as she opened up to me. My pants tightened. Her taste was still unreal, even more delicious than the enchanting scent of her skin. The softness of her mouth unhinged me in a way I'd never felt before. I hungered for her. Oh gods, I wanted, no needed to possess her. Everything else disappeared except for the woman and my white-hot need to devour her.

She slammed her hands into my chest, and we broke from each other.

"Get off!" she yelled, panting and flushed.

I ran my hand through my hair, reeling. Was I losing my mind? Had I kissed her and didn't realize it? I had only moments ago reveled in my control, but I must have imagined it.

Oh fuck, how out of control was I?

She was right. This was a terrible idea. Miranda needed to get out of here. We needed to put the bars between us. We could never do this again. Not while I was so out of mind to get to her. This uncontrollable level of passion would surely lead to me losing control in one way or another. While she hacked away at the beastly parts of me, another kind of beast had reared its head and wanted to take a bite out of her.

Miranda grabbed me by the back of the head and kissed me again.

Okaaay, maybe I'm not the crazy one here. She clawed at me like she couldn't get enough. I met her hungry kisses with my own desperation. I knew she had a deep vein of passion in her and apparently the levee had broken. My hands swept along the curve of her back as she clutched my shoulders. Oh fuck, it felt good. The feel of her body against mine after thousands of years of empty space around me, had something screaming from the center of my chest for more, more, more.

Her leg rose, and I caught it, wrapping it around my hips so my rising hardness could nestle at her center.

"Oh fuck," she whimpered as if the sensation caused her pain. I rocked into her softness and growled. Fuck, I wanted to be in her. I wanted to be in her so deep, she could taste me at the back of her throat. I shoved my tongue into her mouth, deeper. It was an assault, mimicking what I wanted to do to her. Fill her, finish her.

My fingers slipped under her shirt and ran along her warm, bare skin. I let out an even louder groan. I was so fucking aroused and caught between wanting to revel in the sensation of our touching and ripping her clothes off. It both satisfied me and drove my desire higher, hotter, until a sweat broke out over my body.

Miranda's hand slid over my chest and shoulders, gripped my hair as she rocked herself faster against me. She broke our kiss, gasping, her head falling backward. The little minx rode my hardness like a woman possessed. My raging need took a back seat as I watched her get off through our clothes. I placed a hand on her back and pulled her leg and hip forward, forcing her to arch further. I ground into her, feeling so hard I could pound nails with my dick. A wet heat spread between us with each rocking motion.

So close. We were so close.

The erotic vision she presented as she rubbed and groaned, face scrunched in concentration, nearly fucking undid me. If I hadn't already brought myself off by my hand twice today, I would have come right there. At some point, I'd picked her up by the hip, so she was writhing on me midair. My counter thrusts pushed her closer to the edge.

"Oh fuck," she gasped. "Right there, oh fuck, don't stop."

The world could explode around us, burn down, or freeze over and I wouldn't stop. I licked my lips, mouth dry from watching her, wanting her to finish. She had every iota of my rapt attention.

A long guttural moan left her throat before it hitched upward. Her eyes flew open, and her head snapped up as her body shuddered. I held her as she orgasmed, still rubbing against her sensitive cleft.

The sounds she made burned into me. Her scrunched up expression hit me like a sledgehammer. Her lips were parted even as she was locked into her orgasm, like the relief was so intense it was completely wringing her out. I stilled, suddenly afraid of moving. I didn't want this to end. I wanted this to be my eternity. Even with my own erection becoming painful, I didn't care. Not if I could experience this forbidden side of Miranda. My badass was an erotic visage and her clothes were still on.

The power she held over me was unprecedented.

Slowly I tilted Miranda into an upright position, sliding her down my body until her feet touched the floor. When those pretty brown eyes met mine, I realized there were flecks of emerald and gold surrounding her irises. Again, I wondered if she wasn't some kind of supernatural creature based on the hold she had over me.

Her glazed eyes all too quickly returned to their usual sharpness. They widened and her brows furrowed as I watched the uncertainty take hold of her. What I wouldn't give to keep her from where she was about to go.

Miranda pushed away from me gently, and I released her. I wanted to scream, but I swallowed it and fisted my hands to keep from grabbing her again.

I need you. I need you. I need you.

The demand throbbed in my mind, but I shoved it deep down.

It was only because of her and all she'd done for me that I was capable of grabbing hold of my madness with a tight grip.

Miranda's eyes held a strange wonder as if she were seeing

me clearly for the first time. I studied her right back, drinking her in with my eyes, trying to brand the image in my mind. Her breasts rose like waves cresting the shore while sweat glistened on her face and skin like a river of diamonds. I fell into the fathomless black pools of her dilated pupils, while the heavenly scent of bergamot and sex wrapped around me.

Did she also notice the grasp I had on my sanity?

Fuck, not only that, where shards of electrified glass used to travel through my veins, I was now pumping hot with endorphins and desire. Is this what living felt like?

The only pain I felt emanated from hard-on so intense it pinched as well as throbbed. But witnessing Miranda succumb to release was far more gratifying. This might be the best day of my entire existence.

The best day since I met her lips for the first time.

It almost scared me to think of what tomorrow could bring. I'd never expected this. I had never expected *her*.

Her eyes bounced back and forth from each of mine, as if rapidly processing something. Then Miranda dove for her sword, grabbing it before plunging it into my chest.

Shock didn't even register, it happened so fast.

Regret instantly filled her eyes, along with the glassiness of unshed tears. Her hand shook on the hilt of the blade.

I understood. My little badass had let herself be vulnerable, and I'd seen it. She had to kill the witness.

I was always out of control and vulnerable, and it still pained me. It's why I didn't mind my condemnation to solitude. I didn't want anyone to see me like this. It only made me feel crazy.

She looked so scared. Scared of herself? Of what we just did? Of what she felt?

Life leeched out of me, but I reached out and covered her

hand on the blade with my own. I tried to give her a reassuring smile.

It's okay. I'd die for you.

It was the best death I'd ever tasted. Knowing it would ease her pain.

And then I was gone.

CHAPTER EIGHTEEN

THE BADASS

I ran out of there so fast I forgot my jacket. I merely clenched Bob as I dashed for the car. My brain raced. I couldn't get hold of a single thought until I was in my house with the door shut behind me.

Back against the door, I slid down. Strange mewling sounds escaped me. I didn't know what they were until I touched my face. I was crying.

"What the hell is wrong with me?" I asked out loud.

"It's likely all that killing. It can't be good for you," a voice answered.

I froze, fear slicing through my shame. "Who's there?" I jumped to my feet. Bob was poised out in a threatening manner to any intruder. The red of Xander's blood stained the tip and another wave of pain and shame smashed into me. Still, I remained vigilant.

"I'm right here." The voice said again. It was male with a French accent.

I swept my arm to the left and then the right, still seeing no one, though it sounded like it came from right next to me.

"Oh dear, I figured you might overreact."

My heart pounded out of my chest. Where was this guy? Had the thief trying to get in my car returned?

"You see, I've been quiet for many, many years. But it seems this has been damaging both of us."

"What is damaging?" I asked, still not understanding. I backed toward the center of the room, spinning slowly with the blade. The voice moved no further away yet no closer.

"All the killing. Normally I detest it, but Miranda this is really becoming unbearable."

What the fuck? The panic rose faster in my throat. "How do you know my name?"

"Well we have spent months on end together, though really it's only been the last several weeks that we've really gotten intense about this whole killing a god business."

No. No, I must be going out of my mind. Still, my eyes slowly fell to the glint of my blade.

"I've been killing gods, immortals, and fae for millennia but does anyone ask me how I feel about it?"

I dropped the sword and backed up fast as lightning, flattening against the door. "No. Way."

"*Ouch*. No need to be so dramatic."

"You," I said in a shaking voice. "You've been affecting my aim, trying to keep me from stabbing him."

"Well, yes. But can you imagine how it is for me? I may be an enchanted blade that kills immortals, but does anyone ask how *I* feel about it? Does anyone ask how *I* feel about all the blood and icky gore? No. Nobody cares that I'm squeamish or that I'm a pacifist."

My hands clutched my head. In the same day I have now flubbed a date, played monopoly against a god, dry humped him into a mind melting orgasm before I killed him, and now I was having a conversation with a talking sword.

"Bob?" I asked, hoping against hope I only had a mild hallucination and that it wouldn't speak again.

"I can't say I entirely appreciate the moniker, but I do feel it has brought us closer together. And while we are on the subject, I'd prefer you stop referring to me as 'they' or 'it.' I am quite a masculine weapon, and am a 'he.'"

"Oh my gosh, I can't handle this right now."

"Well unfortunately, you are the only one who can handle me, so you are going to have to get it together, Miranda."

"I—I've got to make a call," I said, then shook my head. Why the hell am I qualifying what I'm doing to a sword?

I left Bob there, in the middle of the living room and walked into the bedroom, shutting the door behind me.

I called Vivien. Thankfully, night had fallen, so I knew she would be up. Otherwise, she was dead to the world during daylight.

She didn't pick up. I called twice more before she picked up.

"What's wrong?" she asked immediately. I never called so insistently, so she knew it was urgent.

"Bob is talking to me."

Silence.

Well that's a first, my friend being at a loss for words, but not helpful right now. "The sword, it's talking to me," I reiterated.

"What is the sword saying?" she asked in a tone that suggested she didn't want to set off the crazy person any more than possible.

"He says he's squeamish about blood, that he's a pacifist, and oh also, he has a French accent." Okay. Maybe I did snap. Maybe this was all some fever dream brought on by Jamal's absence.

Or what I just did in the basement with Xander. Fuck, it scared me beyond anything. I'd gladly run back into a warzone than face the feelings that rushed to the surface after what we did. I felt completely wrung out, like something deep inside me had exploded and left nothing of me behind. And then I'd opened my eyes and found Xander watching me, looking at me like. . .like I don't know what. But I felt completely naked and the fear rushed at me a million miles an hour and I had to get away, I had to get him to stop looking at me like that, he had to stop seeing me. The me no one got to see.

So I stabbed him.

A *totally* proportionate reaction to the situation.

And now the sword took issue with my actions.

What the actual fuck?

I rubbed my face, my breath coming in short, panicked bursts.

"So we were wrong about Bob being nonbinary?" Vivien mused.

"Yes, but that's not the point. The sword is literally talking to me or I'm having a nervous breakdown."

"Have you been nervous?" she asked. I could hear she was taken aback.

"No," I answered automatically. "Yes. Maybe. I don't

know." I covered my mouth, contemplating how much to say. Would I tell Vivien? She was my best friend. If anyone taught me it was safe to divulge about sexual encounters, it was her. But that was different. It was her and it didn't seem to make her vulnerable. Something about what I'd just done felt so completely shameful, I didn't know if I could even tell her.

For a brief moment, I was grateful for the talking sword to divert my attention from my issues with Xander.

Maybe it was time to invest in a therapist.

"Okay, okay, okay," she chanted as if trying to pull it all together. "Here's what we're going to do. I'm gonna wrap up my bullshit with the baby vamps and you are going to meet me at Sinopolis and we are going to get some answers."

"Okay," I agreed weakly. I felt lost. I never felt lost. I always had direction, duty, and my shit together. I had it so together, I had it together for everyone else. But in this moment, I could only follow my friend's orders and try not to think about anything.

Thirty minutes later, I strode into the grand lobby of Sinopolis. I tried to ignore the rioting feelings inside me at knowing what lay far below my feet.

Vivien was already there waiting for me, decked out in a red mini dress and knee-high boots.

"So what's the plan?" I asked.

"We are going to take a little visit to someone who would know all about Bob." Then she said in a hushed whisper. "Is he still talking to you?"

Maybe I had overreacted. Maybe it was a little mini mental break after what happened with Xander, and I just needed a chill night at home to restore my sanity. This was all unnecessary and I was being silly.

"Oh, she could put her hands around my hilt anytime," Bob said.

My face scrunched. Apparently, Bob was a bit pervy too. "Please tell me you heard that."

Vivien's green eyes narrowed in confusion. "No."

Dammit.

"Bob is definitely still running his non-existent mouth."

She twisted her lips and nodded solemnly. "I see invisible reaper dogs no one else can see, so I totally get you." Then her expression turned thoughtful as she tapped her lower lip. "Maybe that's why we're friends? Bonded by the crazy."

I was about to respond when a dark shadow advanced from behind her. With a quick look around, I noticed how suddenly empty the lobby was. A spike of cold fear shot through my stomach.

Then the dark mass came into focus, and I recognized Grim in his black suit. He held a finger to his lips, motioning for me to keep silent.

But Vivien already noticed I'd become distracted. Her eyes widened as she whipped around, arm swinging to land a punch.

Grim easily caught it. She threw out the other fist and he twisted her by the first arm until her back was to him. She tried to kick him, but he dodged out of the way. Their movements were concise and supernaturally fast as they fought.

Grim locked down both of her wrists in one hand behind her back, forcing her to face me again. The whites of Vivien's eyes nearly swallowed her irises as if she knew what terrible fate was about to befall her.

A fluffy white pillow poofed against her face with a gentle pat. When it dropped away, Vivien still wore the same stunned expression.

"That makes six to four," Grim said in a low rumbling voice before dropping a kiss on her cheek. He released her arms and turned to me. "Hello Miranda. I'd stay to chat, but my staying would only put me in danger."

And then he was gone, pillow and all.

"That sonofabitch," Vivien railed, throwing her hands up.

"So you're losing the war huh?" I was grateful for a distraction from my talking sword problem. Which was an even greater distraction from getting off on Xander's magnificent boner.

It was a Russian nesting doll of distractions.

"I ain't losing nothing," she said, holding out a finger. Vivien was incensed. "It isn't over until it's over."

As amused as I was by their hijinks, my mind travelled back to the disastrous Monopoly game between me and Xander. Had it been fun?

I enjoyed winning, and it brought out both of our competitive streaks, but I wouldn't necessarily call it fun. It was exciting though.

Then I thought of what happened right after the game. That had been fun. Until I realized what I'd done and it wasn't anymore. Shame washed over me again, but I swallowed it down.

Talking sword first.

Vivien led me to the garage and her cherry red Range Rover with the special tinted windows in case she got caught out in daylight. In no time, she drove us far off the strip to a warehouse. I knew this place. She'd brought me here once before.

We headed to the very back of a dusty factory to a freight elevator. Vivien pulled the cage aside and smashed the button. The cage jerked then descended at a painfully slow rate.

"I didn't bring any Doritos or bananas," I said casually. This wasn't my first visit, but that didn't put me anymore at ease. Vivien had been down here plenty of times before me, but that didn't mean either of us enjoyed what was to come.

"I didn't have time to grab them either." Vivien was silent for a beat. "I'm thinking we won't need a bribe though. Not this time."

She was likely right. If anyone knew about the blade it was the person we were about to see. And based on our past inter-action, this person may have a vested interest in Bob.

When the elevator finished its descent, Vivien yanked the cage open. Overhead fluorescents turned on with heavy ker-chunks, lighting a darkened hallway.

A camera dropped from the ceiling, along with an auto-matic gun. It honed in on us, ready to strike if we made a wrong move.

"What do you want?" A familiar yet irate, tinny voice demanded from the microphone.

Vivien nodded at me.

I stepped forward though my hackles rose under the sights of a weapon. "I want to know more about the blade of bane."

Silence.

I looked over my shoulder at Vivien. She nodded again, encouraging me to go on.

I sucked in a deep breath before saying, "It speaks to me."

Another beat, and then the camera and gun zipped back up into the ceiling. I let out a breath.

We continued to the big double doors Vivien wasted no time sliding open. On one side there was a thirty-foot wall of fifty monitors. Some of them played anime, others played the news, but the majority appeared to be live footage of streets, shopping malls, or other public places.

The other half of the room looked as if someone had plucked a cozy grandmother's room and popped it in here. A girl lounged amidst the floral couches and chairs surrounding an antique coffee table. A large decorative rug cushioned the setup from the cold concrete floor.

A mixture of must and potpourri hung heavy in the air.

The high-backed chair in front of a long table of electronics and keyboards swiveled around.

A heavy-set woman in her late fifties squinted at us suspiciously. She spoke with a thick Filipino accent that was clipped with her impatience. "So, the blade speaks to you, does it?" Echo. We'd met before.

"Oh no, not her," Bob cried, clearly unhappy.

"Oh, quiet you," Echo shot back.

"Hi Echo," Vivien waved cheerfully at Echo, then at Echo's daughter, splayed on the couch. "Hi Aoiki."

Eighteen or so, Aoiki wore a school uniform decorated with chains and goth jewelry. Her wide nose and almond skin tone resembled Echo's, while her narrow yet mischievous, mono-lid eyes matched her Japanese father's.

The young girl waved back with a bright smile. "Hi Vivien."

Aoiki's head rested on the lap of another girl wearing a matching uniform, with serious eyes and a sleek, black bob. She was Asian as well with square features and even thinner eyes. Chinese, if I had to guess. She wore a matching school uniform to Aoiki's and from the way she stroked Aoiki's hair, I got the sense they were more than friends.

I didn't respond to Echo's acknowledgement of Bob's voice at first, unsure of Aoiki's companion.

"She's cool." Aoiki reassured me, as if reading my mind. "This is my girlfriend, Sunny."

"Hiya Sunny," Vivien said with another enthusiastic grin.

Sunny returned a small smile.

"Don't let that mad woman touch me," Bob carried on in a wail. "She's a brute. She tried to sharpen me by grinding me down, and she did it dry no less! Don't let her touch me, Miranda, I beg of you. I'm serious Miranda, take me out of here right now," Bob demanded.

"You are the whiniest weapon in all history," Echo groused. She didn't seem self-conscious in front of Sunny, so I guessed that was good enough.

"You can hear him?" I asked Echo, needing to hear the confirmation I wasn't alone in my crazy.

"Of course, I can," Echo said, getting to her feet and shaking out her brightly colored mumu. She grabbed the cane resting against the table and wobbled toward us.

Vivien and I came here when we'd been looking for the god killer, and Echo used her skills to help us locate it. But she'd made an addendum. She'd only help us find it if Vivien promised not to wield the blade. Not just that, Echo specifically told me I was the only one who could be its keeper, and we'd agreed.

"Don't listen to her, she's a brute," Bob sputtered.

"Okay, one of you needs to explain what the hell is going on, right now," I demanded.

Vivien's eyebrows shot up in confusion before her gaze settled on the blade and she realized she was missing part of the conversation. So she slipped away and crashed on the couch next to Aoiki. It was then a little white wiggling nose poked out from under the couch. A small white rabbit with black circles around his eyes, army crawled out from under the couch and immediately jumped up into Vivien's lap.

"What's up Darth Vader?" she cooed affectionately. He sniffed her in earnest. Then a fawn-colored rabbit the size of a small dog lumbered out from behind the couch. Her big ears stood out tall from her long face and flopped gently as she made her way to over to Vivien as well. "Hi Lulu," Vivien added, reaching over to scratch between the long ears.

The genetically engineered rabbits had been crucial in our mission to retrieve the blade, serving as the perfect distraction.

And though they were adorable, and my hands itched to go pet their soft fur, I needed answers.

"Why can you hear the blade? Why did you pick me to wield it? What aren't you telling me?"

Echo's face tightened. She was a volatile, explosive woman and I expected she was preparing to lash out at me. But then she let out a big breath as if all the fight left her. "I suppose if we must do this, we might as well do it over tea. Ryuki," she bellowed loudly enough to make me flinch.

A sweet smiling man popped out from a door on the far side. His build was sparse, his head almost bald and he wore an apron as he carried a tea tray. There was something about him that reminded me of an imp who lived in an ancient wood from one of Jamal's story books. "Yes, my beloved," Ryuki answered his wife.

"We'll need more cups," she said.

Soon we were all settled in the makeshift living room, everyone holding a cup of tea. Lulu lumbered over to my side and I was happy to reach over and pet her head. She leaned in gratefully.

"Why do you know about Bob?"

Echo's permanent scowl only deepened. "Bob?"

"The Blade of Bane. Bob," I explained.

"Ha!" Aoiki laughed as she put an arm around the very quiet Sunny. "That's awesome, I love that."

Even Echo's lips twitched at that.

"It's not funny," Bob announced with a sniff of offense. I don't know how he managed that without a nose.

Looking at Ryuki and Aoiki, I asked, "Can you hear it too?"

They both studiously averted their gazes. Even Sunny became far too interested in her cuticles.

"What the hell?" Vivien flopped her hands on the couch. "Am I the only one out of the club? I want in on it too."

"Why?" I asked again.

Echo sipped her tea then set it down with a heavy sigh. "I've been alive a little longer than you."

Aoiki snorted and Echo shot her a stern glare. Still, her daughter said, "try a couple thousand years older."

Wait, what?

"Aoiki," Echo snapped in reprimand.

"What?" Aoiki shrugged. "You are beating around the bush which totally isn't like you."

While I was still reeling from the new information, Ryuki reached over and squeezed his wife's shoulder. "My love, she deserves to know."

"Fine, fine," Echo waved a hand, before it settled on her husband's hand.

"Are you gods?" Vivien asked, her jaw having gone slack.

"No, but we have been here almost as long. We are what some would refer to as fae."

"Fae as in fairy?" I asked in disbelief. I knew the term from some of the books I read to Jamal in kindergarten.

Echo nodded slowly while Ryuki smiled at me. Aoiki watched me as if my top might blow. Sunny averted her eyes as she sipped her cup of tea. *Her too?*

My brain hit a brick wall and went splat. I put my tea down and stood up, paced away then came back again.

That's it. Too much for Miranda to handle in one day.

"Oh my god, you have to show me your wings," Vivien said with a squeal.

CHAPTER
NINETEEN

THE BADASS

"Fairies. You are telling me you are fairies?" A bit of hysteria had crept up into my voice. I fought it back down.

Ryuki grinned and blushed in a way that was far too adorable for an old man, while Aoiki watched me with a mischievous sparkle in her eye, as if waiting for me to blow a gasket so she could pull out the popcorn. Sunny seemed more apprehensive about me blowing my top. Echo simply studied me with her usual scowl, waiting for me to accept the truth.

"First vampires exist, then Egyptian gods, and now fairies." Vivien clapped her hands. "There have to be werewolves, ooooh maybe mermaids?"

One of Echo's eyes bulged grotesquely while the other narrowed in displeasure. "We prefer the term fae. And the supernatural has a way of hiding in plain sight, only the keenest can find them."

The hungry look on Vivien's face intensified. "That wasn't a no," she said in a sing-song voice.

I also couldn't help but notice that it wasn't a no.

"Are you going to pop?" a hesitant Bob asked me.

After becoming a vampire, Vivien had embraced the supernatural lifestyle and most of its eccentricities. I'd been on the outskirts of a lot of the immortal battles and in a couple myself. While I learned to be highly adaptable in the Army, I still found this new world pushed my limits.

Focus on what's important, Miranda.

"So the fae are immortal, like gods?" I pulled my shit together and throwing any would-be hysteria in a box and filing it away for either later, or never.

"No," Echo shook her head while rewrapping her fingers around her cane. "But we do live an awfully long time." She rapped the walking stick against the ground with an explosive clack that bounced off the warehouse walls. "And we don't forget easily."

"How old are you? I always thought you were twenty-five." Vivien flattered Ryuki.

The old man blushed at her flirtatious question. He spoke with a heavy Japanese accent. "Oh, you are close. But more like two thousand and twenty-five."

Vivien sat back. "Whoa." Then she turned to Aoiki.

Aoiki still maintained that mischievous glimmer. "I'm the baby of the family. I'm only five hundred and sixty-two. And a couple years younger than this hottie," she said, jerking her head toward Sunny. Their fingers twined and released repeatedly, playing with each other's hands.

Vivien turned to get Echo's age, but the old woman snapped. "It's not polite to ask a lady her age."

Ryuki reached over and grabbed one of her hands. "You age like a fine wine, my beloved." Then he dropped a kiss across her knuckles. Her expression softened and her cheeks reddened like little apples.

Vivien and I exchanged a look, and I knew we were thinking the same thing. The woman acted more like curdled milk, but we would never voice that.

"Bob is a fae blade?" I needed this all spelled out for me. It was too much to comprehend as a grown woman with her feet firmly on the ground.

Who was I kidding? I was spiraling further into a world that seemed to get deeper and darker with every step.

"That is correct," Echo said matter-of-factly, returning her hands to rest on the top of her cane.

"So why me? Why not have a fae wield the blade?"

The weight of something pulled at Echo's features, aging her almost instantly. "Because you are mortal. You know the value of life. Because you are a warrior. You have had to balance the choice before in war. Because you are a just person, Miranda."

My eyes narrowed. "How much do you know about me, exactly?" I didn't like the idea of someone checking up on me. Privacy mattered to me, especially with a young son.

Echo raised an eyebrow in challenge and swept an arm toward the monitors. "I see, and I calculate. It's part of my magic."

"And also, your talent," Ryuki added, beaming at his wife.

Echo jabbed a blocky index finger in the air. "If not for your involvement, I would not have helped unearth the blade of bane."

Vivien stilled, her expression suddenly serious.

Echo went on. "In ancient times, the gods became tyrannical, unruly. They were cruel and callous with the rest of the creatures of this earth. Soon, the fae found themselves in danger of being extinct, as the gods had become greedy and coveted their magic. The fae needed a way to fight back. So the oldest and strongest of us harnessed their powers to create a powerful weapon able to cut down the gods. It cost our fae elders their lives, but the blade of bane was born."

"Next thing you know, she'll pull out my baby pictures," the blade whined.

"Shh," I hushed at him, so she could go on.

"The fae finally leveled the playing field and through an example of force and power, were able to cut down the most greedy and dangerous of gods. It was then that balance was restored."

Ryuki's eyes dropped to the ground, shaking his head. "But the fae warrior grew too powerful with the blade and began to kill indiscriminately, both fae and gods alike. And we had to turn on the fae warrior to take the blade back. It was then decided that the blade was too powerful, and we hid it, even from ourselves. Once in a great many years, the blade will surface at the time it is needed most. And then when it completes its mission it is lost to us all for a time again."

"What is your mission, Bob?" I asked.

"As you may have noticed, I cannot control my comings and goings. But I must concur that I've noticed I am found at pivotal times. I believe that is part of my magic. Though I must say that this is the first time I have been wielded by a mortal.

Inevitably when a fae gets their hands on me, oh it all starts out roses and sunshine. Well except for the murdering bit. But then they grow hungry for power, and they all eventually turn corrupt with time."

"But I can't be corrupted by time because I'm mortal," I added.

"That is what I am hoping," Echo said with a sigh.

Vivien raised her hand. "Question. Does this mean that these little dudes aren't genetically engineered?" She pointed down at Darth Vader who had settled on the couch next to her.

Aoiki laughed. "They are familiars. They are their own kind of magic. We are engaged in a magically symbiotic relationship. They help us and we help them. Not very differently from how the gods and sekhors join to their mutual benefit."

I reached down to scratch Lulu's head. The oversized rabbit pushed her head up, directing me to stroke her nose.

"There aren't many familiars, just like there aren't many fae. Our numbers are few," Aoiki clarified.

"And we like to keep to ourselves." Echo announced.

"Speak for yourself," Aoiki muttered while sharing a look with Sunny, making me think her girlfriend had similar feelings. Her mother sent her a sharp look. Echo barked words in a language I couldn't even begin to identify.

Aoiki's eyes dropped to the ground, but I doubted she'd stay quiet on whatever disagreement they were in for long.

"What makes you think my judgement is so great?" What with Bianca urging me to stop killing Xander as it will bring about the end of the world, and my feelings for Xander, I felt more unsure than ever. "I don't know what I'm doing," I confessed.

Echo squinted one eye at me, studying me closely. Or perhaps trying to see into the secrets of my heart. Who knows all that she is capable of.

"Before you even set foot in here, I knew everything about you there is to know, on paper that is."

By the glint in Echo's eye, I suspected she knew *much* more than just paper judging by the monitors on the wall.

"I calculate, I see patterns, behavior, and trends. I know you, Miranda. You will make the right decision."

I finally gave into my instinct, sliding down to the floor to pet Lulu who happily crawled right into my lap for more affection. For some reason that made me want to cry. "Is this the part where you tell me to trust my gut?" My voice was hoarse.

"No," Echo snapped. "You do not make decisions from the gut. You make your decisions like this one does," she jerked her head toward Vivien. My vampire friend froze petting Darth Vader to pay attention, as if she were an escaping convict caught in a spotlight.

The tight muscles in Echo's generous jaw line relaxed as she leaned in. "With your heart."

The soft long ears slid between my fingers as Lulu set her head on my thigh, leaning into my touch. "You want me to follow my heart? Like this whole thing is a Disney movie?"

Bob snorted. I wasn't even going to begin to ask how the hell he got my reference. When did French-accented swords get a chance to binge Disney movies?

No, I was too caught up on the hard reality of my situation. Extracting myself from the sweet rabbit, I rose to my feet. "You want me to follow my heart? When my whole job is literally to kill others? How in the ever loving fuck weasels am I supposed to do that? Killing and love have nothing to do with each other." My voice had reached a frenzied peak.

"Love?" Vivien echoed. Her eyes were fastened to my face, as if stunned to find something there she hadn't noticed before.

My stomach dropped out from my body with a hundred-mile whoosh. What the fuck did I just let slip out? Did I really say that? "Heart. I mean heart," I corrected far too adamantly and far too late.

Then Vivien and the others averted their gaze as if trying to give me a private moment, which only served to further wash me in my shame.

Love? Was I serious? That was ridiculous. I didn't love him.

I was just lonely, and desperate for some physical connection. Yeah, that's it. I went on one bad date, and it made Xander more attractive. But only temporarily.

The amount of deep, soul moving connection, and excitement I felt when it came to fighting and flirting with Xander had nothing to do with anything. That was a childish notion, and I left childish things behind me when I gave birth to one.

But why the hell would I say *that*? The 'L' word? Is it because I felt I met my match?

Wow, Miranda, we think highly of ourselves, don't we? Our only equal could be a god?

But something in my gut pulsated with an undeniable knowing.

I couldn't shake how Xander listened to my child from a scant few minutes of conversation and then went to the lengths to set up a ridiculous board game, to help me have *fun*. Even if it had been an abysmal failure, the thought he put into it had rocked me. And then he unearthed something far more vital. The sexy, unrestrained woman I wanted to be.

Every time I visited him, he cracked me open a little more. He was fearless in the face of my strength, something that had intimidated others. Rashon, my first husband, had always tiptoed around me whenever I was 'on edge', but not Xander. He leaned into my intensity, eagerly craving more.

But it wasn't just about what he did for me. Whenever his

god-like facade cracked, Xander's vulnerability peeked through, humanizing him in ways I never expected. The dry humor that laced his words, even in the midst of his darkest moments, struck a chord in me, revealing a wit and resilience that I found irresistibly compelling. I craved those glimpses of his genuine self.

Despite his pain, or maybe because of it, Xander's character shone brightly, raw and unabashed. He was a raging storm, yet he had an inexplicable calming effect on me, like the eye of the storm - still and serene amidst the chaos. The raw honesty of his struggle resonated within me, a poignant melody to my own inner battles.

He was a whirlwind of chaos and pain, yet in those moments, I found myself drawn even closer to him. I felt an inexplicable desire to soothe his torment, to stand by him in his battle, to become his rock.

It had grown beyond mere attraction; it was a connection that penetrated deeper, into the very core of my being.

It was fucking exhilarating. It was life altering.

I was the biggest idiot of all time.

While I struggled with my insane emotions, Aoiki was the only one who didn't shy away. She nailed me dead in the eye. "Sometimes it happens like that. Sometimes love smashes into you like a Mack truck, and rationale has no ground to stand on. You can either go with it or dig your heels into the ground and miss the opportunity to fly." Her hand tightened on Sunny's, and the other girl met Aoiki's gaze with a mirror of loving devotion.

The serious admission from a girl who seemed so young— excuse me, a five hundred something year old fae—only unsettled me more.

We had gotten so far afield of why I'd come. I came to learn more about Bob, about why I'd been chosen to carry him. Putting my professional voice back on like one dons a jacket, I said, "Thank you for the information and the tea. I may be in touch in the future regarding the talking sword. I appreciate your time."

Then I shot a hard look at Vivien. She picked up on her cue and extracted herself from Darth Vader and followed me out without another word. Thankfully Bob also remained mercifully silent.

Only when we stood in the freight elevator side by side, did she speak.

"Do you want to talk about it?" she asked, her voice softer and more careful than I'd ever known her to be. It would have been far more normal if she came at me like a battering ram, demanding to know more. It only heightened my awareness of how wrong and screwed up I was.

I said I loved the god I killed every night. Maybe I was as mad as he was.

"Nope," I said, popping my 'p.'

I could feel her disappointment fill the space around us. Great, now I felt guilt on top of everything else.

Vivien was an absolute open book. Everything she thought or felt came out, and I supported that. Her free, open expression was part of her.

But it must look like I didn't trust her, but it was really because I couldn't face my own feelings much less put them all out in the open air. They would solidify, become real, and I couldn't afford that. It was better to keep all my rioting emotions inside under lock and key.

Vivien opened her mouth and then closed it several times as if debating what to say. Finally, she landed on, "You don't have to kill him."

My body nearly sagged with the weight of her words.

Because it was something I so desperately wanted to believe, but at the very center of my heart I knew it was the right thing to do. I had to release Xander from his torment. Even if that meant carving off a piece of myself in the process.

So all I said was. "Yes, I do."

TWENTY

THE BADASS

My heart pounded as I ran through the darkness, my lungs burning with each breath. I stumbled, catching myself just in time before I fell face first onto the ground. The scenery swirled around me. The bright lights of the Vegas Strip, the polished black marble of Sinopolis, and then the vast desert stretched out before me in a barren, deathly wasteland.

Fear had taken hold of me. Something was stalking me, something malevolent, and larger than life.

Running faster, I pushed myself to flee, until I couldn't breathe, my eyes watered and stung.

The sands pulsed and a wave of black rushed over them, turning the hard granules into soft silt, making it even harder to move.

BOOM. The earth shook.

"Miranda." A voice called out my name. I couldn't tell if it was male, or female. All I knew was it hungered to take me. Claim me? Kill me? I didn't know.

Sweat covering me, my legs started to give out, but I pushed on.

BOOM.

Something massive was right behind me. It was too big, too powerful and I wouldn't survive it.

Then I felt it. A pin prick of burning on my back. I instantly felt scorched as it spread. I was an ant under a magnifying glass.

"Miranda." The voice called again, just as my body finally gave up. My knees buckled and I crashed to the ground. I was covered in sweat, every bit of muscle trembled and shook from the exertion. A strangled sob escaped my lungs. I couldn't catch a breath.

As the entity drew closer, the heat from my back spread until it was suffocating, and I felt like I was going to burn up from the inside out. I wanted to scream, to fight back, but I was paralyzed with fear and pain.

My gaze lifted enough to see Xander in the distance. He paced back and forth on the silt, behind his bars. His sapphire eyes burned, wild with fear. He was the only one who could protect me, but he couldn't escape his prison. Xander shook the bars, but they were immovable.

The heat grew stronger, burning me alive. God, it hurt so fucking much.

"Miranda," Xander reached out to me through the bars. "You have to kill me. It's the only way to stop him."

I shook my head, tears streaming down my face. I couldn't do it. I couldn't kill him, even if it meant saving the world.

In my last moments, I turned to face the presence more powerful than the sun. A scream caught in my throat before frying away, my flesh sizzling and turning to ash.

My eyes flew opened. Still covered in sweat and violently shaking, the world came into focus as I woke from my nightmare.

I found myself on my knees, the cold, coarse texture of concrete biting into me. I trembled, disoriented and vulnerable, like a newborn calf dropped into an alien world.

Where the fuck was I?

Harsh, flickering fluorescent lights punctuated the dimly lit cavernous space. The sharp, metallic smell of oil and stale air invaded my nostrils.

A parking garage?

Someone bellowed my name. "Miranda," Bob yelled. I gripped him fast, but he was so heavy my shoulders tilted to one side. His metal shook, as if he were trying to wake me up.

"I'm awake," I said, my words hoarse. Barely able to maintain my balance, I tried to rise, my shaky limbs protesting against the effort. I had to figure out how I ended up here. But first, I needed to stop trembling.

"Oh, sweet Afterlife," Bob breathed. "I couldn't wake you up."

"H-how did I get here, Bob?"

His tone was darkly serious. "You got in your car and drove here. Your eyes were open, but you were unresponsive."

Looking over my shoulder, I saw my car perfectly backed into a spot. Straightening slowly, I noticed it was the parking garage of Sinopolis. On unsteady legs, I made my way back to my vehicle, collapsing in the driver's side. I set Bob down on the passenger side.

"How are you feeling?" Bob asked gently.

My lips twitched at the corner. Yesterday I'd been beyond freaked out by my talking blade, but today I was grateful for his presence.

"Not good, Bob. Not good at all." Somehow being honest with him was easy.

"There there," he soothed. "We need to get you home, with a nice cup of tea. Perhaps. . .perhaps we should find someone to drive us home?"

My knuckles flexed on the steering wheel as I turned the car on with my other hand. I'd left my keys in the ignition. It was just after four am. Cold air blew from the vents and it felt good against my overheated body.

"No," I breathed. "I got this. It was just a nightmare." Still, I didn't put the car into drive. I just sat there, trying to find my footing.

"I've never done any sleep walking before, Bob," I said, voicing my concern.

"I'm not so sure you were sleep-walking, Miranda." he said, still using that gentle tone.

I sighed, resting my forehead against the steering wheel. "I was dreaming. Dreaming of something terrifying, something that was coming for me. It was going to burn me up, burn the whole world up. Like a vindictive sun."

"Sounds frightful."

"Xander can't do that can he?" I was scared to ask the question. It was more for myself anyway. Was my subconscious detecting a danger in him that Bianca had foretold?

"No," Bob said with certainty. "I've tasted his blood many times now, unfortunately," he said with evident disgust. If he had a nose, it would be severely wrinkled. "The god's dominion is water and the seas. While Nun, or Xander, possesses an unsteady current of electromagnetic field of power, it can't do what you describe."

I let out a breath. Since when did I take stock in dreams?

Since you sleep-walked from your house across the strip to work, my brain answered.

"Hey Bob?" I turned the AC off, my sweat having turned ice cold on my body.

"Yes, Miranda?"

"Do you know who tried to break in the car that day I was in the gym?"

"I didn't see their face, whoever it was wore glasses and a bandana."

I pulled the car out of the garage and headed back home to catch a couple more hours of sleep. It didn't make any sense, but I couldn't help feel the strange occurrences were related.

Things had gotten too complicated, and it was far past time that I simplified them.

CHAPTER
TWENTY-ONE

THE BEAST

W ould she come again? Or would she leave me here? For once the pain of my existence didn't hinge on the influx of my power.

It stemmed for my insatiable hunger to rest my eyes on Miranda, hear her voice, eek some bit of personal information about her.

What else did she label other than her lunchbox?

What did she do at work all day?

What did her bedroom look like?

Did she like flowers? And if so, what kind?

I'd gotten a glimpse at the real, unguarded woman and she was even more powerful and ravishing than I first supposed. Nothing else mattered but getting another little piece of her into my damned existence.

I spent most of my day pacing the cage, unable to be anywhere else. I'd lived for millennia but this, *this* felt like eternity.

Come to me, come to me, I chanted even as my eyes remained fastened on that elevator, willing it to ding and announce her arrival.

If it took years to will her back, I would do it. I would pace here day and night until I manifested her return.

The high-pitched chime of the elevator nearly sent me to my knees. My heart threatened to burst out of my chest in the few seconds before the doors opened.

Oh gods, oh fuck, why did I feel giddy and anxious and possessed all at once? I paced back and forth along the bars even faster.

When she stepped out of the elevator, I stopped cold. Miranda had donned casual attire again. Tight fitting athletic pants that rose to her mid waist, leaving a few inches of bared flesh between that and her sports bra. She wore her signature leather duster and a pair of boots. Her deep bronze skin gleamed as if she'd been exerting herself physically, and suddenly I was as parched as a dying man. Whatever activity or workout she'd clearly been partaking in only intensified her scent. I inhaled a shuddering breath as I gripped the bars, my cock hardening. Suddenly, I knew with absolute certainty I could rip these metal barriers out of my way to get to her if I needed.

Despite the energized gleam in her eyes, lines of either worry or exhaustion lined them. Normally she seemed serious and duty driven, but today there was some air of sadness surrounding her.

Was this because of yesterday? What about our interchange could have made her...sad?

"What is this?" she asked, looking past me to the round table I had set up again.

I couldn't tear my eyes away from her even as I answered. "It's a game. It's called Candy Land. I thought we could try again."

"We can't play games anymore, Xander." Her voice was flat and empty.

I instantly hated it. I needed to stoke the fire I knew burned bright inside her.

Sass me, fight me, fuck me, just don't detach.

I smirked, running my hands up and down the bars. "Of course, we can. What else are you going to do with your time off? Not to mention your kid said—"

"Don't talk about my kid," she snapped.

Miranda was strung even tighter than before.

"Is this about yesterday?"

Instead of answering, those luscious, perfectly kissable lips pursed.

It was. I didn't know if she was embarrassed, ashamed, or disgusted of what happened, or because it happened with me.

A better man would tell her what she wanted to hear.

It won't happen again.

We can keep it professional.

But I wasn't a man at all. I was a half-feral god who scented a woman more powerful, more resilient than any immortal I'd encountered. So I wouldn't lie to her.

I *didn't* want to respect her boundaries. I wanted to cross these bars and plow straight through her emotional barriers and get to her the way she got to me. I wanted her obsessed, smitten, and hungry as fuck for more of me.

So I did something else. I pushed one of her big bright red buttons.

"Are you telling me you are afraid to play Candy Land, a child's game with me?" I scoffed, arranging my face in the most condescending smirk, as if I'd known she was a lowly human without a backbone all along.

It couldn't be further than the truth, but Miranda couldn't know that I was a god ready to worship at her mortal feet. For one more kiss, one more death.

The trepidation hardened in her eyes. I'd hit my mark, but I needed another strike or two.

"You're afraid you can't control yourself around me because you are falling in love with me, sweetheart? Because if you can't manage this simple task, we might as well forget about blade training." I let my lip curl in disgust.

Her posture stiffened.

Just one more little push.

I raised my hands as I let my expression smooth with indifference. "But my mistake, I didn't know you'd be so emotional about boardgames. I'll put it away."

Something defiant flashed in her eyes as her nostrils flared.

My heart stuttered at seeing her riled up. It beat out an excited message of anticipation.

Miranda stalked over to the control panel and hit the button opening my cage. "Let's get this over with so I can kick your ass, *after* I finish kicking your ass." She dropped into the chair across from me.

As the doors to my cage opened, I knew I had her right where I wanted her. I grinned, savoring the thrill of the chase, knowing that every move I made was a calculated risk, and every breath I took brought me closer to my ultimate goal.

Time. I just earned myself more time with Ms. Badass herself.

Miranda sat across from me, eyes flashing with defiance as she glared at me over the game board.

I leaned forward, locking eyes with her. "You know I'm going to beat you this time, right?" I said, trying to goad her into a response.

She rolled her eyes, shaking her head. "In your dreams, beast boy. You cheated last time, but it didn't help you then. What makes you think it will help you now?"

I darkly chuckled, picked up and shuffled the cards with colored squares on them. "Oh, you think you're so clever, don't you?" My voice dripped with sarcasm. "I have a few tricks up my sleeve this time. And don't worry, I'll play fair."

"Oh that's reassuring," she said dryly, then sniffed. "Even if you cheat, I'll still kick your ass. Just like last time."

Her competitive mode had been activated and she wasn't even thinking about what had happened after the game yesterday. I liked her in here, in these bars with me, comfortable and unafraid.

But *I* couldn't forget a single sensation about the softness of her full lips or the inferno she made explode to life inside me yesterday.

Miranda pulled a card first, the colored blocks determining how far her little gingerbread man could go. Her face was a tight mask of fierce intensity. We went on for a couple rounds, our cards keeping us neck in neck on the board.

And as the game progressed, I found myself becoming more and more invested in the outcome, driven by a fierce desire to come out on top.

Then I lost my edge, she advanced several spots in front of me.

"Ha!" she exclaimed, giving me a smirk. "Looks like I'm in the lead."

I narrowed my eyes at her. "Don't get too confident, sweetheart. You haven't even gotten to the Peppermint Forest yet."

She raised an eyebrow. "You realize we are taking this game far too seriously, don't you?"

I shrugged, pretending to be nonchalant. "I just don't like to lose."

I was focused on the dark angel across from me rather than the board in front of me. I learned yesterday that playing games with Miranda was more than just a way to pass the time. It was a way for me to push her boundaries without scaring her.

I gave into my long-standing curiosity and asked, "Do you miss him?"

Without even looking up, Miranda responded. "Always. He's the light of my life and while he's away at camp, the house feels colder, emptier. But Jamal loves camp, and he'll be back. I'd do anything just to see him smile."

Something in my chest swelled uncomfortably at hearing her devotion to her son, and how he gave her life. It made me want insane things. Like to meet this kid who she thought hung the moon, or even be like him in making her life fuller, more complete. I wanted to be that reason for the secret smile at the corner of her lips, or the sparkle in her eyes. I was a selfish sonofabitch.

"I actually meant your husband," I corrected.

Miranda's eyes slowly raised up to meet mine, their light brown sugar hue captivating me. Against the smooth, silky texture of her skin, they shone like precious gems, drawing me in closer. "Oh. You mean Rashon." Her voice, soft, flowed over me, sending shivers down my spine.

Jealousy warred with my need to know how she felt about

a dead man. I'd no doubt he was worthy, not just because he died a hero's death, but because he'd earned the respect and love of the woman across from me.

Her gaze fell back to the board game though I know she wasn't actually seeing the brightly colored illustrations. She was looking inward for the answer to my question. How deep did she bury her feelings for him? I knew she'd covered them up and pushed them down like she did all her emotions, but the question was how far? Was she so in love that the pain required a deep grave in her mind so she could function?

That idea created a sour taste in my mouth.

She started slowly. "Rashon and I were very young when we got married. He was a good man." Her expression softened, the corners of her lips curving up as she dove into her nostalgia. "He had the greatest smile."

My fists balled into fists at my sides. How often had I smiled at Miranda? Was it pleasing? Or did it only communicate my bitterness and pain?

Why was I being childish and comparing myself?

Miranda slightly shook her head. "He loved Jamal more than anything." Then her smile disappeared. "But we didn't get enough time to really get to know each other. We both hoped we'd have more time." Her words came slower as she seemed to deliberate each one. "I think a lot of the time I more miss the idea of him. I grieved the future we were going to build together. But we weren't around each other enough for me to miss how he made coffee in the morning or kiss me goodnight. Sometimes I wonder if that makes me a bad person, not missing my own husband. Forgetting about him entirely at times."

Then she jerked, as if realizing I was sitting right there hanging on her every word. She pushed her braids back on one side. I tracked the motion, her elegant fingers moving in slow-motion as they curled around the delicate shell of her ear.

Invisible bolts tightened in my chest. I was half grateful the ghost of her lover didn't haunt her, and half wished she could have had that future. Conflicting thoughts often warred in me, but this was a particularly hard juxtaposition of ideas that I swallowed down like razor blades and cotton balls.

"I've never said that out loud before," she confessed, abject terror entering her eyes making her pupils shrink to pinpricks.

Before she could freak out too much, I said, "You aren't a bad person, Miranda. I think you know that. And from what I can guess, your— Rashon wouldn't have wanted you to love his ghost more than your present." I took a gamble on imagining him to be a practical man, that's who I envisioned Miranda with. Someone steady, who could support her and others, a beacon of strength.

Something in my chest caved in as I thought of how opposite I was to that.

Miranda visibly swallowed before she held out the deck of cards. "Your turn."

I allowed my fingers to stroke hers as I took the stack. For such a small surface area of connected skin, a massive spark leapt to life and travelled through my entire body, warming me.

Our eyes locked, forcing us both to face the vulnerability she exposed. I tried to silently communicate to her that it was safe. I was safe.

Our touch broke and so with it, went my lie.

Who the fuck did I think I was? Trying to convince her I was safe? I wasn't. But thankfully, even in the moments I deluded myself, I doubted she'd forget. Miranda was far too sharp to fall for the bullshit I even fed myself.

We continued to play, both of us getting more and more

competitive as we advanced through the different colored spaces of the board. When she landed on the Molasses Pit, Miranda groaned in frustration as she was forced to miss a turn.

"I can't believe I'm falling behind," she groused, crossing her arms over her chest.

I couldn't help but feel a surge of satisfaction as I danced my gingerbread man past hers. "Looks like the tides have turned," I said with a smirk.

Miranda shot me a glare, but I could see the glint of amusement in her eyes. "Don't get too cocky," she warned.

Was she actually having...fun?

As we approached the finish line, our movements became more frantic, each of us desperate to be the first to reach kastle. When Miranda drew the last card that would determine her fate, she held her breath as she flipped it over.

"It's a red one," she exclaimed in excitement with a fist pump. "I win."

Miranda victoriously marched her little gingerbread man to kastle, beating me fair and square.

I groaned in defeat. For a moment, I felt a twinge of disappointment, a sense of frustration at having come so close and yet fallen short once again.

But then I looked up, meeting her gaze across the table, and something inside me shifted. My ego slid to the side, I saw Miranda not as a rival or an opponent, but as a partner, a kindred spirit who spent all their time feeling this life was about burden. Her burden was duty and responsibility, mine was surviving and managing pain.

Miranda grinned, her eyes sparkling with mirth. "While you are shit at playing games, we've definitely confirmed you are a sore loser."

"Well, you sweetheart, are a poor winner. Do you rub it in

your kid's face when you beat him at a game?" I didn't even bother asking if she let him win. Miranda was too upright to pander to anyone, even a child.

She rolled her shoulders back. "I treat him like an equal."

I scoffed. "I hope your kid doesn't cry easy."

"He is very mature for his age," she said, a little bit of pride sneaking into her expression, a slight smile curving her lips.

Her kid was right. She did need fun. And in that moment, I realized how badly I needed it too. But I also wanted more.

My hunger for her returned with a vengeance. I leaned forward, my eyes locked onto hers. I grinned, feeling a sense of anticipation building within me. Our game may be over, but the real competition had only just begun.

"Let's make a bet this time," I said, a sly grin spreading across my face. "If I win the next game, you have to kiss me."

Miranda's eyes gleamed with ferocity, like a shark smelling blood in the water. A hint of a smile tugging at the corner of her lips. "And if I win?"

My little badass couldn't resist a bet. I wondered how many people knew that?

I leaned even closer, the heat of her breath mingling with mine. "You get to decide."

Her eyes widened in surprise, but I could see the spark of desire igniting within them.

"You're on," she said, her voice low and husky.

Then her expression smoothed as she returned to business mode. "If I win, we skip the sword fighting lesson and we skip straight to me killing you. I'd like to enjoy what time I have left of my day off."

My heart pounded in my chest, heat crawling up my neck with panic. This was more than just about a bet. Miranda was drawing a line. If she won, things would return to a more professional interchange of death between us. If I won, I got to continue to push a boundary I desperately wanted to break.

If she'd really regretted yesterday, she would have run for the hills. But she was still here, and it was game on.

And I intended to win this time.

CHAPTER
TWENTY-TWO

THE BADASS

I couldn't believe I'd agreed to this ridiculous bet over a game of freaking Candy Land. I knew it was a bad idea, and I absolutely knew better. I eyed the colorful board. The truth was skill had little to do with this game. I was really leaving this up to chance, and that wasn't like me.

But down here, in this isolated cell, it was easier to take risks, to throw caution to the wind and just live in the moment.

But Xander still wasn't going to get that kiss.

Then again, I hadn't planned on getting off on his hard body yesterday or talking about Rashon today.

The way I acted around Xander both terrified and exhilarated me. It was like coming to life while realizing at the same time that I could die just as quickly.

Maybe it was all spilling out because I knew my secrets would remain in the walls of this prison, and die with him, or the way his piercing sapphire gaze seemed to drag out all the most important innermost desires like the ocean's undertow. Whatever it was, I found myself wanting Xander more and more with each passing moment.

I partially blamed Jim. What a douche. It's his fault Xander suddenly looked a million times more appealing. It was his fault that I suddenly found this game the most entrancing, captivating activity. It's his fault I was pushed into taking on this bet.

As we set up the board for the second time, I tried to focus on the game. But my body grew hotter, the aching hunger in my chest spread. Xander's scent filled my nostrils, a tantalizing blend of salty ocean air and warm, masculine musk. His eyes bored into mine without reserve, pinning me in the gut.

My lips tingled, wanting, waiting.

Nope nope nope.

The sooner I win, the sooner things can go back to how they were, I insisted to myself.

I ignored the part of crying out that it wanted more. More of Xander, more of the woman I was around him. Around him I felt equal parts sex goddess, clever wit, and absolute badass.

Topside, back in reality, I felt like a workhorse who ground herself to the bone so she wouldn't have to think about her own life.

And in this makeshift dungeon, reality was far far away as I played with my tiny, plastic, red gingerbread man.

The idea of the world ending, or killing Xander also slipped away as we continued to play.

The game progressed quickly, with both of us determined to win.

Our little tokens wound up the board, and headed toward the sweet ending. I was ahead, but he was always right behind me. As the game wore on, I could feel the tension mounting, the stakes growing higher with each turn.

About to move my little gingerbread man, there was something about the way Xander scrutinized me from under his long dark lashes that made me hesitate. His gaze was intense, almost predatory, and it made me feel hot and flustered.

The memory of his lips on mine assaulted my mind in high definition, making my stomach flutter and my heart speed up.

I moved my gingerbread man only one space forward. It was a weak move, but I didn't want to make it too obvious. Xander raised an eyebrow, but he didn't say anything.

His plastic player moved ahead of mine.

I drew another card and played it, deliberately foregoing the yellow square that would have slid me up Licorice Lane and put me in the lead. Xander's gaze was now riveted on the board, while I licked my suddenly dry lips. My nerves twisted into a tight cord at what I was doing.

What *was* I doing?

If he said anything, if he so much as met my eye I would either stop what I was doing, or just get up and leave. Get right back in the elevator and return to reality where life was orderly, if not a little dull.

Xander passed Duchess Gumdrops, while I landed on the Molasses Mudslide and slid back down the board by a considerable distance.

I could feel the tension mounting, both of us silently daring the other to voice what was happening. I didn't have to land on the Mudslide, and could I really say I didn't know better while playing an easy child's game?

I'm not losing on purpose. I'm doing the best I can, I blatantly lied to myself.

Xander drew another card. With only a twitch of his lips did he slide his gingerbread man into the Candy Land.

My stomach dropped out of my body, and I swallowed hard.

"Game over," he murmured.

I tried to keep my expression neutral, but my heart pounded in my chest and I was sure Xander could hear it.

I couldn't meet his eye, knowing what I'd done was so blatant, so foolhardy, so desperate and completely unlike me. Xander slid his chair back with an audible screech before rounding the small table. He held out a hand to me.

Still avoiding his gaze, I slipped my fingers into his, allowing him to pull me to my feet. His strong grip found my hips then tightened, sending jolts of heat straight to my sex. I kept my focus steady on his broad, muscular pecs, marveling at how insanely good he smelled. I don't think I could even imagine him wearing a shirt at this point. My fingers itched to trace the numerous scar lines branded in his flesh.

Xander guided me backward, forcing my feet to shuffle in compliance until my back hit the bars of his cage.

"What are you doing?" I asked, my words coming out breathy. I still couldn't look him in the eye.

Then he encircled my wrists, pulling them up and over my head, guiding me to hold onto the bars. The move caused my chest to push out, my full breasts meeting the warmth of his hard body

His hands slithered down my arms, as his lips evened up to my ear. "I'm going to kiss you, Miranda."

"O-okay." I stuttered. I actually fucking stuttered. Every

nerve ending was screaming for him to do it.

Touch me. Make me lose my mind. Kiss me until I can't think. I don't want to think anymore. I don't want to be responsible anymore.

My eyes fluttered closed as his mouth hovered over mine. Fuck, why did he smell so delicious? The heat of his breath against my overly sensitive lips sent my anticipation through the roof and I couldn't even try to suppress the full body shiver.

Though I didn't open my eyes I felt him smile at that.

Lips brushed against mine. The pressure was so delicate, so teasing, causing the flutters in my stomach to morph into a hoard of butterflies on speed.

How was he so in control? The one time I wanted him to lose control and push my limits, he doesn't even open his mouth to slip me tongue. I'm frustrated and suddenly insulted.

I started to drop my hands but his shot back up, forcing me to hold the bars again.

"No, no," he chided in a low voice. "This is *my* kiss. I'm going to take it how I want it, sweetheart."

The sharp command in his voice belied the tenderness in which he continued to kiss me. Anytime I tried to open my mouth or press in deeper, he pulled back. At last, a frustrated growl escaped my throat.

He chuckled darkly. "I may be a beast Miranda, but look how in control I am right now? It's all because of you. Any other time I would be out of my mind, half feral, trying to rip your clothes off and bury myself into your sweet heat. Fucking you within an inch of your life until you beg me to give you a break to recover."

My breath caught and my lower lips were instantly soaked. I hate that he voiced what I wanted. It's what I'd secretly been hoping for, and I was trying to keep it a secret even from myself.

Shame burned up the heat of my arousal and I moved to push past him. Fuck swordplay today. I'm going to kill him and go.

I'm pushed back, my ass and back slam against the bars but not so hard that it really hurts.

"What did I say?" Xander warned. "I get my kiss the way *I* want it, and I'm not done collecting on my winnings."

I opened my mouth to say something scathing, but before the words could even form in my mind, he grabbed under my thighs and hauled me up so hard and fast, I was shocked to find I'd blinked and my legs rest on his shoulders, my hands now gripping the bars behind me for balance.

For the first time since starting the second round of our stupid game, I meet his eye. Xander's hands gripped my thighs as he gazes up at me with his devastating sapphire eyes.

"W-what are you doing?" I stuttered again, feeling completely off balance emotionally and physically perched on Xander.

"I'm still claiming my kiss." He smirked wickedly up at me, never breaking eye contact as he leaned in and laid a kiss right on my center.

I sucked in a breath so fast my head spun. The intimate touch nearly fucking sent me.

Self-consciousness was a brief thought as I knew he must realize my wetness already gathered where he could feel it, taste it. But then even more moisture shot down to soak through the center of my leggings.

Xander's hands tightened on my thighs.

His words came out careful and low. "I won that one, sweetheart. But I think..." he licked his lips, reminding me of a hungry jungle cat. "I think you want me to kiss you a second time."

He was sin. The literal incarnation of sin and temptation.

Yet my pride fought for dominance over it. It muscled and punched at what he was offering, wanting to order him to put me down so I could march out of here, indignant and independent of his affect.

"Yes," I whispered, even as terror warred with my desire.

Xander's smile turned dark with satisfaction. "Wish granted." Then he pushed his lips to my center again. The pressure was more insistent as he opened his mouth and let his tongue swipe up my cleft through my thin leggings.

My hips jerked forward. A strangled sound escaped my throat as my fingers tightened on the cold metal bars. He continued to open mouth kiss my lower lips, his tongue probing, seeking entrance despite the barrier of the fabric.

"Xander," I gasped as the pressure of his tongue found my clit. All my thoughts scattered like a flock of birds. "*Ungh.*"

His hands moved, digging into the globes of my ass. "Fuck sweetheart, when you moan my name, it makes me hard as steel." Then he went back kissing me deeply, thoroughly until my hips were bucking and I was halfway to sobbing for relief.

"You threw that game, baby," he said in between kisses. "You wanted this. You want me. You want the beast to fuck you."

I was out of my mind with desire, the sounds coming out of my mouth were unrecognizable. Even on the rare occasion I pleasured myself, I stayed quiet, holding it all in.

My feet hit the ground and I was shocked by the literal sensation of coming back to earth.

Xander's face had changed, it was now a feral mask of need and determination. He pushed my coat off and it hit the ground with a thud. I was grateful Bob was in his sheath. I hoped it acted like a blindfold so he couldn't "see" what was happening.

My tight sports bra ripped up and off my body.

"How fucking dare you bind these gorgeous breasts up," he snarled, before attacking them with his hands and mouth. My left breast generously filled his palm as he licked and sucked on the other one. Tingles and heat spiraled out from where he touched me.

It was true. I had shapely breasts but I kept them bound up in sports bras, never going for the lacy, shape-flattering pieces Vivien used on her much smaller ones.

But now that they were out, being feasted on and worshipped, I never wanted to wear one again. Even as I let him run the show, I felt sexy and empowered.

Xander's hand snaked down, fingers skimming under my workout leggings instantly finding the split of my sex without the barrier of panties. I didn't wear them with these pants.

His fingers toyed with my heat. I choked. The foreign and shocking sensation of someone other than myself touching me there completely threw me.

When a long digit slipped up inside my tightness, penetrating me, I stopped breathing all together. My hands clutched at the corded muscle of his shoulders, hanging on for dear life.

He began to make the come hither motion, hitting a spot I didn't even know I had, while his palm ground into my clit. I cried out, my torso trying to curve against the onslaught of sensation.

"That's it, my sweetheart," he breathed into my ear, his hot breath washing across my neck causing goosebumps to pebble the skin of my entire body. "You are going to come for me, aren't you?"

It was all too much, too fast. I hadn't been touched like this, treated like this in so long my brain couldn't digest it.

"No," I ground out. And it was true. My body clenched

down and fought it. It didn't want to let go of control. My brain was rebelling, still trying to bring reason to the table.

"Wanna bet?" he dared me, his tone dangerous. The lights flickered around us and I felt his power crowd into the room, pressing against the exposed flesh of my half naked body. Xander was losing control and I didn't even fucking care.

Then his mouth covered mine and I was lost again. Lost to his passion, his need, and the most delicious taste of a man I'd ever known.

No, he wasn't a man. He was a god. A dangerous immortal of power who could destroy me. Those bars were there to separate us for a reason.

We needed to stop. We were nearing something truly dangerous.

Still my body bucked against his hand as I hyperventilated. My body clenched, working hard to tamp down my rising orgasm.

More than ever I wanted him to wreck me. This beast had clawed his way through walls I'd never intended to let him bypass. He inspired a part of me to emerge that I thought long dead, and now, I was addicted to being that woman.

The lights flickered more violently.

"Fuck," he muttered against my lips before removing his hand.

I cried out at the loss, tears gathering in my eyes, as pressure nearly exploded in my chest. No! I needed him to touch me. I felt starved. I forgot how good it could feel. I needed more. I needed him or I would die.

Xander backed up, sucking his middle finger into his mouth before slowly pulling it out. He still looked at me like he was preparing to devour the rest of me.

A hot shudder tore through me.

"Tell me what you want." Xander's voice was hoarse, either

from desire or trying to stay in control. "Whatever you want, and I'll give it to you."

"Take those off and sit down," I ordered, words bypassing my brain, coming straight out of my mouth.

The fabric of his pants pooled at his feet as he stepped out of them. The rod that emerged was massive, his hand already fisted at the base. My mouth watered, and I instantly wanted to find out how much I could shove down my throat before his toes curled and he groaned. The other part of me wondered if I could fit all of *that* in me.

It had been so long since a man had been inside me, much less a god. I was usually fully in my confidence to handle anything, but he might damn well break me in two.

So why was I so quick to kick off my boots and shove my pants down? Wasting no time, I strode over to him in three steps before settling in his lap. His hands found my hips again, making me feel secure and powerful. My wet center pressed against the length of his hardness, nestling him against me without letting him inside. A thrill swept through me like a wave. Was this really happening?

"Miranda." He gasped my name like it was a prayer as those brilliant blue eyes searched mine, looking for I don't know what. Mercy? Release? Connection?

Reaching down, I encircled the velvet hardness of his cock and lifted my hips. Slowly, I settled onto the tip of his dick. Oh. My. God. Even that small amount had me throwing my head back and groaning at the sensation of being stretched.

So long. It had been so long. And had it ever felt like this?

My name fell off his lips like a never-ending waterfall. Both of us were falling to pieces and he was barely inside me.

I lowered a little more. Fuck, I was already so full. My entire body broke out in a sweat. "Gah," I hissed. Despite my work outs, none of that had prepared my body for this.

"Fucking hell," he said, and dropped his head forward so he could suck on one of my breasts, moaning into me. It sent vibrations straight down into my already sensitized center.

Another few inches and I feared I would die.

When I finally had him fully inside me, my nails broke the skin on his shoulder, my thighs and entire body shook. It was too much. He was too big. And whatever spot he just hit inside me must also be my emotional center because an unprecedented wave crashed over me. I wanted to cry, shout, and scream at the same time. As if all the emotions I'd pushed down, shoved into little boxes so I wouldn't have to deal with them had exploded open at once.

"It's okay, sweetheart," I heard Xander say before he found my lips with his. "I've got you. I've got you," he chanted in between deep, searching kisses. His hands slid up my bare back, soothing me as a couple tears escaped the corners of my eyes.

Fully inside me, Xander didn't move though I knew he must have been desperate to do so. Slowly I adjusted to his size and the wave of emotion calmed a fraction. When I took my first shallow breath after I don't know how long, I rocked my hips.

"Oh fuck," I cried out, pleasure ripping through me in a totally new way.

Xander's teeth pressed into my breast as he panted heavily.

I continued to rock my hips, my head falling back as I surrendered to the feeling of being intimately impaled again and again.

His power still pressed in around us. It pulsed with the rhythm of our bodies. I started out moving gently up and down before his hands gripped my hips, easily lifting and lowering me in longer strokes.

"I could die like this," he rasped. "So very wet. So very

tight."

My eyes squeezed shut as thoughts of reality tried to bombard the moment.

I *would* have to kill him. After this I'd have to pull out my talking, pacifist-sword and run him through.

The absurdity of it all made tears crowd in my throat again.

I didn't want to kill him. The petulant child in my banged her fists on the ground in protest.

"Baby, I need you to come for me," Xander crooned, resting his forehead against mine, still rocking my hips up and down. "I need to see you come again. It's all I want." His words ended between gritted teeth. As if it would kill him if I refused his wish.

My body tightened up, fighting against his words.

My teeth gritted. No. I didn't want to let go. My brain couldn't decide if it's because that would end this moment, or because I couldn't let myself let go.

"Don't fight it," he growled, glaring at me, somehow knowing exactly what I was doing.

"Don't tell me what to do, beast boy," I said, sounding more in control than I felt.

"Oh no sweetheart, now you've done it," he taunted. In a moment we were up and against the room, my back pressed against a cold concrete wall this time. The contrast of his hot body on one side and the freezing hardness behind me only heightened my awareness of how much he filled me. My legs wrapped around his hips.

Xander rocked his hips into me, faster than the slow steady pace we'd been keeping while seated.

"No," I ground out, pulling on the hair at the back of his hair.

"You want me to stop?" he asked, his pace slowed.

"No," I practically yelled.

His pace picked up again, the friction faster and hotter than before. My brain went fuzzy as I screamed incoherently, still fighting the building pressure every step of the way.

I chanted curses, pulling at the hair at the base of his skull.

"You are fucking driving me crazy," he growled.

"You were already crazy," I shot back, barely able to keep my eyes open as he slammed his rock-hard monster cock into me over and over again.

"Give in, sweetheart. Give it to me."

"No," I insisted again. We were fucking and still fighting. He wanted me to give him all of me, unrestrained, but it was too scary. I'd given enough ground. I refused to give any more.

"You want to, I know you do," he gritted through his teeth. My ass bounced off the wall as he pistoned in me. Sweat covered both of us. Pressure built in me, pushing me to heights I'd never known.

And I did. Part of me desperately did, but it wasn't my nature anymore. My nature was to hold things in. It kept me safe. And alone. Alone was safe.

I could stay safe if I kept everything inside.

Suddenly he stopped. I blinked, aware my thoughts had manifested in my facial expression. I must look fucking pitiful.

I couldn't allow myself to let go or give in, even though I balanced on the edge of the most tremendous orgasm of my life. How many times in one night could I want to cry? I never felt like crying. Not at cute commercials or touching movies. But a damn had cracked inside me.

His fingers cupped my jawline, his thumb brushing against my cheek.

"No one has to know."

Whatever reaction happened on my face, he gave a curt nod too. Like he knew what I was feeling, even when I didn't.

Then he slammed back into me over and over, licking up

my neck, fondling my breast and whispering in my ear. "No one has to know."

A wire tripped in my brain as the fight I'd been waging for so long turned on me. Fuck. I realized I'd only made my release ten times more intense, as it built up relative to the fight I gave it. I was suddenly at the top of the highest rollercoaster, locked in, and the clicking to the top had stopped. There was no way to go but down.

I broke into bone wrenching shudders, screaming bloody murder as I bucked and keened on Xander's hard dick. Everything came down to the chaos of pleasure exploding in my body.

I don't know when he moved us, but I blinked and found myself lying flat on the ground, still coming uncontrollably. He drove into me, somehow pushing my release even higher. My legs wrapped around his waist, trying to find purchase, as my mind shot out of my body like a cannon. I was still screaming even as he pumped into me with a roar that shook the bars. The lights flickered and then exploded in a wash of sparks.

His warmth flooded my insides. A flash of panic about protection flashed across my mind before I remembered I was on the pill to manage my period better. And supposedly he hadn't gotten action in thousands of years.

The gentle rocking of his hips on my mind wiped away the worries as aftershock shivers rushed through me again and again until my body was spent and boneless under his.

Leaning over me, his hair hung in his eyes but there was something soft at the center of his ferocity now. "You are the most gorgeous, *impossible* creature I have ever beheld."

The tenderness was too much. It struck me under my ribs and I had to turn my head away.

Out of my periphery, I watched his lips tighten, brows furrowing as if he were in pain. Then he smoothed his expression, his demeanor turning impassive. Xander got up, helping me back to my feet. As soon as he left my body, I felt clearer about things. I could think again. For better or worse.

Cold reality closed in around me. My entire body was numb as I walked over to my discarded jacket and pulled out Bob.

"No, please no Miranda," the sword begged me. "You don't have to do this. We don't have to. Not with the blood and the death. You like him. It's okay not to kill him. We can both be happy."

The lump in my throat was immovable as was my mind. Whereas last night I'd struck Xander in a knee-jerk reaction to my shame, this was cold and calculated.

Xander looked at me in disbelief from under the hair that had fallen in his eyes. "What? No pillow talk?" He let out a dark laugh but there was no humor in it.

"This is why I'm here," I said plainly. "You asked me to do this."

His jaw tightened and his expression flattened, becoming unreadable. "You're right. I did."

I crossed the distance between us, the blade raised. Bob cried out. "Miranda, you can't do this to him. Not after what you just did together."

"Shut up," I said in a harsh whisper.

Xander's brows bunched together, but he didn't say anything.

Bob continued to adamantly plead with me. "Miranda, I know about death. Doing this, now, it will kill a piece of you too. I know. I know death."

I stopped a foot away from Xander. He stood there, hands balled into tight fists, accepting the fate I was about to deliver while still looking pissed.

Sword in my hand, poised at Xander's heart, Bob became

impossibly heavy. My wrist strained to keep the blade straight as it vibrated. Bob was trying to thwart my aim.

The lump in my throat grew. It crowded out my vocal cords. My heart suddenly felt as weighty as my blade, as heavy as a stone. As if it was also trying to drag me down, keep me from doing what I was about to do.

My arm dropped.

Then without a word, I turned, put on my leather duster over my naked body, grabbed my clothes, shut the cage behind me then got onto the elevator. I didn't look back to see Xander's face as I left him there. The doors closed behind me, and I didn't turn around. Clutching my clothes and boots to my bare chest, the elevator automatically started its ascent. I'd need to dress fast before it arrived on the lobby level.

But I wanted it to stop. I needed a minute. A minute or two of safety.

A red button appeared before me. Before I could think, I pressed it. The elevator halted. I should probably freak out about the magic/intuitive elevator, but I was already past full capacity of mental and emotional overload.

Dropping my boots and clothes to the floor, I sat down right there. My arms encircled my knees, pulling them to my chest as I rocked back and forth.

What was I doing? Who was I anymore?

How could I kill him when I lov–

"Don't you dare finish that sentence, Miranda West," I said out loud, my voice hoarse.

"Oh Miranda," Bob said from where he lay on the elevator floor next to me. "It's going to be okay."

I don't know how long I sat there, rocking back and forth while a talking blade comforted me over my fucked up life and the feelings I had for a beastly god who resided in the Grim Reaper's basement.

CHAPTER
TWENTY-THREE

THE BADASS

The next night at Xander's cage again, I dropped my duster to the ground on the chair. I tried to put what happened between us behind me.

"What the holy hell are you wearing?" Xander blurted out.

My head snapped up. "What?"

"You have a line with bunches around your backside."

I twisted around forgetting what I'd even worn today. "Oh, my booty shorts? I got them from a site online."

"They should be illegal."

My eyebrow raised, letting him know he was sidling up to danger. "You got a problem with how I dress? Because I'm a grown-ass woman and I can wear whatever I want."

"Sure, you can, but if you want a bunch of people glued to the ass you're flaunting..."

"Maybe I do. Is that a problem?" I asked stepping closer. My body felt lighter than usual. Almost unreal as I challenged him. I stalked over to his open cage, ready to take this fight to the next level. He met me in the middle, only inches separating us. Heat and intensity vibrated between us.

"Enchanting the masses with your perfect rear can cut into your services for me," he said, voice husky and low. It sent hot shivers through me, which heated into pure desire.

I couldn't tell if we were fighting anymore. Is this how Vivien felt when Grim first realized how provocatively she liked to dress? Granted my friend had the taste of a high-class hooker, but she rocked that shit.

And now that I was getting blowback over a measly pair of shorts, I suddenly wanted one of her skimpy dresses to parade around Xander and give him a coronary.

"The shit you're saying is some masochistic bullshit, you realize." I'd never let my son Jamal talk to a girl about her clothes like this. And I sure as hell wouldn't stand for it. I don't give a damn if he is a big scary, feral god. I deserved respect for my choices.

"The shit I'm saying is that I can't focus if you're going to wear those. It makes me. . ." His eyes glazed over at the same time a supernatural spark ignited in them. "Miranda," he growled. "The things you do to me when you're on the other side of those bars... you could be wearing a paper sack and still drive me right into madness. Have you no mercy for a poor god like me?"

I was stunned. All thoughts of my kid flew right out of my

head as I realized what Xander was saying. He advanced on me, and I didn't retreat. Standing mere inches from me, the heat of his chest radiated into mine. My nipples tightened, but his eyes were trained on my lips.

"Miranda," he rasped. Then he reached his hands around me and grabbed my ass cheeks, dragging me to him. His eyes fluttered shut. "Fuck," he muttered. Then he picked me up and my legs naturally wrapped around his toned waist.

I groaned loudly when his hardness ground into me. His body felt mind-meltingly good. Logic threatened to crowd its way in and ruin the moment, but I managed to keep it at bay. All I could focus on was how his hands massaged my ass, pressing me against the hard length in his sweatpants.

Again, my body took on a weightless feel as if I weren't really here.

He didn't kiss me. Instead, he ran his nose up along the column of my neck. Then his lips skimmed my sensitive flesh until I was ready to beg him to latch onto me anywhere. Suck, lick, bite me anywhere, anyway he could.

A wave of power rippled through the air, beating into my body.

"Xander," I said in warning.

My bones creaked and groaned as another wave of intensity seemed to clamp down on them, making them strain under the weight.

Pleasure was swept away by pain. His name escaped my throat in a breathless gasp.

The heat of desire turned into something else. My skin burned. It burned painfully and I was reminded of the dream I had before. The one where I was running and couldn't get away from an entity far more powerful than anything I'd know.

Forcing my eyes open, I looked down at Xander, but it

wasn't him anymore. He'd changed, morphed into the monster that had stalked me before. It wasn't his signature blue flowing energy that wafted off him. Xander was bright and scalding like the sun. Beams shot from his open eyes into my chest until I screamed from the searing agony.

He set me on fire, my skin bubbling and melting. He refused to release me from his arms. I had to kill him, or I would die. Thankfully my sword was in my hand. I raised my arm before plunging the killing blow into his chest.

"Miranda!" a familiar voice screamed.

The world swirled around me, but the blinding light only grew brighter accompanied by a blaring horn as I realized I was seconds from my end. I dove and rolled away, my skin scraping along the asphalt as I tumbled into the grass. The car sped by, not even slowing.

"Oh thank fae," Bob breathed a sigh. "I thought we were goners for sure."

I blinked hard several times, my fingers digging into the grass and dirt underneath me.

I'd been sleepwalking again. And this time, I found myself on a highway near my house. I clutched Bob but I was still in the oversized shirt I wore to bed.

"What the fuck?" I breathed.

"What the fuck, indeed," Bob agreed. "I think it's time we start discussing the prospect of putting chains on your bed to keep you from taking these little midnight jaunts."

Rolling over until I lay on my back, I let out a heavy sigh. "Bob, I can't believe I'm saying this, but I'm thinking you might be right."

CHAPTER
TWENTY-FOUR

THE BADASS

Today it was back to work, but I could already tell my heart wouldn't be in it. I was exhausted. The nightmares and sleep walking were really wearing on me. How did one treat those things? Therapy?

Pretty sure that wasn't an option for me. Unless the gods had a psychiatrist who specialized in immortal problems.

As I drew closer to Perkatory, I saw Vivien was conversing with someone else at our usual table. The perfectly styled hair and burgundy suit gave him away. Timothy.

I connected eyes with Aaron who was still behind the café counter, making someone's latte. He was likely too far away to hear what they were talking about, but his mouth was turned down. His eyes were serious as they bounced from me the two talking.

Something about his expression told me I was better to skip the Perkatory line, and head straight over there. As I approached, Vivien caught sight of me. Her lips tightened as she leaned back in her chair. A signal to Timothy to stop talking. Something was definitely up.

I stopped between them. "What are we talking about?" I asked in a falsely casual tone.

Vivien pouted off into the plants, while Timothy stared at her with a hard look.

Timothy was a god who knew how to keep things locked down like a steel trap. So I moved my focus onto Vivien and crossed my arms, waiting.

She still stared at a green frond but shifted in her seat.

I could almost feel Timothy willing her not to break.

I simply waited.

Vivien straightened in her seat, still avoiding my gaze. "Nothing," she mumbled, looking down at her barely touched blended sugar coffee.

The tension in Timothy didn't let up. It was a battle of pressures on her, but Timothy didn't know he'd already lost.

"I don't think you should kill Xander," The words burst out of her as her hands flailed in defeat.

"I agree!" Bob practically shouted, though no one else could hear him.

"Vivien," Timothy cried out in exasperation while rubbing the spot between his eyes.

A smile barely twitched onto my lips at winning the battle of wills before it disappeared again. I slipped into the seat, after a quick glance around to make sure no one around paid attention to the vampire casually bringing up the fact I murdered someone every night.

"What is going on here?" I pressed, interlacing my fingers and setting my forearms on the table. And why the hell were they talking about my situation when I wasn't present?

"Vivien asked to speak with me," Timothy said, still shooting daggers at her with his eyes. She was suddenly preoccupied with sucking noisily from her straw.

"She thinks I should let you out of the 'deal,'" he said using air quotes.

I turned to my friend, who avoided my eye like a kid caught with their hand in the proverbial cookie jar. "Okay, first off, why aren't you talking to Grim instead of Timothy? And second, I'm not on the hook to Grim or Timothy about this."

Vivien's auburn mane swayed as she shook her head. "I try to keep personal matters and business separate with Grim. It's better for our relationship." She practically rolled her eyes saying it, which told me it was his rule, not hers. I could only imagine the damage my well-meaning friend could cause when he was trying to judge souls for the Afterlife or obliteration.

"And you are doing it for them. They are the ones who asked you to do this. But you don't have too, Miranda."

"That's what I was telling *you*," Timothy waved a frustrated hand at her. "This is her choice. Hers and Xander's."

"It's a terrible choice," Bob muttered, though no one else could hear. "All that sticky blood. *Gew*." I felt him shudder in my coat. To appease him, I'd spent considerable time cleaning him in the evenings. But my blade acted like a prissy pony.

Not so hard. You missed a spot. We need more oil, don't rub me dry!

Vivien shot a glare at Grim's aide. "Timmy, this isn't so simple anymore."

He visibly cringed at her nickname for him. The two bickered like a couple of siblings.

"They have feelings for each other," Vivien went on in earnest.

"Vivien," I cried out at the betrayal, my palms slapping the table. How could I freaking forget that if the vamp couldn't hold her load for anyone else's secrets, how could I expect her to keep her trap shut about mine?

A serious mask replaced Timothy's ire as he turned to me. "Is this true, Miranda?"

My cheeks heated up and suddenly I wanted to be anywhere else. Thank god, I hadn't yet told Vivien about how physical things had gotten. But it was all a game, and she wouldn't understand that.

"W-w-would that be so bad?" Aaron interrupted. The line for coffee had dwindled, and the other barista was handling it.

Aaron stood by Timothy, and again, a palpable tension of sex, want, and frustration vibrated between the two them. Aaron's brilliant aquamarine eyes pinned Timothy down with a silent accusation.

It made me want to push my chair back a couple inches.

Timothy's tongue poked at the inside of his cheek as if he were trying to compose himself. "Yes. It would be. She is a human, and he is an immortal. Mixing the two worlds is a bad idea."

"Vivien and Grim seemed to have m-managed just fine," Aaron countered.

Timothy was back to pushing at that spot between his brows. "We are not having this argument again."

Though they were clearly having their own not-so-subtextual conversation, I felt chastised by Timothy. It was *my* hand in the cookie jar now. I was making things complicated with Xander, and if I hadn't told big-fang-Macgee over here, no one would have known.

Before they could get into it further, I turned to Vivien. "Xander asked me himself. He's in pain. He needs to be released from that."

Though recently he seemed to be less. He wasn't losing control; he wasn't radiating the small hairs off my body like when we'd first met.

She released her drink to cover my hands with her icy cold ones. "But you are easing his pain just by showing up. He's been an immortal, alone all these years. Do you know every baby vamp fears is? Being alone. They'll watch everyone they care about die. For the first time, you are giving him companionship and maybe. . .more." she threw me a sheepish grin, having guessed what had been going on.

Timothy stiffened at that, as did Aaron for, I'm sure, an entirely different reason.

"He still has to die," I said to her quietly.

Her face twisted up in anguish. "Does he? Even Bianca said killing him could have a catastrophic outcome."

"Bianca?" Timothy asked, his body turning stiffly toward me in alarm.

I quickly explained what she'd told me about killing Xander leading to a terrible, end of the world event.

"But Xander said her visions aren't always cut and dried. That it's too vague. He swore there was no way his death could cause such a thing." I rubbed my palms on my thighs, they were suddenly sweating. Had I been compartmentalizing too much?

I'd told myself she was wrong and I was doing the right thing, but bringing the prediction of doom back up made me question it all over again.

Not to mention a tiny spark inside me came to life, hoping Timothy would agree it was too dangerous. That I needed to stop.

Then what? Xander would remain caged in the Grim Reaper's basement, and I'd occasionally go down to bang the gong with him in between his monstrously painful episodes? A bunch of worms squirmed in my stomach. That didn't feel right either.

Timothy's expression turned to stone, and I could tell he was going inward, debating something. Aaron watched him with rapt attention. The fingers on his right hand twitched, as if he was dying to reach out to Timothy. But the god would keep Aaron at arm's length as long as Aaron was a mortal. Or maybe as long as Aaron was a loose cannon, adrenaline junkie. Timothy liked things orderly, predictable, and under his control.

Aaron wasn't any of those things.

When those dark eyes finally blinked, Timothy said slowly, "Xander is correct. Bianca's visions don't always mean what you think they do on the surface."

"She said my bringing back Grim would have dire consequences."

"Don't you mean pillowy consequences?" I asked, unable to keep myself from the dig to lighten the mood.

Vivien lips parted in surprise even as she glared at me in disbelief that I'd gone there. I half expected Grim to materialize and swat her with another pillow. Or maybe I was just hoping for it to get out of this conversation. I felt pinned and it was hard to breathe.

Then her teeth clicked shut before she went on to prove her point. "Vivien argued, her fingers digging into the table. "What if the end of the world is barreling toward us because of what I did? What if this is another link in the chain to a catastrophic event?"

"Is Vivien right about you and Xander?" Timothy asked, training all his attention on me again, making my skin prickle with an uncomfortable, shameful heat.

"We have spent a lot of time together." I licked my lips trying to buy myself time to find the right words other than, *yeah, we fucked and it was earth shattering and I don't think I can stop it from happening again.*

I was learning the harder I fought him, the faster I fell into him.

"I wish I didn't have too. . ." I quickly redirected my sentence when I heard the affection and sadness mingle in my own voice. Tightening it up, I said, "But I understand my duty, not only to Xander and Grim, but to the blade."

"The *talking* blade," Vivien corrected.

Aaron and Timothy's faces held twin confusion. I slowly turned to stare at Vivien, feeling betrayed for a second time.

"What?" she challenged, indignantly throwing her arms out again before crossing them across her chest and pouting. "You know what I am."

I did, dammit.

"I must have a chat with Bianca," Timothy said, pushing his chair away to stand. Except when he got to his feet, it brought him to eye height with Aaron, their faces inches away.

The smolder in Aaron's eyes was only matched by the intensity of Timothy's. It was like some kind of sexy face off, that Vivien I sat back and watched like a couple of voyeurs with popcorn. Who said women didn't have a thing for watching two impossibly sexy men together?

Aaron's gaze dropped to Timothy's lips, caressing them with a look before meeting Timothy's eye again. The god's jaw tensed and twitched as his hands balled into fists.

Vivien and I had been waiting to see if one or both of them would break for months. And if they did, we weren't sure if they would fuck or fight. Maybe both?

I sure as hell understood the fucked up dynamic now. Xander riled me past my sensibilities. It was intoxicating to be pushed out of control like that.

Get it together, Miranda. You have to stop this. You are going to kill him like he asked, end of story.

As if hearing my internal pep talk, Timothy turned stiffly on his heel and walked away. Aaron closed his eyes, inhaling deeply before his shoulders sagged.

I released a breath I didn't know I had been holding. Even Vivien gave a low whistle.

"He's so f-fucking stubborn," Aaron finally let out between clenched teeth.

"Yeah, but isn't that kind of what you love about him?" Vivien pointed out.

A grim smile curved at the edge of his lips. "Maybe."

Then he left us to go work the line that was forming up again at Perkatory.

Once we were alone, I said, "I love you Vivien, but stay out of my business."

"I can't do that, Miranda," she said, giving me an unusually grave look. "You're my friend. Honestly, the first real friend I've ever had. And I love you too damned much to let you get in your own damned way."

Deciding to skip the line at Perkatory and settle for the subpar coffeepot in the surveillance office, I stood up. "It's already done Vivien. There's nothing to do about it."

She grabbed one of my arms. "He's bringing something out in you. I've seen you smile in a way I've never seen before. I'm also watching you fight it. And I need you to think whether fighting what's happening between you and him has to be this way, or because you are scared of what happens if he lives?"

I gently pushed her grip off me and walked away without responding. I tried to keep from thinking about her words, but they haunted me the rest of the day. A swirling echo in my head.

What would happen if he lived?

CHAPTER
TWENTY-FIVE

THE BEAST

B*ing*. I looked up from the spring where I relaxed. My heart jumped into my throat. It was too soon for Miranda to show up, but despite my best efforts, my hope soared that she'd arrived early.

She'd walked away without killing me for the first time in over two weeks. I'd expected to have a bad night. Not long ago, my powers would arc, shutter, and burn in and out of me until I shifted and went crazy and blind with the pain. But whether she'd carved away enough of my power, or because of the

211

salvation I found in her kiss, in her body, I felt more steady than I had in a long time.

Yesterday had been a mess of competition and passion. I needed Miranda to come back to me so I could soothe it away. And frankly, so we could do it all again. I'd researched another game to play, and I even learned to shuffle the deck of playing cards I procured.

I hadn't decided on our challenge or our game for today. Poker? War? Go Fish? If nothing else, I needed the activity to serve as a distraction to keep me from tackling her the second those bars slid open. All night and morning I'd rolled around in the memory of her scent, her taste, the sinful fucking sounds that escaped her as she slid up and down my rock-hard shaft, finding her pleasure.

The screen up at the top corner of my quarters showed a different person travelling down the elevator to my lair. My good humor and growing erection were instantly shot down.

Still, I surged out of the water and wrapped a towel around my bare waist, not bothering to dry off. I padded my way across the stone path up to the cage. The door opened with a heavy metal groan as I pushed my way through.

There I found Timothy standing on the other side of the bars. Hair perfectly gelled in a pseudo-messy coif, today he wore a silken burgundy suit with his usual tie clip. The uptight ass always looked perfectly put together. Not that I despised him, but his perfectionism gave me annoying pin-prickles in my forehead.

"How may I assist you?" I taunted with a grin, knowing that was usually his line.

Except today, instead of the usual matter of fact, down to business attitude, Timothy's mouth with a thin slash of displeasure.

"I need you to back off," he said without preamble.

I opened my arms to the bars separating us, wordlessly stating the obvious.

"You know what I mean," he countered.

He hadn't come right out and said it, no, but I was beginning to suspect. . .

"Miranda," he clarified, raising his chin. "You need to back off."

Timothy and I rarely got along, and part of that had to do with him thinking he could tell me what to do to fit into his tidy little boxes. I didn't fit in boxes, I tore them to shreds until there wasn't one left. And him getting involved in my business, intensified my dislike.

"Our arrangement isn't your business."

"Maybe not, but Miranda is my business."

My hackles rose faster than a rabid dog's. "Go on," I dared him, my tone dangerous. My sanity suddenly slipped and slid across the thinnest of ice that separated me from violence. If there was something between these two. . .no, I couldn't even imagine that or I'd lose all control.

"Not like that, you idiot," he chided, instantly seeing through me. "My proclivities don't lie there." His dark eyes darted away as if he were thinking of someone else in particular where his proclivities did lie. But I didn't care about that.

"Well then Thoth," I said dryly, using his ancient name, "why don't you spell it out for me, on account of the fact that I'm fucking crazy, and beating around the bush only compels me to want to beat you. . .with a bush."

He gave me a curt nod. "I understand you need Miranda."

The way he said it struck a chord deep inside me. But it wasn't just about her killing me. Miranda was more than that. She tasted like life and hope, and looked at me like I couldn't get away with shit. I was addicted.

Thoth went on. "But keeping her down here for extended

periods of time isn't good for either of you. Getting involved with you in any other way, isn't good for either of you."

I had to suppress the snarl. "And what makes you think you know what's best for her or me, Thoth?" I demanded in open challenge.

He sniffed. "I know you are a fiery train wreck barreling toward the edge of a cliff. Miranda is my friend. I don't want to see her trapped on your ride and plummet over with you."

A sick feeling filled me. The imagery of what he described was far too accurate. I didn't want to do that to her.

I had no words. No snarky comment. No hateful things to spew at him. Because he was right, and I wasn't sure which I hated more. The fact that Timothy had a point, or that I'd not given any consideration to hurting Miranda in lieu of chasing the short-term pleasure I felt with her.

I melted back into the shadows.

Timothy took his cue and pressed the elevator button with a ping. Then he looked over his shoulder. "And if you do hurt her. I'll make you really wish you were dead."

I knew he meant it. And what more, the scrap of respect I had for the uptight priss rose considerably. Fuck.

CHAPTER

TWENTY-SIX

THE BEAST

E ven before Miranda breached my territory, I was already against the bars, bracing for the final blow. Today, she wouldn't step inside my cage. The playing cards, diminutive table and chairs had been tucked away. There would be no idle conversation or games. Just business, then she could return to her normal life, while I confronted the remainder of my death.

Miranda stood immobile. She didn't reach for Bob.

Avoiding the allure of her breathtaking visage, I fixed my gaze just beyond her left shoulder and waited.

"No game today?" Uncertainty tinged her voice.

"No games."

"Why not?" Indignation underpinned her query.

A crushing wave of realization, triggered by Timothy's words, made my heart implode. I had wanted her to long for me, even depend on me. And now it was clear, I had succeeded.

But my need for death surpassed my desire for her. I was betraying her by drawing her in, knowing I was on the precipice of my exit from this life.

I was truly detestable. A harsh, manic laugh erupted from my throat, uncontrolled and uncontained.

Miranda's eyes narrowed. "What's going on, Xander?"

"What's going on?" I parroted, my focus still off her face to avoid falling under her enchantment, "is I'm waiting for you to fulfill our agreement and end my life."

"No games, no sword lessons, no. . ." Her voice trailed off, unable to encapsulate our shared past.

The knowledge that she wanted to spend time with me, that she wanted me, was as heart-wrenching as it was exhilarating.

"You're lonely," I declared, my voice as icy as I could manage.

"I'm not lonely," she replied, her words automatic.

"Sure, you are." I shot her a condescending smirk, no longer able to keep my gaze from meeting hers. A surge of desire and resentment swelled within me like a tidal wave, ready to decimate a city of reason. If I couldn't have her, I'd burn everything down.

"See this cage?" I gestured to my surroundings. "It keeps me separate from everyone. It ensures their safety from me, but it also keeps me alone. And there?" I pointed directly at her.

"That space in front of you? You've enclosed it with bars. You've created a cage for yourself, and you carry it everywhere you go."

"Don't be ridiculous. I haven't done any such thing," she retorted, even as her pupils contracted in fear. My words had hit the mark so accurately, she couldn't even accept it.

Cocking my head to the side, I persisted, "You've grown so accustomed to loneliness, you don't even notice your cage anymore. But you can't come play in mine anymore. Because soon, it's going to be vacant here, and I won't have a single thought or memory of you." I pointed upwards. "You need to venture out there and free yourself. Because there won't even be a ghost of me to comfort you."

"I don't need your ghost. I need—" she stopped herself.

I decided to take a different angle. "I don't need you, Miranda. Even if I live, what happens after you are gone? Do you have any idea what it's like to watch everything you love die?"

"I have some idea," she said quietly.

Her husband. A mortal who couldn't survive the passage of time. It was a wound that would never fully heal.

She licked her lips and spoke. "When I was a child, I begged my parents for a puppy. For a full year I worked to convince them that I could handle the responsibility. I did double the chores. I saved up my money. I even treated one of my stuffed animals like it was a real dog and carried it around with me. Still, they always said no. But that didn't matter to me, I kept pretending that little stuffed dog was real. And then my ninth birthday came. They set down a big box on the kitchen table after I'd blown out my candles. I still remember the light blue wrapping paper with balloons on it, and the way my heart leapt when I saw the big airholes on the lid."

I had no idea where she was going with this. I should stop her, but I couldn't.

"And damned if it wasn't the cutest puppy with the biggest doe eyes."

"Why do I get the feeling this story doesn't have a happy ending?" I said dryly, even as my heart strings pulled.

"Because it doesn't," she said, her face clearing of all expression, a mask she painted over her emotions. I had come to recognize it well.

"I weirdly grew too used to the stuffed animal. The puppy was so full of energy, he was always stepping on me, never giving me a moment alone. I'd been alone a lot before then and I didn't know how to handle him constantly being in my face. One day I was in the backyard, and I just wanted to play with my dolls without him biting off their heads or running off with them. I got so frustrated I sent him away. I wasn't watching him," she whispered, and I could feel her pain in the air as sharp as a knife. "The puppy walked out into the road and got hit by a truck."

Fuck. That was terrible.

I frowned. "That wasn't your fault, Miranda. You were a kid."

It's not like she wanted something bad to happen to the dog. She just needed some space. I understood that. Not just because I required an inordinate amount of alone time, but from what I'd learned of Miranda there was a quiet stillness at her center that needed to be respected.

Then again, I spent most of my time riling her up. But I was playing with the parts of her that were long neglected, that clearly wanted to come out and play.

"Of course, it was my fault. I didn't protect the puppy, I was too busy playing instead of taking care of it. And the dog died because of me."

"And you've been trying to make up for it ever since."

A wan smile spread across her face. "I suppose I have." The smile disappeared. "But I've learned from that not to let things in that will hurt me in case I lose them. That if I relax or have fun, everything will fall apart. Fun is for my child, not for me. And while I loved Rashon, he never really got inside me, not to the parts he could potentially destroy. But you've somehow gotten inside me," her fingers pressed to the center of her chest.

Despair wailed up from my depths. This is what Timothy warned me of. I was doomed to hurt her.

She was handing over her most private, vulnerable parts on a silver platter to me. I might as well be a butcher, ready to hack it all into pieces.

The reality of what a disaster this was, fully hit me. I might as well be one of the gods of chaos. And it sickened me.

Miranda closed the distance between us until her hands wrapped around the bars beside my face. Her light brown eyes searched mine as she whispered, "Sometimes I forget what these bars are for. Because when I part them, I know you won't hurt me. You won't hurt anyone, Xander. Not anymore."

I stepped away, though every nerve in my body screamed in protest at the increasing distance. My voice was flat, emotionless. "Miranda, I don't want to live."

"But you're getting better. You don't have to die. Don't you see? You can control your power, you aren't out of control anymore."

My hands slammed on the bars so hard they shuddered, and lights flickered all around us. "I am not in control," I bellowed.

And I wasn't. Perhaps I'd gained a modicum of control over the pain of my overflowing power, but when it came to her, I was entirely out of control. I wanted her more than reason.

Maybe even more than death, but I wouldn't hurt her. I absolutely refused to do that. I'd much rather die.

"Yes, you are," she stubbornly countered, sticking out that tempting lower lip. She stalked over to the control panel and hit the button, opening my cage.

Damn it.

"You won't hurt me," she declared. "Come with me." She extended a hand. "Let's go aboveground. If you step out of line, I'll kill you, and we'll try again tomorrow."

How dare she?

How dare she tempt me with a dream long dead and buried? After so long, I'd have no idea how to return to the world. I was meant for shadows and solitude, or death.

Spinning on my heel, I retreated back into the shadows of my cage.

My spirited little badass had lost all sense and reason. This was evidence that Timothy was right; things had gone much farther than they should have.

If I have to hurt her, to sever this bond that I've foolishly entangled her in, then so be it. I pivot once more and strode toward her, falling back on my bitterness, my resentment, all the pain that had turned parts of me dark with cruelty.

"Miranda, I am not safe. You are not safe with me."

"Yes, I am." She fully believed it, her hand still extended with unwavering confidence in me. She walked further into my cage, ready and willing to trust me. It repulsed me.

I let out a harsh laugh. "You think you want this? That makes me wonder then. Did you ever even love your husband?"

The change in direction was so sudden, her hand dropped. "How can you say that?" Pain saturated her words.

I shrugged. "I'm just saying, it sounds like you chose him because he was safe and self-sufficient. You thought he could take care of himself, and you wouldn't have to. But then he died."

Miranda shook her head. "Shut up. You don't know anything about me or Rashon. He was a good man, and he shouldn't have died."

I had my foothold now. I advanced on her, sneering. "That's the thing, Miranda. Of course, he should have. It's what mortals do. No one makes it out alive. Or rather, no one should."

"I know what you are doing." She tried to act like my words didn't affect her, but the quiver in her voice told me her subconscious was shaky at best on the topic.

I circled her with slow, predatory strides. "If you loved him, you could never want me, Miranda. I am the opposite. You want to take me out into the world? He saved people, I would hurt them. Sometimes it would be an accident, and sometimes. . .not." That at least was a truth I was certain of. Captivity and pain had stripped away the remnants of humanity I possessed as a god. "Rashon took care of himself, but you would always have to watch me. Make sure I didn't hurt someone. Hurt you." When I circled behind her, I whispered in her ear, "hurt your son."

Miranda shook her head hard, as if trying to dislodge my words. But I knew the fear I was planting in her would grow. She could put herself in danger, but not her child.

The idea of harming a child revolted me, but I had to lean into the idea to convince her.

"It's best for everyone, Miranda," I said, reaching into her jacket. I reveled in the warmth of her body and her scent far too much as my hand withdrew her blade. She took it from me, and I backed away, adopting a combative stance.

"Kill me," I commanded. "And this time, you are going to chop off my head. Perhaps that will do the trick."

Miranda's brows were furrowed in a mix of anger and pain.

"Do it," I growled when she didn't respond.

"No," she shot back, even as her grip tightened around Bob.

"Do it," I yelled, taking a few menacing steps toward her. My movements were jerky and unpredictable. I would never hurt her, but I needed to provoke her.

"I don't want to," she said, something sparking through her anger. Fear?

Yes, fear. It's what I needed. I could break her bond to me with that.

I retreated to the far side of the room, melting into the shadows.

"Fucking do it," I roared, letting my body partially shift into the monster I truly was. Then I rushed straight at her. The whites of her eyes were all I saw before her blade slashed through the air. Suddenly, I found myself flying until my head slammed into the ground. I felt both heavy and light at the same time.

My brain took another second to register that she'd done exactly what I asked before everything went black. I hoped this would be the last time, so I wouldn't have to live with the terrible things I said to her.

I BLINKED. I blinked again. The concrete wall of my cell came into focus.

Godsdammit.

I was hoping decapitation would do the trick.

Apparently not. My head throbbed, and my throat was sore. Still, another piece of the all-consuming magic has been chipped away.

A sniffle caught my attention. Pushing myself up off the

ground, I found I wasn't alone. Miranda sat, curled up in a ball on the far end of the room, her arms wrapped around her knees. Tears streamed from her red rimmed eyes as her body shook.

I'm next to her in an instant. Without thinking, I wrapped my arms around her.

I hushed her in soothing tones, trying to generate some kind of heat in my body so I could envelope her in warmth. The wretchedness I felt was nothing compared to any death she had bestowed upon me.

I'd meant to hurt her, and I had. I truly was a fucking beast.

Miranda worked to gain control of her hiccuping sobs but failed. Still, I understood her words. "Please don't make me do that again."

I'd been so focused on getting her to kill me, I didn't think of the horror she might witness at taking off my head. She was supposed to separate my head from my body and separate herself from me at the same time. But she'd stayed. That hadn't been the plan.

"Why didn't you leave?" I asked in frustration, rubbing her arm. She felt cold, too cold.

She shook her head. "I couldn't leave you like that. I was too scared to leave. And then when you started too. . ."

She stayed. Miranda stayed and watched my decapitated body slither towards my head until I knitted myself back together.

Her head shook more vigorously. "I couldn't leave you like that." She wiped her nose on her arm. "Please don't make me do that again," she repeated, her voice so hoarse it threatened to shatter my heart.

Oh gods. I pulled her until she was forced to unravel from her ball and plaster against my chest. My arms wrapped tightly around her, as tears soaked my chest. "I won't. I won't make you do it again. I'm so sorry, sweetheart." Then I pulled her into my lap so I could hold her more completely. To my surprise, she let me.

We stayed that way for a long time. Me rocking her and holding her tightly. My senses filled with the salt of her tears, and bergamot oil. Eventually, Miranda stopped crying, but I didn't even think of letting go. She continued to tremble for a long time after. Even when that stopped, I continued to hold her against me.

I broke my badass. I couldn't forgive myself for that.

Only when her breath evened out, did I realize she fell asleep. I didn't want to wake her. So I stood up, with her still in my arms and walked to the back of the cage. I opened the door and left the cell behind us.

CHAPTER
TWENTY-SEVEN

THE BADASS

Even in Xander's arms, the stress didn't leave my body. I stayed partially aware, afraid I'd forget he was really alive. I needed to keep a part of my consciousness on to cling to that fact.

If we had left off like that. . .if he hadn't healed and woken up. It would have been like being stuck inside a nightmare. My heart thudded dully, grief still welling inside me though he was fine.

I suddenly understood Vivien better when she lost her shit over Grim getting hurt. He was a god, he couldn't die. Or not in the conventional ways. But while immortals were used to the occasional stab wound or car explosion, my human brain wasn't conditioned to be 'okay' with it. Everything in me had twisted up in sickening knots.

Xander was awake and whole, but my brain and body wouldn't calm down.

At one point, I felt Xander pick me up and move us onto something soft and comfortable. Exhausted and tense, I couldn't force myself awake for what felt like a long time. I only cracked open a lid when I no longer felt the warmth of his embrace.

"Xander," I cried out in a panic, jerking up, my eyes flew wide. I couldn't comprehend what I was seeing, or figure out where I was, at first. Then everything slowly came into focus.

I sat up on a massive bed in a huge rocky cavernous grotto. Several pools of water reflected against the stone walls with a magical shimmer of light. The room was lit by soft, warm torches that cast dancing shadows across the walls, somehow creating a cozy, intimate feel in the cavernous space.

I breathed in the scent of the warm, humid air, and my eyes drank in the beauty of the many pools, each one unique in its shape and size. Some were small and circular, while others were long and winding, stretching off into the distance like a river. The pools were filled with crystal-clear water.

I slipped out of the bed, covered in supremely soft white sheets. My bare feet met rocky ground, but it was smooth and somehow warm. I only wore my camisole and panties. My clothes were neatly folded in a pile by the bed.

The walls of the grotto were rough-hewn and uneven, giving the space an ancient, timeless feel. And yet, despite the ruggedness of the stone, the entire space was infused with a sense of tranquility and peace.

As I walked around, I could hear the sound of water trickling from a nearby waterfall. The sound was soothing, and it drew me closer until I was standing in front of it, watching as the water cascaded down over the rocks and into the pool below.

An inexplicable warmth crept over my shoulders, the distinct signature of Xander's presence. I swiveled around. His gaze was a penetrating mix of shadow and fire, casting sparks that caused the very air to bristle with energy. Yet, in this tranquil space, he seemed strangely soft, his strength manifesting as a protective veil rather than a threatening force.

"How are you feeling?" he asked. Apology was etched deeply in his eyes as his fists closed and relaxed repeatedly, like he needed to let off nervous energy.

The need to throw myself into his arms was overwhelming, but I was so thrown by my surroundings that I crossed my arms over my body. "A little cold, but I'm okay."

I hadn't been cold when he'd been in bed with me. And some part of me recognized the temperature of my body was directly related to the stress I'd been undergoing lately. If I didn't watch it, I was going to get sick. When I was younger and I got too stressed out, I'd get colds. But I'd learned to manage my emotions so well, I hadn't been sick in many years.

Xander took my wrist, unfurling my arms. "Come here," he said.

And like a little idiot, I went with him, following the beast to wherever he led.

I was guided up to one of the medium sized pools. With a push from his thumbs, his pants slid off his hips and puddled on the ground at his feet. Then he stepped into the water and it instantly began to bubble as if jets had been turned on.

God, he was fucking beautiful. My scarred, broken god. Regret and pain radiated from his eyes, as his face shone with hope that I would follow him in.

I shouldn't forgive him. I should stick Bob right in his heart and stomp away. But I'd been broken down into little pieces when I'd— Jesus, I could barely say it in my mind—chopped his head off.

It really put the horror in horrible.

His hand stretched out toward me, inviting me to join without pressing the issue. It was my choice.

I slipped mine into his before stepping into the water, not bothering to take off my garments.

A smile flickered at the corner of his lips. Gorgeous bastard. I shouldn't give him relief after what he put me through, but it was more like I couldn't deny myself comfort. And the hot water lapping against my legs instantly made me feel better. I followed him further in until I could crouch down and the water line stopped at my neck. It was like some giant, ancient hot spring and I instantly felt soothed by the heat working its way through my muscles.

Xander watched me carefully, slowly approaching, neck deep as well. His hands wrapped around my waist, and he floated me until my back was pressed against the pool wall.

His gaze dropped to my lips, leaning in but giving me plenty of time to protest. Plenty of time to shove him back, call him a monster, and storm out of here. I didn't though. I told myself again, I needed, no, I *deserved* the comfort.

Xander kissed me so tenderly, my toes curled, and my heart swelled. His mouth opened and slanted against mine, filling unexpected parts of me with his depths. He kissed me like. . .like he loved me.

But I knew it was just an apology. An immortal couldn't love a mortal, I told myself. Just like Candy Land, I was a game.

I may be his favorite game, but a game none the less. I melted, letting his kiss wash over me, feeling my heart ache with the longing I'd been trying so hard to suppress. I knew it was wrong to let him touch me, wrong to let myself be vulnerable to him again, but I couldn't help it. The warmth of his lips, the heat of his body, all of it was too much to resist. I wanted him, needed him, despite everything that had happened.

Xander deepened the kiss, exploring my mouth with his tongue, his hands roaming over my body as if he couldn't get enough of me. I moaned, my body responding to his touch, despite the doubts that lingered in my mind.

For a moment, I let myself forget about everything else, lost in the sensation of his touch, the feel of his lips on mine. The way his fingers grazed and massaged my neck so he could gain better purchase on me, molding me to him. But reality soon came crashing down, and I pulled away from him, breaking the kiss.

"Don't you ever make me do that again," I barked at him in my sternest tone.

He shook his head. "Wish granted," he confirmed.

Then I grabbed him by the back of the neck and hauled him down for a deeper, searching kiss. I wanted to disappear in him.

The water bubbled more emphatically around us. Xander took my arms and splayed them on the edges of the pool. I was impatient and wanted to fight him, but something about his expression stopped me. He swam back a few feet then raised his hands. His palms glowed blue before they lowered into the water.

Shoots of water connected with my body. Swirling vortexes caressed my breasts, varying in temperature from cool to hot, making my brain turn fuzzy with arousal.

A shoot of water licked up and down my cleft through my

sodden panties that suddenly felt heavy and cloying. I let out a gasp, as my center became molten.

"Did I mention," he said casually, "That I'm god of the seas?"

"You might have," I said breathlessly. My panties were slowly pushed to the side to make way. Then another tiny vortex found its way around my clit while there was still the sweeping motion up and down my pussy. My jaw parted as all my muscles turned liquid.

There was a parting of the seas joke tumbling around my sex-addled brain, but I couldn't catch it and pin it down.

My head fell back as the magic jets held me captive, playing me like an instrument.

"Fuck, Miranda," Xander growled. "You don't know how fucking incredible you are."

"Sure I do," I shot back, then let out a high-pitched moan as what felt like a column of water penetrated me.

"WH—," I asked.

The column of water was moving inside me. I was panting now. I put my hand against the side of the pool and tried to hold myself up.

The heat of the pool had made me pliable, and the pressure was as soothing as it was insistent in pushing my arousal higher.

Xander directed the column of water deeper and faster. It curled up and hit a sensitive spot in me that had my rocking my hips riding the sensation that coiled tighter and tighter in my lower stomach.

"I've thought of you in a bubble bath, more than once," he confessed, his irises blown out as he watched me with blatant hunger. "I've thought long and hard of how I could top your lavender scented froth to get you to relax.

The vortex quickened around my clit, and I gasped again. Xander finally drew near, kissing me, filling my senses with his power and masculinity.

I came for him then. I came hard and long. And I just kept coming. He didn't stop. The water continued to invade me, hitting a specific spot I didn't know I had, again and again.

The climax was beyond anything I'd ever experienced. I couldn't have imagined it. I was floating and was slowly drifting in and out of consciousness.

When I'd finished, the pool stilled around us. Xander pulled me close. My body was limp as he swam me to the edge. My arms reached for him. He scooped me up but kept me in the water, floating to and fro.

"Is that your version of an apology?" I asked, trying to sound coherent and alert.

"Gods don't apologize," he explained, even as a smile tipped up one side of his mouth.

"Well as nice as your apology was, it's not a substitute."

Deep blue eyes met mine as his grip tightened around me. "I'm sorry," he whispered in a ragged tone that begged forgiveness. "I'm so very sorry, sweetheart."

"I meant it's not a substitute for this," I said, pushing away so I broke from his hold. Then I reached down and encircled his long hard cock with my hand. Even the feel of him made my mouth turn dry as the anticipation built around how I was going to fit all that in me, again.

"Miranda," his tone was still a plea, begging for me to stop, or for me to continue. I wasn't sure.

The words crowded in my throat again, wanting to work at convincing him that he didn't have to die. I kept them stuck there, not wanting to ruin the moment.

"While your power is epic, I just want... I just want you."

When did my voice get so raspy? Xander's eyes lit up with surprise.

And then we were out of the pool and he was carrying me back to the bed at the center of the grotto.

CHAPTER
TWENTY-EIGHT

THE BEAST

She wanted me. *Me.*

Even when I freely roamed the earth, the humans would prostrate themselves before my almighty power, but not before *me.*

I lay her dripping body down on my bed, my chest squeezing so tight with the prospect of having another being here. I'd resigned myself to the doom of remaining in my prison alone. But suddenly, my cave didn't feel so oppressive.

Leaning over Miranda, I captured those full, sensual lips in a kiss.

I thought I'd found salvation in the death Miranda would serve me, but this was so much more than I could have ever dreamed. My hands slid up her bent legs, starting at those perfect ankles, smoothing up her muscular calves and gliding back down her sinful thighs.

Miranda shivered, her long dark lashes fluttering. She must be cold, still wet from the spring. I needed to heat her up, but I didn't plan on using a towel, and she was going to be wetter than when we started.

The pads of my fingers played along the slit of her mound until her hips bucked.

This wasn't a game though. Right now, we were just two beings who wanted each other. Nothing else mattered.

I'd show her. Show her that while I was the god here, she was the one deserving of worship. I'd slay her with pleasure and draw her blood out with a kiss.

I kneeled and spread her legs wide. I brought my lips to her pussy, and with my tongue, I licked away the water. The saltiness of it tingled my taste buds and whetted my appetite.

Her hips shot off the bed as she cried out. The sounds made my cock rock hard. I found the sensitive bundle of nerves between her folds and swirled my tongue around it. I was obsessed, addicted, and ready to drown in her pussy. Without preamble, I stuck three fingers up into her slick channel. She squealed and squirmed at the sudden invasion, but they were instantly coated with her desire. So I brought them up to her hot mouth, sticking them down her throat, forcing her to taste herself. Her body undulated as she sucked my fingers while I continued to devour her sex.

Her sultry groans vibrated through me. I savored every

moment of her enjoyment, something I hadn't experienced within the chaos and darkness my life was consumed by.

I licked and sucked and teased her until she was a quivering, slippery mess. Until she gripped my hair in her fists. Then I plunged my tongue into her, fucking her in earnest. The sound Miranda made made me feral. I drove into her even harder, faster, penetrating her delicious, sinful center.

Nails scraped along my scalp, urging me on. And yet, she was fighting it. I could feel her body brace against me, struggling to maintain control, trying not to fall over the edge I desperately wanted to push her over.

Why were we always fighting?

And why did I love it so much. Reaching out and gathering my power, I pulled it to me until I moved it all into my mouth, wrapping it around my tongue. I unleashed the power to follow the rhythm of my tongue, sending shockwaves and pressure into her, bombarding her.

"No, no," was all she got out before her knees jerked up, her upper body curling forward as she screamed. Her muscles rippled with release around my tongue, her hips and thighs jerking and shaking, completely overtaken by pleasure.

I backed off as she rode out the end of her orgasm, delighting in the mess she made on my face. I licked my lips, feeling way too fucking satisfied with myself despite my hungry, hard cock still demanding attention.

Miranda tugged me up for a kiss. Her mouth opened for my tongue and I happily swept inside, letting her taste herself — sex, the sea, and citrus.

My hands gripped her hips and I brought her to the edge of the bed. My cock pulsed at the entrance to her sex. Her glassy eyes widened, her ragged breath hitched. We were far from done.

Her head fell back and her hands roamed over her breasts,

plucking and pinching her nipples. I watched her for a moment as she pleasured herself for me. She was magnificent. Her full, pouty lips pursed as I eased into her willing body. Her inner muscles clamped around my cock and I groaned at the sensation.

"Oh no. Please," she begged, still not wholly giving in to what she wanted.

"A god could get confused with how many times you say no opposite to the all the other ways you tell me yes."

Her eyes opened to glaring slits.

So now was *not* a good time to go over her psychology. Right.

My hands grabbed her hips and I slammed into her, over and over. I was going to bury myself so deep inside her I could never leave again.

She cried out and grasped the sheets, clutching them tightly.

Even as she said it, her body tensed against me. I knew. I knew though she wanted every bit of me, she would yet again fight her desire every step of the way. But I also knew if I didn't let up, that her resistance would turn against her and drown her in pleasure. I intended to do just that.

I let go of her hips and she wrapped her legs around me so I could better drive into her.

"Miranda," I whispered into her ear again. "No one has to know. Just give it to me baby." My cock slid through her wetness as she clenched and contracted around me. So close. . .

A seemingly endless moment passed as our bodies melded together, sweat sticking us together. Her breasts pressed against my chest. I didn't want to stop, but I'd been holding back my release so long, it was going to rip right through me. I stilled and felt her tense.

My angel of death groaned, turning her head to side. She was fighting her release.

I'd have to take it from her. The more she fought, that harder, the faster I pounded into her. She was close. I could feel it. I could tell by the way she held her breath, poised on the edge.

I bent my head and sucked on her elegant column of neck. Her head turned away, eyes clenched shut. She was on the edge, fighting tooth and nail to maintain control.

"Xander. . ." she gritted between her teeth.

"Give it up, sweetheart. Come for me." I wanted to swallow her scream. I wanted to drink it down and die happy.

I reached out and rubbed her clit, my thumb pressing into it just so. I felt her shudder and watched her as her body gave over to what I'd made her feel.

I kissed her, drinking in her scream of pleasure. Her body shook for me and I felt so alive.

Driving into her once, twice, and my own head snapped back as my release shot from me so powerfully, I couldn't see straight.

Somewhere at the back of my mind, I feared hurting her with my power, turning into a monster. But no, I would never fucking hurt my goddess of death. My enchantress. My badass with a sweet heart.

When I came too, we were both panting, my dick softening in her. The feel of her fingers gently stroking my hair relaxed me so completely, I never wanted this moment to end. Not for life, not for death. Just this, forever more.

"So that's how you know about Batman?" She asked after a while.

What?

I pulled back to look into her face. I twisted to follow her gaze. A cluster of monitors showed the empty elevator, the entryway of my cell, and the third one played a 1960s episode of Batman on mute.

Looking down at her again, my lips morphed into a crooked grin. "You thought I was down here for millennia with no means of connection to the outside world? You should see my library. You'd be impressed."

With a glazed, satisfied look in her eye, Miranda nodded. "I bet I would." She sighed a little. "I have an ever-growing stack of books on my bedside table. When I was younger, in high school, I loved to read. But since Jamal. . . I keep buying books that I swear to myself I will make time to read, but the pile continues to grow as I never make time to actually read them."

I pushed back several glistening braids behind her ear, absorbing everything she said.

We drifted into awkward silence. Not about what we'd just done, but because we hadn't resolved anything. Not really.

I'd never make her behead me again, but I didn't believe in me like she did. I'd lost sight of what I was doing and Timothy pointed that out.

Did I want to die anymore? Could I be allowed to live?

To change my mind after wanting death for thousands of years was too severe and violent a turn for my mind to take.

Slipping my soft member from her hot body with a dual groan of protest, I pulled her body against mine, drifting into a light sleep.

I could live, for tonight anyway. Tomorrow I'd deal with Timothy's threats, the madness of my broken brain, and the woman who was making me question everything.

CHAPTER
TWENTY-NINE

THE BADASS

There were no dreams, no nightmares, in Xander's arms that night. For the first time in what seemed like forever, I felt rested to the marrow of my bones. It was comforting to fall asleep in one spot and wake up in the same place. I was already stirring from slumber, cocooned against a firm chest, arms wrapped around me like a protective barrier, when the intrusive ding of an elevator forced my eyes open.

My gaze snapped to the flurry of movement on one of

Xander's security screens. A parade of all too familiar faces had me springing upright.

"Oh, fuck," I blurted.

Xander made a half-hearted attempt to pull me back into our shared warmth, but I swiveled and swatted him away. "Xander, get up. We've got company."

His brows knitted together, a crease of confusion forming between them before his sapphire eyes flickered open. "What?" he rumbled, his voice laced with suspicion and displeasure.

As I fumbled into my pants with frantic haste, Xander took in the animated scene on the screens.

"Fucking hell," he echoed, a growl rumbling in his throat as he raked a hand through his tousled hair

Fully dressed, I snatched up my duster with Bob safely nestled inside. I pivoted around, searching for an exit. Strangely, until that moment, the thought of wanting to leave hadn't crossed my mind.

Xander was up, his pants slung low around his chiseled hips, a sight that kindled a familiar warmth coursing through my lower body, stirring memories of our shared intimacy. But I pushed all arousal and emotions aside. A storm was about to hit, and I needed to stay focused.

"This way," Xander said, leading me to a stone staircase that curved around and up a wall. With each step, I slipped more into battle mode. By the time we stood in front of the large steel door, I was ready.

As it swung open, a tumult of yelling and arguing assailed us, hitting like a sucker punch

Silence dropped like a curtain as I stepped into the room, Xander right on my heels, his hand a comforting weight against my lower back. Yet, no amount of preparation could brace me for the confrontation ahead.

Bianca, Grim, Timothy, and Vivien were scattered around

the room. Confusion creased Grim's brow at our arrival, while Bianca's eyes ballooned in shock. Vivien, however, couldn't mask her triumphant smirk, her eyes dancing with delight. As if she had been in on my secret all along.

She was my friend; I shouldn't have felt embarrassed. But so many people charging into my private, intimate moment made my skin crawl and my heart pound. My stomach knotted up, then knotted again.

"What is this?" Grim asked, looking back and forth between me, Timothy, Xander, and Vivien. It seemed my friend had kept some secrets after all.

"See?" Vivien said, pumping her fist in the air. "No one has to die."

Bianca watched me closely, and I tried to avoid her gaze.

Xander stepped forward. "What brings you all here?" he asked, sounding unimpressed. "I haven't had this many visitors since we moved from Egypt."

Timothy's mouth tightened, and I suddenly felt like a teenager caught sneaking a boyfriend into my bedroom. Except his disapproving look was aimed at Xander.

Grim gestured at the goddess in the soft pink dress. "Bianca came to me insisting that I put a stop to our arrangement."

"Hear, hear," Bob chimed in.

I bit my lower lip to keep from shushing the blade, as no one else could hear him. At least he'd remained silent during my other, more intimate moments. Who knew I'd appreciate a blade's discretion so much?

Bianca's light blue eyes darted between me and Xander. "Then you can't do it? You can't go through with it?" The conflict in her eyes told me she didn't necessarily approve of our relationship, but I think she was willing to accept it if it got her what she wanted.

"Miranda will follow through as planned," Timothy interjected.

Vivien's impish smile transformed into a displeased frown. "Hey, just because you aren't getting any, Timmy, doesn't mean you have to dampen other people's happiness."

I tensed. Was this happiness? Was that what I'd experienced in Xander's strong arms, in his bed, in his cave? Or was it merely a fleeting moment of peace?

Timothy whirled to face Vivien. "Quit stoking the fire, Vivien. Can't you see this is a recipe for disaster?"

"That's exactly my point," Bianca interjected, her voice tense. "If she ends Xander's life, catastrophe will follow."

"That's as vague as saying if you toss a coin, you might hit a leprechaun or just get a heads or tails," Vivien shot back.

Bianca's nose wrinkled as her brows knit.

It was a weird saying, but I completely understood her meaning. That's part of why we were friends.

Grim's voice, steady and low, cut through the escalating tension. Acting every bit the judge he was, he commented, "Bianca, your prediction could use more specificity and clarity if it is to hold any weight.

"I'm telling you," Bianca urged, "if he dies," she pointed at Xander, "we are going to face a world-ending threat."

"You also said that would happen if I revived Grim," Vivien countered, stepping protectively in front of Grim. She wouldn't change anything about what she did and dared Bianca to say otherwise. Vivien seemed to have forgotten they were on the same side.

Bianca brushed her hair back from her face. "That's what I'm telling you, Vivien. This is all connected. Bringing Grim back has tipped a line of dominoes into motion that are falling faster and faster, bringing us all here. And it very well may take us to the end of days."

"Bianca," Timothy snapped, his voice tinged with frustration. "Xander deserves death. It is his right. He has been denied all these years, and the world has only suffered from his presence."

Xander's spine curved as if he'd been physically hit.

Timothy kept going though. "He is the reason we left our home and came here, to get far from the ocean. He causes brownouts with his overflow of power and is one step away from being a nuclear bomb."

"But he's better," Vivien said, her tone pleading. "Miranda has been cutting a lot of his power away, and he is better. They can have a happy ending."

"Xander has been too far removed from the world," Timothy chided, his eyes narrowing at her. "He cannot reintegrate, not after so long. It would be a danger to everyone. It's not just his power that makes him dangerous."

I nervously licked my lips, watching the battle unfold, feeling excluded. I had been prepared to be thrust into the melee, but it felt worse being left out of it.

All this time, Grim had been silent, his gaze heavy upon me. He was studying me, like he could see all the mistakes, all the strange games, and the bizarre dance I'd engaged in with Xander. I'd started out as a professional, but now I'd fallen into another mode altogether.

"Love," my brain whispered. "You've fallen in love."

Or was it Bob that whispered that?

But Grim had also forsaken all the rules because he loved Vivien. I was ready for him to take the work out of this, tell Timothy that it was clear I couldn't go forward with this. Not with Bianca's vision. I was going to be released here and now from my duties by the Grim Reaper himself, and then we'd go from there.

"You are such a baby," Vivien said, wheeling on Timothy,

her stance defensive. "This feels way more about your piss-poor excuses to keep Aaron at an arm's distance than it is about Xander and Miranda's situation. Do you just not want anyone to be happy if it can't fit into your little boxes?"

Timothy's face flushed fully red. I'd never seen him so out of sorts. A crackling power filled the room, different from Xander's. It was more lightweight and nipped at the skin like little sparklers that almost, but didn't, hurt.

"That's enough," Grim bellowed, his face flickering into a skull of deep, sucking darkness. It made the pit of my stomach drop out, as if my body anticipated instant death. But Grim's face cleared back into the whiskey-colored human eyes, gaze still trained on me and Xander.

"Bianca, I give your visions great credence, but if there was one thing I know, it was that death was necessary for the health and wellbeing of this entire realm. Xander's anomaly threw even the elements into chaos. And as the protector of humanity, I could not condone his existence to continue in such a way. Miranda swore she would uphold the duty of her blade and made the judgement that it would be so. I trusted she would abide by her judgement without emotions clouding the matter."

The breath was sucked straight out from my lungs. Instead of grabbing and clinging to Xander's arm protectively, I curled my hands into fists. My boss's eyes were a mix of disappointment and regret. Disappointment in me, regret for having to be the enforcer in the situation.

"Grim," Bianca breathed sharply as if he'd slapped her. The god of the dead held dominion over all other gods, and what he said, went. She'd been shut down, and there was nothing she could do about it.

Vivien's expression was crestfallen, her shoulders curved in disappointment. Her eyes welled with tears, and I knew my best friend well enough to sense she was taking his judgement personally. While she was a vampire, she still had an overabundance of humanity and did her best to influence him with it, but it was clear he would not be swayed on this matter further.

Timothy adjusted his cufflinks, avoiding my gaze. He'd gotten what he wanted. But a bitter seed of resentment in me agreed with Vivien. Timothy had made my situation with Xander some strange avatar of his own issues with Aaron. He wanted to ruin our chance because he didn't have one of his own.

No, that wasn't fair. Timothy was my friend.

It was me. Me who wanted Grim to change his mind. But there was someone else's will I answered to over Grim's. My shoulders straightened. I told Grim I wouldn't do it for him. I would judge based off the plea of the god himself.

"I agree," Xander said. "Thank you for making this simple, Grim. I've always appreciated your sound judgement."

I pivoted to Xander, incredulity contorting my features. My eyes, usually guarded, laid bare the sting of betrayal. I expected him to be defensive and cold like he usually was when he was trying to push me away. But instead, I saw sound logic and agreement with Grim.

I could fight him on being stubborn, but I couldn't fight this.

"Xander, I—" I couldn't. I couldn't do it. I couldn't kill him because I loved him.

My throat closed around itself, strangling the words out. I could barely admit it to myself, much less in front of so many others.

Xander gave me a half-smile and grabbed my shoulders, kissing my forehead. "This was always the plan," he said, reaching for my duster and pulling out Bob.

Bob cried out in protest, "No, no, no! Tell him, Miranda! Tell him you can't kill him because you love him. That every time you end his life, you kill a little bit of yourself. And tell him I don't want to taste his blood anymore. It's. . .it's icky."

Despite Bob's childlike whines, his words struck me in the heart, but I couldn't bring myself to say it. So, I took Bob's hilt from Xander while the god urged me on silently, and everyone stood there waiting for me. My throat tightened, and my chest felt heavy.

Xander tried to comfort me, saying, "It's okay, sweetheart," with a crooked smile that held both swagger and resignation.

I knew Xander would wake up again, and I would have to kill him again. Each time, he would be closer to his final death until it was the last time.

Vivien was right. He was less powerful than before. The city hadn't been plagued by brownouts. He didn't mutilate himself or lose control. But I was only one piece of this decision, and I was judging it with my heart.

In a raspy voice, I replied, "Wish granted," and then stabbed him in the heart, in front of the other immortals. Every part of me iced over as I made myself cold to his death, to his fate, and my hand in it.

My job had gone from helping an immortal find relief from an eternity of pain to killing someone I loved. And right now, it was me who was dying inside.

THIRTY

THE BEAST

I t has been two days. Two near eternal days since Miranda killed me, or even fucking showed up.

I hadn't slept, hadn't eaten, I hadn't even gone back down to my chambers. I simply stalked the bars of my cage back and forth, minute after minute, hour after hour, waiting for her. My angel of death.

Without an explanation of her absence, I wracked my brain for a suitable substitute. Is this because she didn't forgive me for forcing her to decapitate me? Is this because she saw another side of me, and she couldn't stand me now?

I thought turning into my godlikeness and losing control in front of her was a vulnerability I couldn't bear. But taking her into my inner sanctum and experiencing bliss with her in my bed, in my personal springs where no other being visited, had been a whole new level of vulnerability for me.

Or was this a rebellion against Grim's judgement and my desires? Was she flat out going to defy the death order?

Was she right? The blade had killed off so much of my excess power, I felt almost…normal.

Whatever that was.

It was a time where I was a powerful god, in control of my faculties.

It felt far away now, but I knew the times I'd sparred with Miranda, the times we'd played our games, I'd exhibited a control I couldn't remember having. She truly was safe with me. The need to protect and be with her magnetized my shattered pieces, bringing me into a new kind of wholeness. They didn't fit together like pieces of a puzzle; it was a clump of shards. Was that enough? Was that enough for an existence?

But an existence without Miranda—I was falling apart at the very idea.

I thought living in pain and power was hell, but it was nothing compared to this new prospect. Living an eternity, being denied death, and never seeing Miranda again.

I'd be trapped down here, thinking of her sweet taste, her seductive eyes, her strength and softness. I'd be haunted by her, yet never getting to see her again.

My hands trembled violently as emotion surged in me. I'd been teetering on a thin edge, but my control snapped like a brittle twig. A roar exploded from my chest and throat as the lights blew in a tremendous display of sparks.

Images of Miranda taunting me from outside the bars, continually walking away to the elevator to leave played on repeat. My skin thickened with rage and blue energies surrounded me as I was stuck in the loop of pain and rejection.

I needed her. I fucking needed her now.

If I could just get to the other side of the bars, I'd grab her, shake sense into her. Tell her she can never leave again. Not until I was dead.

She could dance on my bones. She could carve out my face.

Thoughts jumbled and jammed together as my vision filled with flickering hallucinations of black sands, harsh sunlight, and all-consuming darkness.

Something let out a roar exactly like mine from nearby. Or was that me?

Bars bent under my strength, freeing me from my confines. I exploded forward like a cannon ball.

The hot black sands of Egypt, my homeland, scorched the soles of my feet. Bright lights and screaming sirens and horns assaulted my senses.

Words tumbled out of my mouth, but they were other words from the other people, the power of other gods. They were all here, crowding me out, threatening to explode my brains.

"They want her blade. They want her hands. They are in her brain and her mind and her brain. They toy with her, wind wind wind, chatter chatter chatter."

My heart pounded so hard and fast, I feared it would break through my chest. Rage and need collided; two powerful tidal waves smashing into each other, rocking the entire ocean.

Miranda came into view, throwing a terror-stricken glance over her shoulder. She was being chased. A bright blazing heat followed her. She was going to burn. Like I did. My throat turned dry.

249

Then she blipped out of existence. She'd been taken. I cried out in rage. I had to get her. Had to get her back.

An oak door appeared before me.

She was through the door. I had to break it to get her. I'd break everything and everyone to get to her.

My foot kicked into the wood, and it crashed open.

"Miranda," I roared, slamming the door open. I had to find her. I had to find who took her. If they so much as frayed one of her braids, I would rip their eyeballs out and eat them.

A voice broke through my insanity. "Xander?"

All my broken pieces slammed together, yanking me into the present, grounding me in reality. And I found myself inside a house I didn't recognize, facing a completely shocked Miranda.

CHAPTER

THIRTY-ONE

THE BADASS

I blinked.
This wasn't my cage.
This was a house. I was outside in the real world. The air was different. There was so much of it, and it blew all over the world before ruffling my hair up off my forehead.

Miranda's house emanated a comforting blend of practicality and warmth, its earthy tones and inviting furnishings creating an inviting atmosphere. Framed photographs of her son, Jamal, adorned the walls, capturing his radiant smile that

251

radiated joy and innocence. While his eyes and mouth mirrored Miranda's, the distinct features of a wide nose bridge and darker skin tone clearly bore resemblance to the man depicted in the well-framed, official army photo—his father.

I blinked.

What the fuck had I done?

Miranda stood halfway between the kitchen and the living room of her house. She wore purple sweat pants and a black tank top. The coffee table was littered with used tissues, and it looked like she'd made a cocoon of blankets around her on the couch earlier and could return to the same spot later. Half empty mugs also covered the table, while the television flickered colorful light into the room. The sound of rushing water from a faucet filtered in from another room.

Miranda stared at me wide-eyed.

"You're okay," was all I could manage to say.

Her brows furrowed, as if she couldn't understand how I stood inside her house.

I didn't understand either. But I was here.

"You didn't come to kill me," I explained lamely.

She started to say something but was overtaken by a sneeze. Grabbing first one, then two tissues, she blew her nose. When she got hold of her sneezing, she answered in a nasal, congested voice. "I have a cold, so I called into work."

For fucks sake.

"No one told me." My tone was defensive. Suddenly I felt foolish standing there at her threshold.

"You left your cage?" she asked, jaw still hanging in disbelief.

"Yes, well. I thought something had happened to you."

She shot a look over my shoulder. It was then I realized I left the door open. It barely hung from one of its hinges. I closed it as best I could, not entirely sure I was on the right side of it.

"How did you know where I live?" she asked.

How did I know? I searched my addled mind. Had I found her by pure instinct? Or was it something more tangible?

"You have it neatly labeled inside your lunchbox." And I remembered it. I remembered everything about her.

She spoke again, slowly as if trying to make sense of things. "You broke out of your cage because I didn't come to kill you, and you thought you needed to come rescue me?"

Okay well now I felt absolutely stupid. My overreaction was of epic proportions.

"I didn't know where you were," I said with vehemence. Was I defending my intrusion to her, or my out-of-control reaction to myself?

Yet, her expression softened. As if she was touched by what I'd done. Then her eyes shut as she swayed a little on her feet. In a flash, I was at her side, easing her back onto the couch. I laid my hand on her forehead. Heat radiated into my palm even as she shivered. "You are burning up."

She was ill. I shouldn't take such great pleasure in touching her but hell if it wasn't the most soul-satisfying thing in the world right now to hold her.

"I'll be better by tomorrow. But I guess I can kill you now since you are here," she said even as her teeth chattered, trying to get up.

I gently guided her back down.

"No, that's not why I came." It pained me to think she believed I may have come here just to make sure she performed her duty to me. Who knew how many more blows it would take to kill me? It could be a hundred, it could take only one more? Either way, it was more important she take care of herself first. If I'd known what was preventing her to come to me, I would have waited.

...probably.

"You need to rest," I assured her.

Miranda let out a loud sniffle, momentarily giving the impression that she wanted to speak. However, she shook her head ever so slightly, as if rejecting the notion. "You should go. I don't want to get you sick," she said.

Without thinking, I replied, "I can't get sick."

But then it dawned on me, her unspoken consideration. I asked the question tentatively, my heart swelled with hope, almost fearing her response. "Would you like me to stay by your side?"

"No." She said it so fast, I knew that was exactly what had been rolling around her brain.

Game over, sweetheart.

I stood abruptly, with purpose. "Too bad because I'm not leaving." Walking to the kitchen, I picked up the steel tea kettle and filled it with water from the sink."

"Even if you can't get sick, I can't...entertain you," she said.

I raised an eyebrow at her. "What do you mean, entertain me?"

"I'm not up for, you know." She coupled her incoherence with waving a hand back and forth between us.

"For fucks sake," I said, horror dawning on me. "I didn't come here for sex, either."

I followed the sound of running water to her bathroom. She'd been preparing to run a bath. Noting the water was hot, I stopped up the drain. A variety of bubble bath serums sat around the edge. I instantly grabbed the lavender one and dumped half the bottle in. Fuck, I loved this scent on her skin.

Miranda stood in the doorway; a large blanket wrapped

around her shoulders. She frowned at me as if I were a misbehaving child. "What are you doing?"

"You may have a fever, but you are also chilled. We need to get you warmed up."

"I can take care of my—of my—*Achoo*."

"Has anyone told you that you sneeze like a mouse?" The woman suppressed all of her instincts, even her sneezes. It was unexpectedly adorable.

The brows over her eyes furrowed deeper. Her pallor was ashen even as she defied me. "I do not."

She didn't shy away when I drew near, but she clung to the blanket even as I tried to remove it from her shoulders.

"Let me help you," I said, softly.

Miranda's full lips parted a moment before closing. Knowing her, she was caught between saying no or she didn't need help from anyone. Playing dirty, I yanked the blanket off her. Then moving in a most unthreatening manner, my fingers went to the hem of her shirt.

I waited, silently asking for permission. Though she still remained pensive, she lifted her arms as I pulled the shirt off.

Fucking hell, her nipples tightened in response to the cold air. I wanted to taste them again. But I wasn't a beast in that respect. I would never maul her when she was in such a state. Not until she was just as hot and willing as the last time.

As Miranda pushed off her pajama pants, she swayed again. I grabbed her, keeping her upright. It also brought her naked body flush against mine. The heat of her chest on mine felt so fucking good.

Her eyes turned up to meet mine. They were bleary and bloodshot, but I could see a heat behind them. "I can take care of myself."

"Of course you can," I assured her. Still, I walked backward, drawing her with me until we were next to the sudsy water.

She licked her lips, slowly, and I expected her to kick me out any second. "Let me help you in."

"Okay." The word was so soft, I needed to rely on my supernatural hearing to catch it.

I held her hand, guiding her into the half-filled tub. Bubbles built at an incredible speed. She sank into it with a groan, and her shivers intensified. With her knees up she leaned her head on them as if trying to warm herself.

"C-can y-you hand me that wr-wrap?" She asked through chattering teeth, pointing to the counter.

I grabbed the purple silk cloth. Miranda had already begun to twirl her braids up into a bun. Before she could stop me, I put the cloth over the back of the bun and tied it in the front.

"Is the water too cold?" I asked, watching her continue to shake.

"I'll warm up soon. You can go." Her voice was strained. But I didn't want to go. Instead, I grabbed a hand cloth and dipped it in the water. I smoothed it over her back, trying to help warm her. Her lids fluttered shut as I continued the ministrations.

"This is really weird," she said, cheek resting on her knees, eyes still closed.

"I'll say," I muttered in agreement, watching the water rivulets trickle down her perfect smooth skin. Then I set the rag aside and raised my fingertips over the water. I drew it up in a sheet over her back, like a cloak. To keep the water from cooling, I directed it into a continuous running fountain so hot water was always covering her skin. I became mesmerized by its motion over her strong, elegant back.

Cracking one eye open, she said, "I'm still convinced this is some kind of fever dream."

"Do you often dream of men bathing you?"

"That is none of dream Xander's business," she slurred.

I failed to suppress a smile. Miranda was in a bit of a delirious state. I liked it far too much.

Over and over, I wet the rag in the bubbles before running it over her back in tandem with the water I commanded to surround and caress her. Steam curled up from water and around her body, obscuring the mirror. It wasn't long before she stopped shivering and her breath evened out.

Something in my chest squeezed so tight I almost wondered if Bob hadn't run me through. Being alone all these years, I'd been denied companionship, physical touch, and the ability to care for another. My fingers dipped through the layer of water to stroke down the bare flesh along the ridges of her spine. Having the opportunity to indulge all three, it made me feel...important, connected, and mortal.

Or how I imagined a mortal might feel.

Truthfully, I was bitterly jealous of humans. Their lives were so much more precious than immortals simply because they were finite. They were a song with a beginning, a middle, crescendos, and refrains before they ended on a furious dramatic timbre, or on a soft fading note. An immortal's life was continuous, monotonous, and unchanging. We didn't age, we didn't die, and we didn't have the opportunity to experience that same level of meaning.

This was beyond dangerous, but I was so far away from that basement, that cage, and the version of me that knew my place.

Something stung behind my eyes, causing my lip to curl. Each time Miranda had buried her blade inside me, she'd left a piece of her in there as well.

I lifted the dozing woman out of the water, waving all the moisture away from her body with my power, sending it back into the tub so she was instantly dry. I carried her to the bedroom. She didn't rouse from slumber, even as her arms curled around my neck. The tightness in my chest twisted tighter. Laying her down in her bed, I pulled the sheets up and around her. Then I slid in next to her.

She moaned and turned to wrap her arms around me. Her body molded into mine, a perfect fit.

"Miranda," I said just above a whisper. I half expected her not to hear me.

"Mmm?" she didn't open her eyes.

I swept my hand down her bare arm, enjoying the silky feel of her skin.

Something pressed up against my rib cage. The words I'd been denying. The thing I'd been most afraid of. I was more afraid of the sentiment lodged in my throat than I ever was of not getting a chance to die.

I thought that had been my worse fear, never dying.

But this, this, I was one thousand times more afraid of. It was only into Miranda's ear that I could whisper it.

The words came out shaky. "Miranda. I want to live."

She didn't respond or open her eyes, but I could feel her thinking, hard.

"You're right. For a while now, I've been in control. That is, until tonight. I want to live, but I need you. Without you, my demons will still eat me up from the inside. Say you'll stay with me as long as I live, and I can do it."

Her eyes opened at that. She sniffled, clearing her stuffy nose. "Are you proposing?"

I pulled her against me tighter. "Maybe I am."

She frowned and tried to move away, but I wouldn't let her.

"Xander, this is crazy. You are outside your cage. You aren't thinking right. You've had a taste of freedom and now you have lost it."

"You're right about one thing. I'm crazy. I've been crazy for as long as I can remember. But even all the voices in my head love you and would never hurt you."

"They love me?" she said in a strained voice.

"*I* love you, sweetheart," I clarified with vehemence. "I know all that came out jumbled and backward, but like you said, I'm crazy." Then I flashed her a grin meant to devastate her resistance.

"You've made me so different," she confessed in a whisper filled with fear and awe.

"Any version of you is the right version," I said, my arms tightening around her. Suddenly I was afraid. Scared she didn't like what she'd turned into around me. Maybe she'd rather be something else with someone else. I honestly couldn't blame her. Shackling her to a crazy, feral god was likely a punishment.

Then after a pause, she said, "I love you too." Her words tripped on emotion. Or congestion. I didn't mind either.

I kissed her softly, sweetly, with all the aching tenderness threatening to crack in me. I kissed her with a promise that I would reward her love her and trust.

"As soon as you are feeling better, I'm going to show you exactly how much I fucking love you, sweetheart."

"Promise me one thing," she said, her fingers curling into my chest.

"Anything." And I meant anything. I'd fucking rake down the moon from the sky if she wanted it. I knew a guy.

"No more board games," she said, closing her eyes and snuggling into me.

A laugh rumbled through my chest. "Deal."

THIRTY-TWO

THE BADASS

"Something bright flashed through the window. The heat of the light was scalding, and I shied away from it. The room was bathed in an eerie, fiery glow. It seemed almost alive, pulsating with an insidious intent. This wasn't the gentle caress of dawn's first light; it was a harsh, consuming blaze.

Beside me, Xander was a comforting presence, lost in the serenity of his godly dreams. The way his chest rose and fell, the soft, almost purr-like snore he gave every third breath, it was all so normal. It was at odds with the lurking threat I felt seeping into the room.

"Bob," I whispered, reaching for the sword I kept by my bedside.

"What is it now, Miranda?" it muttered, the sarcasm in its voice almost tangible. I wasn't even going to try to figure out how or why a sword would sleep.

"I think we have a problem," I replied, clutching the hilt of the blade. The metal was comforting and cool, the familiar grooves fitting perfectly into my palm. "Something bright."

Bob let out a sound akin to a snort as I hastily pulled on a pair of panties and oversized tee-shirt. "You woke me for a lightbulb? Really, Miranda?"

This wasn't just any bright light. It was malevolent. The room seemed to shrink around it, as if it were absorbing the life force of everything around. I slipped out of bed, careful not to wake Xander, and moved stealthily towards the window. The light outside was blinding, but I forced my eyes to adjust.

Suddenly, the light morphed into a fuzzy, glowing entity, its brightness a cruel mockery of the sun. It was all consuming, eating up the darkness, consuming the night. I gripped Bob tighter, my knuckles white with the intensity. The Blade of Bane hummed, as if sensing the impending danger.

"All right, I see your point," Bob finally conceded, the tone of its voice changing from its usual dry wit to something more serious. "That doesn't look like any lightbulb I've ever seen."

Summoning all my courage, I crept out of the bedroom to the living room. Scalding brightness shone in through the front windows and cut in from around the edges of my front door, trying to get in, trying to hurt me.

There was a presence on the other side of that door. And I held the only weapon that could destroy anything and anyone.

A certainty settled into my gut. If I didn't cut this thing

down now, everything was going to burn up. Me, Xander, and everyone I cared about.

I could feel Bob's energy coursing through me, a tingling sensation that spread from my fingertips to the soles of my feet. I could kill it. I knew it in the marrow of my bones that this was the moment to do it.

I threw the door open and leapt out of my house. Bob and I flew through the air with a true strike that would kill the enemy.

A high-pitched scream reverberated, jolting me from my brave attack. My eyes snapped open, the glow of the fuzzy entity fading as I blinked in the face of Xander. Surprise widened his eyes, a flicker of astonishment dancing within them. I wasn't outside at all. I was still in the living room of my house.

I looked down at the sword in my hand. Bob was buried deep in Xander's chest. The menacing, world-ending entity was just another dream. And I had been sleep walking again.

But more than that, behind Xander cowered a small figure. My son, Jamal.

My son. Home from camp?

Confusion and panic grappled for control of my brain.

What was happening? Nothing made sense. "What. . .what are you doing here, Jamal?" My voice was rough from sleep and confusion.

My words hung in the air, unanswered. Jamal was frozen in place, his eyes wide with terror. His gaze flitted between me and the stranger I'd run through in our living room.

Oh my god.

The realization hit me like a ton of bricks. I'd been about to hurt Jamal. I'd almost killed my own son. But Xander jumped in the way.

Glyphs lit up along Bob's blade. That hadn't happened since the first time I used the sword to kill Xander.

Xander crumpled to the ground, and I fell to my knees with him, trying to hold him up as best I could.

I pulled the blade out of Xander's heart, and a blue glow of energy shot out, winding around the blade, traveling upward and winding around my arm. It was the same hue as Xander's power.

What the hell?

A strange buzzing thrummed through my bones, spreading out to my entire body. I'd only felt this one other time. When the goddess Bast threw herself on my blade, and died.

"Oh Miranda," Bob said in a way that made my stomach drop out of my body.

No. No. It couldn't be. This wasn't it. This wasn't the one that did it.

Xander's eyes met mine, an inexplicable sadness mixing with his pain.

"Miranda," he rasped, his voice a mere whisper. "I. . . I couldn't let him get hurt."

"Xander," I choked out, tears blurring my vision. His life force was ebbing away, his divinity dimming with each passing second. "What. . .what have I done?" Panic rose in my throat like a pile of bugs growing higher until it was in my mouth. I had to push back the urge to throw up.

Xander's pained gaze flickered to Jamal. My son didn't know him, didn't know anything about him. And yet Xander had sacrificed himself for him.

"You made me want...to live, sweetheart," Xander admitted, his voice barely audible.

"I know," I replied, my voice a broken whisper. "We get more time now. We get to have more time. You changed your mind. This can't count."

Wetness covered my cheeks as my tears spilled uncontrollably. This couldn't be it. This was a nightmare too. It was a mistake. I needed to take it back. Oh god, why couldn't I take it back? It was only a short while ago Why couldn't I reach back just a little and take it back? A sob wracked my body as I clutched at Xander.

"But you. . .you'll still live . . ." His hand weakly reached out, brushing against my cheek.

His hand fell away, his eyes losing their spark. His chest heaved one last time before falling still. The unkillable god who had once been too powerful, too vibrant, lay lifeless in my arms.

A deafening silence filled the room. I clutched Xander's form to me, a raw, deep pain tearing through my heart. I had killed him, night after night, chipping away at his power, at his life force. And now, in a cruel twist of fate, I had delivered the final blow once he'd decided to live.

The sound of Jamal's quiet sobs filtered through to my ears. He didn't understand. He couldn't. I still didn't know what he was doing here, but he knew his mother had been about to kill him before a stranger jumped in and sacrificed himself. I held Xander closer.

Two words kept circling my brain, taunting me, shredding any remaining pieces of my heart.

Game over.

CHAPTER
THIRTY-THREE

THE BADASS

T he next couple days were a blur. Half clouded by grief, half from the cold medicine I was taking.

It turned out someone had contacted Jamal's camp, posing as me, insisting Jamal needed to return home because of a family emergency. Whoever had called had even sent a plane ticket and instructions for Jamal's trek home.

My kid's plane landed late, but I'd supposedly even arranged for a rideshare. When Jamal let himself in the house with his key, he found his mother charging at him with a sword. Xander had awoken and had gotten up to look for me just as Jamal arrived. Seeing what I was about to do, he jumped in between us, taking the killing blow.

I'd numbly managed to call Timothy who said he'd be right over and not to move.

Jamal apologized over and over again, his backpack still on and luggage by the door. My heart broke further. None of this was his fault. He didn't know who Xander was but that didn't matter. He still thought it was his fault Xander died.

I took Jamal into his bedroom and tried to explain as best I could who Xander was. An immortal I had tried to help, who I cared about very much. Then I had the even tougher job of explaining my nightmares and the sleepwalking. I was adamant that I would never knowingly hurt him.

"I'm sorry I came home early," Jamal sniffed as he cried. I heard the front door open and the sounds of many feet and shuffling. Timothy had arrived with help, to clean up. The thought made me sick.

I pulled Jamal tightly into my arms, my head lightheaded from the cold medicine, and fighting back tears. "Oh baby, never apologize for coming home. You should always feel safe to come home. I—I don't know what happened."

And I didn't. But I was going to find the fuck out.

Uncle Javier was over a lot after that. He'd been one of the ones to show up at my house that night along with Timothy to clean up. He came to me and asked me *the* question, once Jamal was out of earshot.

"You steady?"

The lump in my throat almost kept me from answering. "No. I'm not steady."

He nodded and squeezed my hand. Then just like the last time, he showed up at my house the next morning to make coffee, eggs, and bacon. He played video games with Jamal while I rested in bed, still sick and grief stricken. I was so very grateful for Javier. He wasn't just a friend. He was family and he acted like it. I'd die for him back in the day and I still would today.

I still kept Bob nearby out of habit though I half hated him. He did his best to cheer me up and reiterate it wasn't my fault. And that at least we don't have to kill anyone. I didn't have a lot to say to him.

It took days longer than I planned, but when I was well enough I set up a meeting. Six am sharp, I arrived at Perkatory, to get my to-go mug filled with a strong americano.

I hadn't brought Aaron up to speed, but based on his soft, pitying expression and saying my coffee was on the house was all I needed to know Vivien spilled everything.

She'd forgone baby vamp duty as much as she could to come be with me. It wasn't that long ago our roles were reversed.

But she wasn't the one I asked to meet with this morning.

Timothy slipped into the seat across from me. He wore a dark purple suit today. Stress and responsibility pulled at the lines around his eyes.

"I'm so sorry Miranda. I never wanted it to happen like that," he started.

I held up my hand, stopping him. I wasn't here for that.

"I've been having nightmares for a couple weeks. They've caused me to sleepwalk."

"Yes, I heard," he murmured.

"They started after someone tried to break into my car. I think they were trying to get the blade. And Jamal was sent home because someone posed as me. I don't have many vulnerabilities other than my child. Do you see where I'm going with this?"

His dark eyes studied me closely. "I think I'm beginning to."

"Someone orchestrated this. Someone wanted Xander dead too." The pain under my chest was sharp and unforgiving for days. It flared at my words, but I muscled past the feeling.

Timothy pressed at the spot between his brows as if trying to dig for some information. He already knew what I was going to ask.

"Who? Who would care if Xander lived or died? Or who would want the blade?" I still didn't fully understand what this entity wanted. Maybe they wanted to break my spirit so I'd never use the blade again and they could take it? Or maybe it was about Xander the whole time. It was all muddled, but a single thread of connection was clear.

Timothy shook his head after a while, dropping his hand. "I couldn't say. Xander has not had any enemies since Aten. And the sun god was slain by the blade you wield."

"Maybe someone who cared about the sun god then?" I asked, pressing him for more.

Timothy bit the inside of his cheek, his eyes glowing a light green for a moment. It was if he was accessing some information from an internal database. It was why I chose him.

Then coming back to himself, he frowned. "No one I can think of. You must understand, Aten changed everything."

"Xander said he thought Aten was getting too powerful, but no one paid attention until it was too late." I added.

Timothy nodded solemnly. "Before Aten, we were a polytheistic society. Everyone prayed to many gods. Aten thought he deserved more than that and influenced the Egyptian pharaoh and all their followers there was only one true god. Him." A dark shadow passed over his face. "When Aten killed Xander, he went too far. We all descended upon him, but the damage had been done. It was then that Osiris forbad any god from taking on worshippers ever again. We couldn't recruit, we could use the old names anymore. It is why our identities have morphed amongst the Greeks, the Romans, and into the present-day celebrities. We were to be stripped of power equally so that humanity could rise to power."

"Who was angry about that? Did anyone blame Xander? Was anyone on Aten's side?"

Timothy shook his head. "We were all guilty of Xander's demise having let him face Aten alone. None of the gods supported Aten's lunacy, and he was hated in death for the price he all cost us. There is no one would help him to this day and age."

The gung-ho parts inside me wilted. None of this was helpful. It was a history lesson without any clues to who tried to steal the blade from me. Who had been fucking with my head. Who made me kill the crazy god I loved.

Seeing my despair, Timothy reached a hand across to pat my arm.

"There are many gods who possess the power to design dreams and hallucinations like the ones that caused you to sleepwalk. I'll make a list and we'll start investigating them."

I swallowed hard and nodded. Timothy understood I needed to do something, anything, or I'd fall apart. But I could already tell by his demeanor, it wasn't likely we'd find anything pertinent among the gods.

Clutching my cup, I started toward the security office.

Timothy was at least trying, and I felt his sincerity. While I didn't agree with the stance he took, I knew he'd only wanted to protect me. I was still pissed at him, but I'd get over it.

The person I wasn't a fan of was Bianca. Resentment stewed in me. She promised the world would end if Xander died. And while I didn't want that to happen, I found her baseless ravings to grate on my nerves even though she didn't show up to press upon the matter.

My booted steps angrily echoed across the lobby of Sinopolis as my duster swept out behind me. Judging by the looks of others, I was a dangerous, moving thunderstorm.

It wasn't enough that I lost a future with one man I loved, but now, twice. It was cruel. It was almost too purposeful not to be fate. It reminded me of what Xander said about being punished? By Osiris or some larger consciousness that thought this was what I deserved?

"Miranda," a voice called out, stopping me.

I turned to find Aoiki running up to me. She wore her school uniform per usual, hair up in pigtails with big pink fluff balls decorating each dark waterfall of hair. Her hands clutched the straps of her cute kitty backpack as she hurried over. Without preamble she threw her arms around me in a tight hug. "I'm so sorry. I'm so so so sorry."

My arms remained at my side as I violently fought back the tears she forced to the surface. I didn't want to do this right now. Not here, not like this.

Finally, she let me go. I'd be cold and put her off, if it weren't for the compassionate look on her face. "You loved him, didn't you?" she asked.

I could only bring myself to nod stiffly. Aoiki was a lot like Vivien. Not really aware of boundaries or conscientious to tip toe around painful subjects.

Aoiki grabbed my free hand with both hers and shot a look around as if to make sure no one was listening. "There's a way to bring him back," she said in a hushed voice.

All my attention perked up at that. Suddenly, I was squeezing her hands back. "What?"

"The blade, Bob, has a way to call back the entities it kills. You can bring Xander back."

"I can what now?" Bob asked in a muffled voice from where he was tucked in my coat.

Excitement and hope welled inside me, nearly bursting through my chest.

I tried to tamp it down. "That's not true. The blade of bane is the only weapon able to permanently kill any immortal."

A sly smile crept up her face. "Miranda. I take the same high school physics class year after year. Some of the shit they teach is totally off the mark, but they are right about one thing. Matter can ever truly be created or destroyed. Things merely change. There is a way to change him back into a god again."

I deliberately tried to numb myself against the hope Aoiki was dumping on me. It was too much, and I wasn't thinking straight, "Why are you helping me?"

She shot me a look like the answer was positively obvious. "Because I know what it's like to be in love. If I were to lose that love, it would break me."

Sunny. She was talking about the quiet fae girl with a bobbed haircut. How long had they been together out of her five hundred sum years?

If I had five hundred years with Xander I doubted it would be enough. I missed him so hard it made my bones brittle. I missed his touch, his eyes, his wry sense of humor. Hell, I missed his crazy. I knew I could help him control it, and I felt robbed at not getting more of a chance.

Then Aoiki whispered while looking around to make sure no one heard. "Can I meet you tonight? Where he died?"

I immediately made plans to have Jamal stay with Uncle Javier. "Yes," I nodded.

"Good," she said, with a nod. "I'll see you at nine PM."

Then she ran off, mentioning she couldn't be late for school *again* and risk detention.

The idea that I could get Xander back made the minutes of

the rest of my day crawl by. What if we were going to be reunited in a matter of hours?

That would change everything.

It wasn't over until it was over.

And when I got him back, I was sure Xander would help me figure out who set me up to kill him and why.

CHAPTER

THIRTY-FOUR

THE BADASS

A oiki was an hour late, but when she arrived she had
Sunny in tow.

"Sorry about your loss," Sunny murmured
avoiding eye contact with me as if she was painfully shy.

I only nodded, unable to respond to yet another person's
sympathies. I hated it. And if tonight went well, they would be
unnecessary.

The girls set down their backpacks in the corner of my

living room. "Sorry it took us a while longer, we had to sneak out."

"Your parents don't know you are here?" The mom alarm went off in my head.

"I tried to feel them out on it, but I didn't get the sense they'd exactly approve."

"Why not?" I asked, feeling suddenly uneasy. They had helped me find the Blade of Bane, they had ultimately helped Vivien resurrect Grim.

Aoiki rolled her eyes as she tightened a pigtail. "Who knows. My mom was in one of her moods today. You know how she is."

It was true, Echo was temperamental to say the least. And she was the one who told me to follow my heart. Everything in my chest screamed at me that bringing him back was the right thing to do.

So even though she wasn't here, I might as well have had her blessing.

"So what now?" I asked, suddenly feeling nervous.

Aoiki smiled at Sunny. "She knows what to do. Sunny can call Xander back."

"Do we need his body or something?" I said, still unable to shake the nerves in my stomach.

Sunny shook her head. "That's not necessary. Matter will regroup when I call it. I just need the sword."

Something flip flopped in my guts. I wasn't supposed to give the sword to anyone.

"What do you need the sword for?" I'd let Xander hold it when we'd sparred, but he truly had no desire to wield it. It felt safe. This...didn't. I didn't really know this fae girl. I would have felt more comfortable if Aoiki asked to hold, but still, even then the idea squirmed in my guts.

"My ancestor was one of the fae that wielded the sword before me," Sunny explained with a small smile of pride. "I know what to do with it. I know that it is capable of more than people think."

"She's very smart," Aoiki nodded with beaming pride.

I slowly drew Bob out from my duster jacket.

"Are you sure this is wise?" he asked quietly.

"You don't think it is?" I asked in turn.

"I honestly couldn't say. Like any being, even I lack the full perception of my full potential."

"You wouldn't be killing anyone," I said, feeling the need to soothe him for some reason.

"I suppose so. And if it will make you happy, I can try."

Something pinched in my heart. How strange was it to bond with a sentient weapon. To have it care for your wellbeing.

"Thank you," I said. I laid Bob out across my hands before passing him over to Sunny.

Her eyes gleamed with intensity and reverence as she took the sword.

Sunny dropped down her knees and continued to hold the sword as it laid across her palms. She closed her eyes and began to chant in another language.

Aoiki grabbed my arm and pulled me off to the side but didn't let go of me. She held me fast while Sunny continued to speak.

After a few minutes, a low pressure built in the air and the smell of ozone rose. Aoiki's grip only tightened on my arm with excitement.

Then sparks shot off Bob's blade. He yelped in surprise a couple times but settled after a while.

This is the right thing to do, I repeated to myself. *The world of immortals doesn't abide by the same rules as mortals. Xander shouldn't be gone for all time. He was ready to live. He deserves a chance.*

Still, something I couldn't name wriggled in my belly. So I focused on what it would be like to be in Xander's arms again. Hell, I'd even break the promise and play a board game with him if he wanted. As long as he came back to me.

The pressure built and built, the ozone smell growing so strong it stung my nose. Sunny continued chanting, her voice growing louder and louder.

A rushing wind picked up in the room despite there being no windows open. It swept at my face and tossed Aoiki's pig tails around.

Soon it felt like being in the middle of a tornado. The wind roared in my ears so I could barely hear Sunny scream over it.

I wouldn't be surprised if the neighbors called the cops. Not that law enforcement would know what to do about this.

Then another shooting spark lept off the blade, bigger than the first mini ones. Then another, and another. They shot out of Bob like shooting stars.

Another sound pierced through the howling wind. Bob. Bob was crying out. "No. No no no!"

I started forward but Aoiki pulled me back. "She's not done yet," she screamed in my ear.

"Something's wrong," I yelled back.

Aoiki's brows furrowed in confusion before she regarded Sunny again.

The girl was lost in concentration, as if she were searching internally for something even as words spilled out of her mouth.

More shooting stars exploded from Bob as he cried out in protest. Aoiki's certainty seemed to falter as her lips twisted. She could also hear his screams.

She released my arm and took a couple steps forward. "Sunny," she yelled to her girlfriend.

Sunny either didn't notice or pretended not too. She chanted faster and bigger, brighter shooting stars escaped Bob's blade.

"Sunny, stop," Aoiki cried out, also realizing something wasn't right.

Bob screamed out, "Miranda, help. Help me."

Okay, that was enough. I started forward, ready to wrench Bob out of Sunny's grip when an explosion of light went off.

I threw my arms up to protect my face even as I was thrown back against the wall. I hit it hard before sliding to the ground. I instinctively curled into a protective ball. It wasn't just any light. I'd felt this before. It was powerful, malevolent and gleefully destructive. It was the entity from my dreams. Except this wasn't a dream. It exploded to life in my living room, searing my skin, my mind.

I felt phantom fingers sear my arms, my legs, as if it was exploring me, studying me. I trembled, unable to move, unable to fight.

After I don't know how long, it receded. I blinked hard against the fading brightness. I sucked in deep breaths, trying to calm the panic that had overtaken me.

Wha the fuck had that been?

"Sunny," Aoiki cried. I barely caught her running out the front door of my house. It slammed shut behind her.

Despite her exit, I wasn't alone.

A naked, muscular figure lay on the ground next to Bob who had fallen silent. Despite lacking all the scars that had marred it before, I recognized the body instantly.

I scrambled to my feet and ran over to the man on my carpet. He pushed himself up onto his elbows, those intense sapphire eyes met mine with a burning intensity. Xander's expression radiated cold hatred and it was directed right at me. It stopped me in my tracks, several feet separating us. My stomach dropped out of my body as heat and panic prickled the skin on my forehead.

"Miranda." My name came out a raspy accusation. "What have you done?"

The gravity of his words told me everything was not alright.

Not by a long shot. And it was all my fault.

EPILOGUE

BIANCA

"I s this what you saw?" a low, masculine voice asked.

I didn't pause brushing my hair from where I sat in front of my vanity mirror. The piece was from the baroque period, one of my favorites. So much champagne, cake, and opulence. The bright lights and hedonism of Vegas was not so different from such a time.

Fallon, formerly known as the god Horus, hadn't knocked, even though it was my bedroom. Presumptuous as always. I met his gaze in the mirror of my vanity. His one blue eye gleamed brilliantly against his rich black skin. His other brown eye did not hold the same magic, but held a different kind of power. Hands tucked in the pockets of his slacks, suit coat open, his white shirt was unbuttoned at the top, revealing a swath of muscular skin that made my skin heat up. Though I'd never let on that he had such an effect on me.

Fallon was beautiful like the other gods, yet so different in his fierce power. To most I was considered the darling of the

279

immortals, but to Fallon I was frivolous and naïve. He never passed on a chance to make me feel less than. I hated him for it.

I went on brushing my hair where I sat at my vanity. "I suppose so." In my vision, I'd seen bright white death. It hadn't made sense then, but hindsight brought all of this into terrifying focus.

"You should have come to me. You know I've always seen the future more clearly than you." There was a harshness in his tone I didn't appreciate.

My hairbrush slammed down on the vanity. "And why couldn't you have seen this for yourself? Why couldn't you have gone to Grim and told him to stop her." I'd believed Xander's death would trigger the end of days, but I didn't realize it would actually be his resurrection that would release fresh hell upon all of us.

Fallon remained silent, leaning against the doorway.

In that silence, I reflected on my hatred for him. I hated how my heart beat faster when he was near. I hated how he always disapproved of me. I hated how he'd come here just to censure me.

"You're scared," he said finally.

I swiveled around on my ottoman. "Of course, I'm scared." I couldn't keep the tremor out of my voice. "Every entity ever slain by the god killer has been released back into the world. Monsters we long thought we'd never have to contend with are out on the streets doing Osiris knows what. And *he's* back." Fear gripped my chest and I forced myself to say his name. "Aten is back. He won't be satisfied until he's killed us all. He wants to be the one true god."

"That will never happen, Bianca," Fallon said in a surprisingly soothing voice.

I got stiffly to my feet. "How helpful you are now, with your empty assurance based on what? Nothing."

I tried to walk past him, but Fallon's hand shot out, grabbing my wrist and pulling me to him. "Bianca," he said, his gaze dropping to my lips for a long beat that made me forget how to breathe. Heat tingled at the back of my head. When he met my eye again there was determination in his expression.

"He won't hurt you," he promised in a low voice.

I jerked my arm out from his grasp. "You're right. Aten won't. The glimpses I've seen, incoherent and unhelpful as they are," I said, taunting his assessment of my power, "I get to witness it all. I'll watch everyone burn." Tears crowded into my throat. My heart squeezed so hard I feared it would pop. "Even you." The last part came out a ragged whisper.

With that, I fled my own bedroom. Fallon didn't need to go on. It was because of my own inability to see, to articulate, that we would all suffer.

Especially Miranda.

And for that, I could never forgive myself.

WANNA KNOW **what happened after all hell broke loose? Grab a coffee and join the gang at Perkatory for a post loss therapy session.**

Go to hollyroberds.com for the bonus epilogue.

WANT A FREE BOOK?

Join Holly's Newsletter Holly's Hot Spot at www. hollyroberds.com and get the Five Orders Prequel Novella, The Knight Watcher, for FREE!

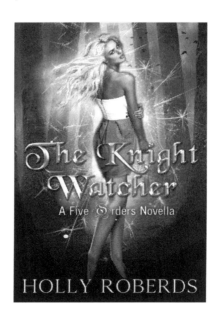

Plus you'll get exclusive sneak peaks, giveaways, fun lil' nuggets, and notifications when new books come out. Woot!

A LETTER FROM THE AUTHOR

Dear Reader,

Thank you for reading!

I loved writing this story and have more in store for Miranda and Xander. There will be more games, death, and debauchery.

Loved this book? Consider leaving a review as it helps other readers discover my books.

Want to make sure you never miss a release or any bonus content I have coming down the pipeline?

Make sure to join Holly's Hotspot, my newsletter, and I'll send you a FREE ebook right away!

You can also find me on my website www.hollyroberds.com and I hang out on social media.

Instagram: http://instagram.com/authorhollyroberds

Facebook: www.facebook.com/hollyroberdsauthorpage/

And closest to my black heart is my reader fan group, Holly's Hellions. Become a Hellion. Raise Hell. www.facebook.com/groups/hollyshellions/

Cheers!
Holly Roberds

ABOUT THE AUTHOR

Holly started out writing Buffy the Vampire Slayer and Terminator romantic fanfiction before spinning off into her own fantastic worlds with apocalyptic stakes.

Recently relocated to New Hampshire from Colorado, Holly is exploring the possibilities of become a witch (as one must consider when living in New England) and is hard at work implementing the word "wicked" into her vernacular.

She lives with her husband whose handsome looks are only out done by his charming and wicked supportive personality.

Two surly house rabbits supervise this writer, to make sure she doesn't spend all of her time watching Buffy reruns.

For more sample chapters, news, and more, visit www.
hollyroberds.com

Made in the USA
Monee, IL
20 July 2023

622ac3e2-deb1-4365-a241-cb13b852eaccR01